Into a
Cornish Wind

Also By Kate Ryder

Summer in a Cornish Cove
Cottage on a Cornish Cliff
Secrets of the Mist
Beneath Cornish Skies

Into a Cornish Wind

Kate Ryder

embla books

First published in Great Britain in 2022 by

embla books

Bonnier Books UK Limited
4th Floor, Victoria House, Bloomsbury Square, London, WC1B 4DA
Owned by Bonnier Books
Sveavägen 56, Stockholm, Sweden

Copyright © Kate Ryder, 2022

All rights reserved.
No part of this publication may be reproduced, stored or transmitted in any form or by any means, electronic, mechanical, photocopying or otherwise, without the prior written permission of the publisher.

The right of Kate Ryder to be identified as Author of this work has been asserted by them in accordance with the Copyright, Designs and Patents Act 1988

This is a work of fiction. Names, places, events and incidents are either the products of the author's imagination or used fictitiously. Any resemblance to actual persons, living or dead, is purely coincidental.

A CIP catalogue record for this book is available from the British Library.

ISBN: 9781471415548

This book is typeset using Atomik ePublisher

Embla Books is an imprint of Bonnier Books UK
www.bonnierbooks.co.uk

Praise for Kate Ryder

'Searingly emotional, compassionately told and wonderfully uplifting, this is one book you will remember long after the last page is turned.'
Julie Bonello, NetGalley.

'The author has a deft touch in handling emotion – her characters are totally sympathetic and believable, surprisingly and satisfyingly complex.'
Anne Williams, NetGalley.

'A fantastic read… If you are looking for some heat in these cold days of spring then look no further as this is the book for you. Warmth, romance and the Cornish breeze flow from these pages.'
Michelle Russell, NetGalley.

'Absolutely loved it: friendship, romance, wonderfully described scenery, a well written story – what more can one ask for?'
Donna Orrock, NetGalley.

'Really enjoyed the characters and plot of this book.'
Jamie Dyer, NetGalley.

'I look forward to more from this author and maybe get to "visit" the Cornish cove again!?'
Sharley Phillips, NetGalley.

'The storytelling in this book is first class.'
Jane Hunt, NetGalley.

Reviews for *Beneath Cornish Skies*:

'A wonderful story of finding love, freedom and oneself with a little help from friends, ancient magic and spirits in the landscape. Uplifting, romantic and perfect for anyone who loves Cornwall!'
Christina Courtenay, author of *Echoes of the Runes*.

'I absolutely adored this beautifully written book. A magical and deeply romantic read.'
Georgia Hill, author of *On a Falling Tide*.

'A beautiful story of love and self-discovery. Evocative, haunting and magical.'
Nicola Cornick, author of *The Forgotten Sister*.

'An absorbing tale of romance and deceit, layered with supernatural magic and impressively researched historical fact.'
Carol Lovekin, author of *Wild Spinning Girls*.

'A lovely and atmospheric read, filled with magical moments.'
Samantha Tonge, author of *The Winter We Met*.

'An evocative and powerful ode to Cornwall, its magic and mysteries, and the power to start over again.'
Nancy Barone, author of *New Hope for the Little Cornish Farmhouse*.

For Rosy
Guardian of the spark that ignited the flame

'Let there be spaces in your togetherness,
And let the winds of the heavens dance between you.
Love one another but make not a bond of love:
Let it rather be a moving sea between the shores of your souls.'

Kahlil Gibran

1

'You know he's married, don't you?'

The blood drains from Kat's face. Clutching the phone, she concentrates on steady, even breathing. In for three, hold for four, out for five . . .

'You didn't. I'm so sorry.' The woman's voice holds no guile.

Kat closes her eyes. How could she have been so stupid – falling for the oldest trick in the book? She usually prides herself on her savviness, but Colin has successfully undermined that particular accomplishment.

'Are you OK?' The voice at the other end sounds concerned.

Opening her eyes, Kat summons the ability to speak. 'Who did you say you were?'

The woman gives a soft laugh. 'I didn't, but I thought you should know before you're too deeply entrenched.'

'A well-wisher then?' A frown creases Kat's brow.

'Yes. I've known Colin for a while. He's a lovely guy, but he's *taken*.'

Kat shuts her eyes and pinches the bridge of her nose. Why hadn't she read the signs? During the course of their seven-month relationship, Colin has rarely stayed over during the week. Foolishly, she believed it was because he felt uncomfortable in her flat, and whenever she suggested staying over at his place he's always made the excuse of a loud and messy housemate. How stupid is she? She should have heard the warning bells, but she was falling in love and so deaf to their clanging.

Pushing back her chair, Kat gets to her feet. 'Do I know you?'

'We have met, briefly.'

'Where?' Kat's voice is insistent.

The moment stretches before the woman answers. 'The Old Swan.'

'What? Last Wednesday?'

'Yes.'

Kat casts her mind back. Colin had arranged to meet her after work for a quiet drink, although it had turned into anything but when several of his workmates suddenly appeared and hijacked the evening. Now she thinks about it, Colin had seemed uncomfortable when his colleagues approached their table. Recalling the women among them, she wonders which one she's talking to now.

Suddenly, the room is plunged into deep gloom as black clouds obliterate the sun. Kat shivers.

'Looks like we're in for a storm,' comments Kat's colleague, Gemma, sitting at the only other desk in the narrow office. Rising to her feet, she walks towards the door and switches on the headache-inducing, overhead fluorescent light, which snaps into life with a loud buzz.

Kat turns and gazes out of the window at a bank of menacing clouds sweeping across the sky that only five minutes earlier held the promise of a beautiful, early spring day. Raindrops fall and swiftly gather force. In the road below, an array of umbrellas spring open under the deluge unleashed from the sky and people scurry along the pavements heading for the nearest cover. Absent-mindedly tapping the phone against her chin, Kat watches the city street quickly turn into a river.

A man dressed in casual attire catches her eye. Incongruous in the busy London square, and seemingly unconcerned by the onslaught of rain, he holds a briefcase above his head and calmly hails a taxi. This is no city gent or office worker. His deep, early tan and the wild dark hair curling at the nape of his neck speak of foreign holidays, distant shores and an altogether more abandoned existence; not one confined to office hours and endless meetings. As a black cab slews across the road in deepening water, the man takes an unhurried step back from the spray that threatens to soak him. Kat watches as he opens the car door and climbs in.

A sudden clap of thunder sounds overhead and the fluorescent light flickers.

Crap! That's all she needs . . . a power cut.

She still has to complete the illustration pinned to her easel before the day is through.

As rivulets of water stream down the windowpane, obscuring the street scene below, Kat becomes aware that she is still holding her phone in a vice-like grip.

'Hello?' The woman's voice cuts into her thoughts. 'Is everything OK?'

'Oh . . . Yes.' Kat frowns. 'Just how married is Colin?' she asks quietly.

The woman sighs. 'His second son is due any day.'

Kat's eyes widen. *Second* son! He's covered his tracks well. She had no idea he wasn't single, let alone a father . . .

'Are you sure we're talking about the same man?'

'Absolutely. Colin Andrews is my brother-in-law.'

Kat inhales sharply.

'When I saw you two together the other evening,' the woman continues, 'and how you were with him, I knew I had to say something. I couldn't let you be drawn deeper into the deception. You see, it's not the first time this has happened. He's prone to wandering during my sister's pregnancies. This will be the third time.'

'Third?' Kat's voice is barely more than a whisper.

'Yes. This is child number three.'

Good God! He's definitely packing them in.

'Thank you for the heads up,' she says stiffly.

'I'm sorry if this has come as a shock but it's unfair of him to take advantage of you. I've seen it happen too many times.'

Aware of intense curiosity coming from the other end of the

room, Kat stares straight ahead at the numerous illustrations plastering the walls of her workspace.

'Anyway, I wish you luck,' the woman says. 'You seem nice and you don't deserve to be treated like this.' She ends the call.

The complete and utter BASTARD!

No wonder Colin has never invited her to his place. Seven months she's wasted on him!

Sitting down again, Kat slowly replaces the handset.

'You all right, Kat?' Gemma enquires. 'You look as if you've had some bad news.'

'I have.' She glances over at her colleague. 'And, no, I'm not all right, but I will be . . .'

The girl rises to her feet. 'I'll grab us some coffees.'

Kat throws her a weak smile. 'Black please . . . strong.'

As Gemma exits the room, Kat's mobile alerts her to an incoming message. In disbelief, she stares at the screen.

See you at Luigi's at seven. Don't be late. Col xx

'Bastard!' she shouts.

'You OK, Kat?' The art director's disembodied voice drifts over the partial screens dividing their offices.

'Bloody men!' she exclaims in response, quickly adding, 'No disrespect, Hugo.'

'None taken. They can't all be like me.'

Despite her tumultuous feelings, Kat's mouth twitches into a smile. 'Sadly, it seems all the best ones are taken.'

'Now, that's where you're wrong,' Hugo assures her. 'Somewhere out there . . .'

She considers Colin's message. What should she do? Not turn up and leave him wondering where she is, or respond with a short, sharp text saying she's aware of his sneaky assignations with her? No, let the sodding man stew.

She glances out of the window again. Flash floods, but the rain has stopped and the sun is doing its best to disperse the ominous clouds. She checks the time on her mobile – 11.40 – and rises to her feet. The unfinished illustration beckons but it can wait; there will be time this afternoon to put the finishing touches to it.

Grabbing her jacket from the back of the chair, she turns and sees Gemma in the doorway holding two steaming mugs.

'Sorry, Gem. Change of plan.' She smiles apologetically. 'I'm taking an early lunchbreak.'

2

Kat climbs the steps to Tate Britain, and as she enters the marble foyer, a sense of calm descends. Art always does this for her, helping to put whatever challenges she faces into perspective. However troubled or anxious she feels, being surrounded by masterpieces carrying centuries of history within them reminds her that life goes on and she is but a mere speck in the overall scheme of things.

Her heart rate settles further as she wanders through rooms filled with important art dating from the 1500s to the present day. Gazing at the incredible talent on display, she knows she can only ever hope to emulate this in her own small way, but is comforted by the knowledge that she is part of a greater whole. Fortunately, there are not too many people about and, unhurried, she enjoys the masterpieces of such eminent artists as Turner and Constable. However, mindful of her lunch *hour*, it's not long before she makes her way through to the Pre-Raphaelite section.

Apart from half-a-dozen chattering Japanese tourists, Kat is alone in this gallery. Immediately she crosses over to Sir John Everett Millais' painting of a scene from Shakespeare's *Hamlet* – '*Ophelia*'. Upon discovering Hamlet had murdered her father, poor Ophelia turned insane with grief, and in her distraught state fell into a brook and drowned. Kat grimaces. With her latest, less-than-successful relationship with Colin to add to her disastrously long list of exes, this painting hits a nerve. But refusing to dwell on such grim thoughts, she examines the background of the masterpiece that Millais had created from real life. At the time, it was thought to be one of the most accurate studies of nature ever painted. Her gaze alights on Ophelia's face. Dante Gabriel Rossetti's lover, wife and muse, Elizabeth Siddal, had posed for the painting and in her hands are flowers that include poppies, symbolising death.

Poor Lizzie Siddal, having to lie for hours on end in a bath of cooling water.

Kat knows the painting was created in the artist's studio, and that lamps placed beneath the bath to keep the water warm had gone out. Subsequently, Millais' model had become dangerously ill.

Continuing around the gallery, Kat gazes at each painting in turn until reaching the works of Rossetti, in front of which a bench is conveniently placed, and she sits down to study the portrait, *Sancta Lilias;* the abandoned first version of one of the artist's most important pictures, *The Blessed Damozel.* It's the only one of Rossetti's paired pictures and poems, in which the poem was completed first. She contemplates its neighbour – *The Beloved* ('*The Bride*') – the best known of his poems and inspired by the biblical *Song of Solomon.* The painting tells the story of a young woman preparing to marry. Rossetti has portrayed her surrounded by attendants, with a young, black child in the foreground holding a gold vase of roses, and as the bride lifts the head covering away from her face, her eyes are fixed directly on the beholder.

Oh Dante, you did have a liking for redheads!

Kat glances down at her own lustrous locks falling over her shoulders. She'd hated the colour growing up. Children can be *so* callous. Carrot-top, ginga, ginger nut, firecracker, tomato . . . She'd been called them all and made to feel like a freak. But as the years passed, the name-calling naturally receded, and thanks to a certain young actress exploding onto the nation's TV screens as Demelza Poldark, Kat's colouring has caught on, and numerous women now dye their hair shades of fire-red through to autumn. No longer does she stand out.

A movement at the entrance makes her look up and as a couple enter, Kat's eyes widen. It's the man she'd spied from her office window only half an hour before! He's ditched the briefcase . . . but it's definitely him. She observes the woman at his side. Smartly dressed in a navy pinstriped skirt-suit, her high heels elevate her to almost his height. They make a striking couple, even though he's casually dressed by comparison. His linen jacket is crumpled, no doubt from having been caught out in the rain and then sitting in a taxi, and there are watermark stains at the ankles of his pale blue trousers. But a sense of freedom envelops him and, as before, Kat is reminded of sunnier climes.

She watches a while longer. The man and the woman are obviously at ease in each other's company and the overriding impression Kat has is one of mutual respect. Oh, how she longs for a relationship like that, not some sordid fumble after work knowing that Colin will rarely, if ever, stay the night to welcome in the morning with her. Why has she been so foolish? As she thinks of her deceitful lover, Kat decides not to stoop to his level. She will let him know she won't be meeting him tonight for a cosy supper at his favourite bistro. She's about to text him when the man glances over in her direction. The inquisitive look from a pair of hazel eyes lasts no more than a few seconds, but as his attention returns to the woman at his side and they move on to the next exhibit, Kat takes a deep, shuddering breath.

As the couple work their way around the gallery she is unable to tear her eyes away. Everything about the man speaks of capable masculinity. His movements are easy yet controlled, reminding her of a panther, and the hushed conversations he has with his companion reveal a delightfully deep, warm voice. An air of confidence surrounds him and she can imagine him taking calculated risks whilst leading an adventurous life.

As her senses heighten, Kat's fingers begin to tingle, and she feels the blood start to fizz in her veins. A dazzling light suddenly falls upon him and as she glances up at the ceiling to find its source, she thinks she hears a seagull's cry and the snap of a sail caught by a gust of wind. And there's another distinct noise, too. *Wap, wap, wap.* What is that – rigging lines slapping against a mast? Kat shakes her head. She's always been accused of being ultra-sensitive and having an overactive imagination, and growing up she was constantly reprimanded for embellishing the facts. She'd learnt to keep her thoughts to herself. However, as her artistic skills developed and her imagination conjured up images that translated into her drawings and paintings, her tutors had despaired and questioned why she was unable to simply draw what was in front of her. She'd never understood and would look back at the subject she was tasked to paint and wonder why her teachers were unable to see the living, breathing scene as she could.

Dragging her eyes away from the man, with a shaking hand Kat responds to Colin's text.

No go tonight or any other night. Thinking of your family.

She hits 'send' and glances up again.

The atmosphere has returned to normal and no strange lights or unusual sounds invade the hushed space. Kat knows she should head back to work but decides to sit for a few minutes longer, absorbing the peace and serenity of the gallery.

The couple are about to exit the room, when suddenly the man turns and silently observes her sitting motionless on the bench, like a statue. Kat stops breathing, stilled by the depth of his gaze.

3

'Honestly, Tara, I had no idea!'

The general buzz of the wine bar is uplifting and life-affirming, despite Kat feeling weighed down by this latest calamity to arrive at her door. She refuses to let Colin's deception send her hurtling into depression. She knows only too well what that feels like, and the last time she'd arrived at that particular destination she'd made a promise to herself to *never* visit again.

'What an absolute sod.' Reaching across the table, Tara takes hold of Kat's hand. 'I'm so sorry you've been messed around, but you know it's not you. It's that philandering rogue who has the problem. Personally, I pity the wife.'

Kat nods her head slowly. 'I never suspected a thing. He gave me no cause to, apart from a general reluctance to stay over.' She gives a small, ironic laugh. 'I thought it was because he didn't like my *flat*!'

Tara squeezes Kat's fingers. 'Womanisers rarely give themselves away, but as charming as Colin is, I always suspected he was too good to be true . . . And now he's been found out.' Letting go of Kat's hand, Tara picks up her wine glass and takes a sip. 'That sister-in-law of his has done you one humungous favour.'

'I guess so, but it doesn't feel like it at the moment. However, I refuse to be brought to my knees.'

'That's the spirit!' Tara considers her friend. 'You know what you need? A change of scene. Let your hair down and have a bit of fun.'

'A change of something, that's for sure.' Kat pulls a grim face.

'Well, for an immediate fix, how about another bottle of this delectable Pinot Grigio Rosé? It's slipping down a treat.'

As her friend rises to her feet and heads towards the bar, Kat contemplatively swirls the pink wine around her glass. What an idiot she's been. Unsurprisingly, Colin hasn't responded to her text message – she suspects the coward has run home with his tail firmly between his legs. She wishes she could feel pity for his wife, but the stabbing pain in her heart only reminds her of her own loss. Refusing to let the feeling work its way up and strangle her, Kat considers her track record with men and wonders why she's so unsuccessful. Take Tara for instance – her best friend since primary school and now a badass marketing manager with a London advertising firm – she and her partner, father of her two young boys, manage to successfully juggle their careers and bring up their children.

Kat sighs. The big *four-oh* is only a couple of years away and what exactly has she got to show for it? Yes, she owns a flat, albeit mortgaged, has a great job as a commercial illustrator for an established publishing house and a varied circle of friends. But as far as romance is concerned, it's a disaster zone. It's not as if she hasn't had a number of 'suitors', as her father refers to the men that make it as far as introductions to her parents, but for whatever reasons, the relationships always fizzle out . . . or she's not particularly into her partners in the first place. It was only when Colin came along that she dared believe that maybe . . . just maybe . . . this relationship could go the distance. What an absolute fool! Kat's cheeks flush with emotion. He'd seemed everything she was looking for – good looking, successful, bright, amusing, great with her friends and, being six years her junior, a bit of a toy boy. Why had she not seen the blatant lie? OK, there was no telltale indentation of a wedding ring having been hastily removed from his finger, but foolishly she'd ignored the insistent niggles. He was *never* available at weekends. When she'd quizzed him about it he'd said the amount of time he spent with her during the week meant he had to work over the weekend. She'd chosen to believe it. But rarely had he stayed over, preferring to leave even if it was two in the morning. How could she have been so idiotically naïve? In denial probably . . .

'Here we go.' Tara places a bottle of wine in the centre of the table and hands Kat a menu. 'Shall we order? I'm starving.'

Fifteen minutes later, a waiter delivers plates of tapas to their table. Kat picks up a fork and spears a deep-fried calamari, dipping it into a bowl of garlic-and-lemon mayonnaise.

'What are you doing for Easter?' Tara asks, spooning grilled aubergine with garlic, parsley and feta onto her plate.

Kat chews and swallows the squid with difficulty. Blasted Colin! Not only has she lost him – not that she really ever had him – now she's lost her appetite, too.

'Well, now that *you-know-who* is off the menu, although I doubt he'd have been around much anyway . . .' Kat pulls a face, 'I'll probably visit my parents. Sandra and the girls are staying so it would be a chance to catch up with them.'

'How is your sister?' Tara asks, adding a generous handful of carrot, parmesan and chilli fries to her plate.

'Good. Thriving on being a doctor's wife in deepest, rural Suffolk.'

'And the girls. How old are they now?'

'Madeleine's ten. Georgina's coming up eight.' Kat spears another calamari. 'My parent's youngest daughter has done them proud.'

Tara contemplates her friend. 'Why don't you come to Salcombe with us? The boys love you and there's enough space in the cottage if you want to escape and have some quiet time, although I think that's the last thing you need at the moment.'

'That's kind of you, but I doubt Niles would want an ageing spinster tagging along.'

Putting down her fork, Tara fixes Kat with a stern expression. 'Will you stop doing that?'

Kat glances at her friend in surprise. 'What?'

'You *know* what! Putting yourself down at every opportunity. There's nothing wrong with you, Kat Maddox. It's simply that none of the men you've dated have deserved you. They're all idiots in my opinion, blind to what they've let slip through their fingers.'

Kat's throat constricts. Picking up her glass, she takes a sip of wine.

'And, anyway, men on the whole are overrated in my opinion,' Tara continues, stabbing at a ham croquette.

Kat laughs drily. 'Not your Niles, though.'

'He's a rare exception.'

'Let me think about it and I'll get back to you,' Kat says, teasing a garlic mushroom around her plate. 'Are you sure Niles wouldn't mind?'

'He would positively embrace it.' Tara grins at her friend. 'He loves a bit of intelligent company.'

Kat raises her eyebrows. 'He's got you for that.'

'These days our conversations tend to be about school timetables, homework and which one of us is ferrying the boys to football practice . . . or is it gymnastics? He'd *love* to discuss something else.'

'Well, if you're sure.'

'I'm sure! Now Kat. Tell me, are you going to chase that poor mushroom around your plate a fourth time or will you eat the damn thing?'

4

Kat comes to with a start, the details of the vivid dream still fresh in her mind. Her heart beats furiously against her ribcage and she lays a comforting hand on her chest, attempting to bring about a sense of calm. The dream seemed so real, tricking her into believing they are still together. Disorientated, she peers into the shadows of her darkened bedroom and checks the alarm clock. It's not long past three in the morning. She groans and covers her eyes with a hand. How can she prevent Colin infiltrating her mind when she's asleep? Not only has he rocked her world, knocking her confidence and self-esteem, but now he won't leave her alone during the small hours.

'It was *only* a dream, stupid,' she mutters. 'Get over it.'

But she doesn't feel stupid so much as inordinately sad.

Leaning over to the bedside table, Kat switches on the lamp and sits up. Scooping up the leaflet from her visit to Tate Britain, she opens it to the centre pages where several paintings by the Pre-Raphaelite Brotherhood are displayed. An image by Dante Gabriel Rossetti gets her full attention – a painting of a young woman with long, wavy Titian hair draped over one shoulder and mesmerising, emerald-green eyes. It's a portrait of a woman very much in love and her gaze, full of warmth, captures the feelings Kat experienced during her dream. As she recognises the model's emotions, a lump lodges in her throat and, without warning, a sob escapes from her lips.

'It's over,' she whispers. 'Accept it.'

Throwing back the covers, she clambers out of bed. It's

too early for the central heating to have kicked in and she shrugs on a dressing gown, tying the belt loosely around her waist as she makes her way to the small kitchen at the rear of the flat. Switching on the light, Kat crosses over to the fridge and takes out a carton of milk. Maybe a hot drink will help her sleep. She places a pan of milk on the hob and as she waits for it to come to a simmer, she refuses to allow more thoughts of duplicitous Colin to further derail her. Instead, she considers what she would like in her life. Certainly a man who actually has some substance as well as charm, someone cultured and respectful . . . All at once, a keen longing for something Kat has never encountered takes hold. Oh how she yearns to experience that in *real* life.

'Serves me right for visiting art galleries and those romantic Pre-Raphaelites,' she mutters.

All at once she recalls the man from the art gallery. Who *is* he? He'd gained her attention the minute she'd first spied him out of her office window. Something about him piques her interest.

Removing the saucepan from the heat, Kat reaches for a jar on the shelf. As she unscrews the lid she stills, the poignancy of her understanding stealing her breath. The man at the Pre-Raphaelite exhibition *was* beautiful to her, but with the millions of people in London it's unlikely their paths will ever cross again. There's no denying it, though . . . they had shared a moment . . . and now she's floundering under the certain knowledge she'll never be with him. Deep in thought, Kat pours the milk into a mug and stirs in a spoonful of honey.

Despite the hot drink, she knows sleep will evade her now, and wonders what to do to fill the hours before it's time to head for the office. As she enters the living room, Kat places the mug on a side table and settles into an armchair. Picking up the sketchpad on the coffee table, she selects a 2B pencil from her box of drawing tools and absentmindedly stares into the distance. Decision made! She starts to draw and the hours tick by. Kat is so absorbed in her work that she doesn't hear the dawn chorus or notice daybreak arrive in the London suburb she calls home. It's only when the occupants of the flat above stir and their footsteps sound across her ceiling that she looks up from what she's doing. The clock on the mantelpiece tells her it's almost eight.

Damn! Now she's going to be late for work.

She glances down at the sketchpad and frowns. It's filled with a number of illustrations she has absolutely no recollection of drawing. She scans the sketches. The first one is of a pair of securely chained and padlocked, wrought-iron gates set in a Gothic-style archway with a bell tower above. One eyebrow arcs as she recognises it as one of the entrances to Highgate Cemetery. The next is of a woman clutching a parasol and looking very seemly in her Victorian dress. Immediately Kat identifies her as the sitter in Dante's painting from the leaflet. Another depicts three, young Victorian men enjoying a picnic on the banks of a wide, sweeping river; the outlined impression of the domed tower of St Paul's Cathedral in the background giving away the setting as the River Thames. Scrutinising the figures, she realises she's drawn members of the Pre-Raphaelite Brotherhood. She pauses at the next illustration. Partly framed by unkempt, floppy locks, two mischievously twinkling eyes gaze out at her, and here they are again, only this time filled with desire and a promise of things to come. Colin! The next sketch is of her ex wearing a Victorian painting smock and a frown of concentration as he paints a canvas propped on an easel. His charisma leaps off the page and Kat gives a deep sigh. The mind is a wondrous and mysterious thing, but it has a penchant for playing wicked tricks. Obviously it doesn't do to visit a Pre-Raphaelite exhibition just as you break up with a cheating lover . . .

Noises from outside penetrate the quiet stillness of her front room and she hears someone whistling. In the distance a dog barks. Glancing at the clock again she sees it's now ten past. No time to dawdle. She has that illustration to complete for the children's book she's working on. Rising from the chair, Kat is about to close the sketchpad when curiosity gets the better of her. Was that the last of her drawings? She flips over the page and inhales sharply.

Recorded on the page is the man she saw in the art gallery. A beautiful smile lights up his face . . . but it's something else that steals her breath. As with her first impressions of him leading an altogether more abandoned existence, he stands in the bow of a boat. In the background are several yachts, peacefully moored in a wooded estuary, their tall masts reaching to the sky, and wheeling overhead are half-a-dozen seagulls. Although it's only a pencil sketch, she has captured the suggestion of strong sunlight highlighting the glorious planes of his masculine face.

5

'Kat?'

The man's voice sounds a long way off and she discounts it. She's flying somewhere high above the clouds, gazing down upon a beautiful wooded, river valley, its waters a deep shade of turquoise. Below her are softly billowing, pink-tinged cotton-wool clouds, and flocks of seagulls fly on invisible thermals above a town that spills down a hillside and hugs the river's edge. Someone sets off from the town's quay in a rowing boat, heading towards a handful of yachts moored in a hidden inlet. As she watches the oarsman's competent progress, something heavy lands on her shoulder. A seagull?

'Kat. Wake up!'

'Hmm . . .?' Reluctantly, she stirs. Lifting her head, she gazes bleary-eyed at her art director, Hugo.

'Late night?' he enquires.

Quickly, she sits up. 'Sorry. Must have drifted off.'

'How's the school-outing illustration coming along?'

'It's finished,' she replies, gathering her thoughts and sifting through the papers she'd been resting her head on. Extracting one, she presents it to her boss.

Hugo pulls up a chair, sits down and picks up the illustration. Silently, he studies it. Kat steals a sideways glance. His face gives nothing away and she looks back at the sheet of paper. Over the past week she's worked hard on the visual and believes she has accurately interpreted the author's story, but Hugo's silence is unnerving. He's usually so vocal. She sneaks another look.

Laying the illustration back on the desk, Hugo turns to face her.

'Is it OK?' she asks, uncertainly.

'It's more than OK, Kat.'

She lets out a long breath.

'As usual, you've more than fulfilled the brief. Thank you.'

She smiles.

'I wondered if you were free for a quick drink after work this evening?' he asks. 'There's something I want to discuss.'

In the six years she's worked at Bryanston Publishing, Hugo has always treated her with respect. His is the voice of reason, always there with a comforting comment and a reassuring smile when her disastrous personal life predictably staggers towards rock bottom, once again. However, although the department occasionally meets for drinks outside work, Hugo has never once suggested a rendezvous with just the two of them. Kat knows he has a long-standing partner, who's deputy head of an inner-city school. Is all well with them? Glancing at him now, she gives a small frown.

What does he want to discuss? She's never considered he'd be interested in her and she's not sure she wants their working relationship to change.

'Don't worry, Kat. It's nothing alarming.' He pats her arm.

'Give me strength!' Gemma exclaims, as she barges into the room and throws her handbag down on her desk. She looks across at Kat and Hugo. 'Can you believe it? My frigging flatmate has only gone and buggered off without paying the rent. He's cleared off without a word!'

Hugo glances at Kat.

'What the hell am I going to do? I can't afford to pay the *full* blimmin' rent!'

'I'm sure the agency will have contact details for him,' Hugo says reasonably.

Gemma blushes. 'They won't. I didn't tell them I had someone sharing.'

'Oh, I see.' Hugo raises his eyebrows.

'You've tried phoning him?' Kat asks.

'Yes. It goes straight to messages.'

'What about his friends? Can't you contact him via them?' Kat suggests.

'He didn't have many. I mean, he never brought any back to the flat. Sod it! What am I going to do?'

Grimacing at Kat, Hugo rises to his feet. 'I'll leave you to it.'

She nods.

'It'll be OK, Gemma,' he says, making his way to the door. 'Deep breaths, and tackle it a bite at a time.'

Planting her elbows on the desk, Gemma groans and holds her head in her hands.

'Can anyone bail you out this month, at least until you find another flatmate?' Kat asks.

Gemma turns towards her with a haunted look on her face. 'I'm so sick of having to find new flatmates. I tell you, Kat, as much as I love living there, I'm seriously considering finding somewhere I can afford on my own.'

Kat contemplates her colleague. Here they all are, trying to make a life for themselves in the capital and earn enough money to pay their way, but it seems they're only a pay cheque away from an ever-spiralling descent into catastrophe. London is *so* expensive, especially if you want to do more than simply exist.

'Do you think HR would agree to a loan?' Gemma muses. 'Just to tide me over.'

Kat purses her lips. 'No harm in asking.'

The girl lets out a loud sigh. 'I guess there's no time like the present.' Rising to her feet, she marches from the room.

Kat glances back at her illustration on the desk. It's full of movement. Animals dressed in shorts and summer dresses climb aboard a school bus as their teacher, Mr Bear, ticks off names on a clipboard in his hand. Cheeky young rabbits and a group of meerkats hang out of the windows, calling to their classmates standing in line and waiting to board. She's pleased with the way it's turned out and relieved it has Hugo's seal of approval. The author has woven a delightful story and Kat's various line drawings perfectly complement the tale.

Picking up her mobile, she checks the screen. Still no text from Colin. What did she expect?

Kat glances at Hugo standing at the bar ordering drinks. This feels downright weird! Just by accepting his invitation to drinks after work, the dynamics of their professional relationship have been thrown into confusion. What does he want to talk to her about? He's not going to tell her the company plan to lay her off, is he? If so, she will be in the same situation as Gemma. As her anxiety mounts, Kat tells herself to get a grip.

A few minutes later Hugo returns. 'Bit of a bun fight up there,' he says, handing her a glass. 'Cheers!'

Perhaps she shouldn't have ordered a gin and tonic so early in the evening, but for some reason she feels on edge and in need of Dutch courage. She takes a large mouthful.

'So, Kat, we never get a chance to chat at work. How are things?'

Hastily, she swallows.

'OK, I suppose,' she says, unable to meet his gaze.

Hugo considers her over the rim of his beer glass. 'OK, you suppose. What does that mean?'

'Well, you know . . .'

He shakes his head. 'Not really.'

She looks up at him, heart thumping; her mind in overdrive. But there's nothing to get worked up about. Sitting opposite her is the kind, supportive man she's come to know over the years. Perhaps she's misjudged his reason for suggesting they meet after work and she's not going to be let go after all.

She sighs. 'I guess life is OK . . . apart from being single *again*.'

'Don't worry about that, Kat. As I said, somewhere out there . . .'

She gives a weak smile, wishing she could share his conviction.

'How about work? Are you happy?'

Irrational panic takes hold. 'Very,' she says.

'That's good to hear.' Hugo takes a sip of beer. 'But have you ever considered a change of scene?'

She stares at him wide-eyed. He *is* going to dismiss her.

'No.'

Why is she answering in monosyllables? She never normally has difficulty speaking to him; Hugo is easy to talk to.

'You know, Kat, life should be exciting and experimental, especially during our younger years. Don't misunderstand me, I totally enjoy working with you – your ideas are fresh and your work is exemplary – but I worry about you. Over the years I've listened to you and Gemma talking about your various romances . . .'

Kat's eyebrows rise.

He gives a sheepish grin. 'It's difficult not to hear conversations over those ridiculous screens that *the powers that be* think are a good idea in the office. I can understand Gemma's messy love life – she changes her mind with the wind – but you . . .' he gazes at her with affection. 'You deserve so much more.'

Kat stares at him, at a loss for words.

'I have a proposal for you.'

Dread strikes again.

What is the matter with her? Why is she so on edge?

'I have a cousin who lives in America,' Hugo continues. 'She's Professor of History at Harvard and is currently writing a book about the landed gentry of Britain through the ages, concentrating on those that inhabited the West Country. She wants the text interspersed with images but she's not keen on photographs. I suggested illustrations and she asked if I knew anyone suitable.' Hugo fixes Kat with an intense gaze. 'I recommended you.'

Kat exhales, only then realising she'd been holding her breath.

So that's what this is about! Why does her imagination always run away with her and cause unnecessary alarm?

'That's thoughtful of you, Hugo.'

He smiles. 'Stella's book is a non-fictional account of the shenanigans nobility indulged in to get what they wanted and achieve positions of power. Your sketches have the lightest of touch, full of romantic charm, and I believe they would not only offset the stark reality of the subject matter but also complement the history. I hope you don't mind, but I took the liberty of sending her a couple of books from the flower series you illustrated last year, as they also include a number of drawings of historic houses.'

Kat gives a small laugh. 'Ah, yes, those flower illustrations. That sure was a steep learning curve for someone who doesn't even own a garden! But at least I can now identify a good number of wildflowers and coastal plants, although I can't see what use I will ever put that to.'

She'd enjoyed that particular assignment, adding charming images of various properties in the background of her flower illustrations, but it was the handsome, period house with its granite quoins and mullioned windows that had intrigued her and monopolised her drawings; in fact, she'd had to make a concerted effort to include other styles of houses. It wasn't a property she knew, it was simply one conjured from the deep recesses of her imagination.

Kat takes another sip of gin. 'How many illustrations does your cousin want, and what's the deadline?'

Even though she has plenty of spare time in the

evenings – especially now with Colin's departure from her life – the thought of committing to months of additional work fills her with dismay.

'If you're interested, I'll set up a Zoom meeting for you to discuss all that.' Hugo takes a swig of beer. 'Stella wants whoever takes on the assignment to visit the sites and produce the works *in situ*.'

Kat frowns. 'How could I do that, working full-time?'

'Stella owns a property in Fowey,' Hugo replies. 'She and her family use it when they come over to the UK. She says that whoever undertakes the work can stay there for the duration of the assignment, free of charge. She envisages it will be an approximate six-month contract.' He watches her expression closely. 'What do you think?'

Kat's mind goes into a tailspin. She can't deny it, the idea interests her. What Hugo has suggested is an opening door, and the fresh breeze blowing through it is intoxicating. But how can she accept the offer? She has a mortgage to pay and a job to hold down.

'It's tempting, but I don't see how I can take six months off and still expect to be employed by Bryanston Publishing at the end of it.' Kat bites her lip.

Hugo smiles. 'You could always suggest taking an unpaid sabbatical. Stella will pay well for your services.' He takes another swig of beer. 'Think about it, Kat. I'm a fair few years older than you and, take it from me, it's good to take risks, shake it up a bit and experience new things. Otherwise, if we're not careful, life has a nasty little habit of passing us by.'

Swirling ice cubes around her glass, Kat watches as the slice of lemon succumbs to the whirlpool. Is that what she should do? Swim away from the safety of the shore, catch the current and allow herself to drift, not knowing where she may end up? A ripple of excitement stirs deep in her belly. What Hugo says is true – life does have a habit of rushing by. As she considers her life ten years before, she realises with shock that her situation then wasn't so dissimilar to the one she finds herself in now.

'You've given me a lot to consider. Let me think it over.'

'Of course. It's not something to make a snap decision on.'

6

'OK, boys, grab these and follow your father.' Tara extracts a couple of canvas bags from the boot of the car and holds them out to her sons.

Kat watches as Tyler, the younger of the two, struggles up the path. The over-filled bag bangs against his legs and half-swinging, half-dragging it, he refuses to let the holdall get the better of him. Kat smiles. He's only six but he's not going to let eight year old Gulliver outdo him.

Tara pulls out Kat's bag and passes it to her. 'Fancy a cuppa?'

'Lovely. Breakfast seems a long time ago.' Grabbing hold of the handles, Kat takes the bag from her friend and turns to face the river. Under a sun riding high in the sky, the clear blue waters of the Kingsbridge Estuary glitter enticingly, beautifully offsetting the whitewashed cottages that line the street. She watches as a yacht motors through the water on its way to the sea, its crew preparing to unfurl the sails.

Tara gathers up the remaining contents of the boot and glances at her friend. She follows her gaze. 'Doesn't that look exhilarating? I wish we sailed, but we can always hire a dinghy and explore the coves and beaches while we're here.'

'It does look fun,' Kat agrees.

She watches the yacht a while longer before turning and following Tara up the path towards the cottage. As they enter its cool hallway, the boys bound down the stairs and land heavily at the bottom.

'Mum, there's an enormous spider in our bedroom,' says Tyler, his eyes round with apprehension.

'I tried to catch it,' says Gulliver, 'but it went under the bed!'

'Not to worry, I'm sure your dad can sort it. Now who wants a drink of orange?'

'Me!' both boys cry.

Tara carries a cool box filled with provisions towards the kitchen and calls over her shoulder to Kat. 'Your bedroom is the second door on the left at the top of the stairs. The bathroom is immediately opposite. I'll make a pot of tea while you unpack and settle in.'

Ascending the stairs, Kat walks to the room allocated to her for the duration of the Easter break. It's usually Gulliver's bedroom, but he's sharing with Tyler while she stays. Pushing open the pine door, she enters and glances around, a smile playing on her lips. Tara has given the room a coastal theme perfectly in keeping with the property's location. The pale-blue chalk walls remind her of kind summer skies, and the cream-coloured cotton curtains are adorned with sailboats, lifebuoys and seagulls, reflecting the area. The furniture is minimal: a stripped-pine wardrobe, matching chest of drawers and a white, cast-iron single bed. An unfussy but comfortable room; after all, what more does one need when on holiday?

Placing her bag on the bed, Kat walks to the window and opens it. The room is situated at the side of the house with the neighbouring property set back a few feet. From here, over rooftops, is an oblique view of the mouth of the river where a number of motorboats and yachts mingle, either heading out for an early evening sail or returning to Salcombe. Tara and Niles had purchased the cottage the previous year, as they wanted to give the boys an alternative life to living in London, and since then, the family has spent as much time as possible in their *home away from home*. As Kat gazes at the view, breathing in the fresh sea air, she can understand why.

Startled by a raucous cry, she watches as a large seagull swoops past the neighbouring property and alights on the slate roof of a cottage on the opposite side of the street. Settling on the ridge tiles, the gull's beady eyes scan the estuary.

'Mum says tea's in the garden,' Gulliver suddenly announces from the doorway.

Kat turns and smiles at the blond-haired, blue-eyed boy. 'Sorry you've had to give up your room for me, Gul.'

The boy shrugs. 'It's OK. I don't mind sharing, although Tyler's a wuss with spiders.'

'Well, at least he has his big brother to fend them off.'

'Yeah. Or put them in his bed!' He grins.

Kat chuckles and glances at her bag. She hasn't unpacked yet, but it can wait. 'Come on. Show me the way.'

As Kat follows Gulliver downstairs, the boy excitedly explains what his parents have planned for them over the following four days. Crossing the kitchen and out of the back door, they enter a charming, gravelled, walled garden surrounded by flowerbed borders filled with an array of shrubs. Butterflies and bees flit from one open bloom to the next and at the far end, draping its foliage over the garden wall, is a glorious magnolia in bloom. It's not a large area but it's private, and in the centre is a white wrought-iron patio table, around which Tara, Niles and Tyler sit.

'I thought we all deserved a cream tea after that long journey,' Tara says, pouring tea from a white china teapot into cups. 'But remember, we must put the cream on first!'

'Why, Mummy?' asks Tyler.

'Because we're in Devon. If we were in Cornwall it would be jam first, then cream.'

The boy pulls a bemused face.

'I know, Tyler, it's all very odd,' comments Niles, helping himself to a fat scone.

'Does anyone know the origin of the cream tea?' Kat asks.

'Yes!' Niles dips his knife into a large pot of clotted cream. 'It originated in the eleventh century at Tavistock Abbey with the tradition of eating bread with cream and jam.'

'I wonder why the Cornish dispute the way it's eaten?' Kat says, accepting the cup Tara offers.

'No idea, but if you think about it, cream is like butter and you wouldn't put butter on top of jam,' Niles responds. 'There's also an argument that it originates from when jam was expensive, so you'd just have a small amount on top.'

'It stops cream going up your nose,' pipes up Gulliver.

Tyler giggles.

'And if you're sharing a cream tea with a Cornishman, although that's highly unlikely, you get first dibs on the cream.' Niles winks at his sons, before concluding, 'It's a debate that has run for millennia, but I always think it's better to simply enjoy it, however it's served.'

'Probably just as well for our waistlines that we're only here for four days,' comments Tara drily.

7

Lying on a towel propped on her elbows, Kat watches the boys and their father messing about in the water, as Niles teaches Gulliver to dive from his cupped hands, while Tyler doggy-paddles around them. It's a glorious day and the midday sun beats down from a cloudless sky. As ripples reach the shoreline, Kat wiggles her toes in the pristine golden sands of South Devon and a gentle breeze teases tendrils of hair from her loose topknot. It's peaceful here, in one of the less-visited sandy coves, which they have mainly to themselves and is only a stone's throw from East Portlemouth beach.

'This is bliss,' Kat murmurs. 'Why don't I do it more often?'

'Exactly! Why don't you?' asks Tara beside her, shaking open a tartan rug and spreading it out on the sand. 'As you know, you're welcome to use the cottage whenever you want, and if your visit coincides with one of ours then Gul can always shack up with Tyler.'

'Thanks. That's so generous of you.'

Tara makes a dismissive sound in the back of her throat. 'Not generous, Kat, you're my dearest friend. Do you remember our pact back in the day?'

'Of course, how could I forget?' Shielding her eyes, Kat glances at Tara. 'It was sealed in blood!' she says, in a piratical voice.

Tara laughs. 'What *were* we thinking using that rusty old penknife? It's lucky we didn't get tetanus! But as we promised each other then, we will always share our good fortune.'

Kat considers her high-flying friend. 'I'm just sorry I haven't had much good fortune to share over the years.'

'Good fortune comes and goes,' Tara says, producing a bowl of tomatoes from the cool box and placing it on the rug. 'It ebbs and flows like the tide. But as long as we have each other's backs we'll be OK.'

Kat smiles and pushes herself up to a sitting position. 'Here, let me help.'

Tara passes over a knife and a baguette, still vaguely warm. They'd bought it that morning fresh from the bakers on their way to the passenger ferry and their day at Small's Cove. As Kat cuts the bread into manageable pieces, she glances across the waters of Salcombe Harbour to the pretty resort town on the opposite bank.

All of a sudden, Tyler rushes up the beach. Shaking himself like a dog, he covers Kat in droplets of cold water.

'Oi!' Tara admonishes. 'Careful of Kat!'

'Sorry.' The boy pulls an apologetic face.

'Skin's waterproof, Tyler. I suspect I'll survive.' Kat smiles at him.

'I'm starving!' he announces, plonking down on the rug beside her.

'You were doing well out there,' she says.

The young boy beams. 'I only have to put my feet down every six paddles now.'

'Good to hear those expensive swimming lessons are finally paying off,' Tara says wryly, as she hands her youngest son some French bread filled with ham and pickle.

'Soon you'll be treading water! Then you won't have to put your feet down at all,' Kat encourages.

Tyler frowns. 'Treading water?'

'Yes. It's a way of keeping afloat when you're out of your depth.'

The boy takes a bite of his baguette. 'Auntie Kat,' he says, cocking his head and looking up at her. 'Why don't you have any children?'

She glances over at Tara, who raises her eyebrows and mouths, '*Sorry*'.

'I don't know, Tyler. But you know what?'

The boy shakes his head.

'If I ever do have children I would want them to be exactly like you and your brother.'

As Tyler grins at this, Kat sees Gulliver and his dad approach up the beach.

'Brrr . . . That was a bit fresh!' Niles exclaims, as he approaches. 'Mind you, plunging your body into ice-cold water is apparently good for you.' Taking the towel Tara hands to him, he starts vigorously rubbing his skin.

Gulliver sits down on the rug next to his brother. 'What's for fillings, Mum?' he says, grabbing a piece of baguette.

'Ham, pickle, tomatoes, Cheddar and coleslaw. Help yourself.'

Picking up a knife, Gulliver haphazardly cuts a thick slice of cheese.

A sailing dinghy tacks across the river and a man's instructions carry clearly on the breeze. Kat watches as the occupants dodge the sail and scramble to the other side of the boat.

'Can we have sailing lessons?' Gulliver asks.

'Don't see why not,' replies Niles. 'We'll check it out on the way back.'

'Cool!' Gulliver grins broadly.

Rifling through the cool box, Niles produces a bottle of wine. 'Want to wet your whistle, ladies?'

'An excellent idea,' Tara says.

Kat agrees.

The afternoon passes in easy companionship with the boys managing to entice Kat and Tara into the cold waters of Salcombe Harbour. It's too early in the season for the sea to have warmed up, but once in – after energetically swimming from one side of the cove to the other – Tara agrees with Kat that it's passable. For a while they play water polo, and

Gulliver demonstrates how well he can now dive as he makes impossible moves to outmanoeuvre his younger brother and prevent him from getting the ball.

The sun arcs across the sky and as the day nudges towards late afternoon, dusky shadows elongate and creep across the sand. As the family tidy away the remains of the picnic and roll up rugs and towels, a sudden billowing sound makes Kat's scalp tingle. Wind catching a sail. Not unexpected in this location but something about it gives her a keen sense of déjà vu. Straightening up, she turns in the direction of the noise. Half a dozen seagulls circle high above the mast of an elegant, dark-blue-hulled yacht gliding by towards Salcombe.

Shielding her eyes and standing with feet apart, she watches.

'She's a beauty,' comments Niles.

Kat nods, but it's not the boat itself that has her attention. The figure of a man standing at the helm seems familiar. As the yacht heads into a gust of northerly wind, his dark hair blows back and sunlight accentuates the glorious planes of his masculine face.

Surely it can't be?

The tingle spreads to the rest of Kat's body, and she watches transfixed, only half-listening to Niles and Tara discussing the desirability of the yacht passing by.

It is him!

Even though it was only a pencil sketch, she captured his features perfectly.

Who is he?

Tearing her eyes away from the man, she scans the boat. Three other people are on deck; a dark-haired woman and a teenage boy and girl.

Who are they? And who was the woman she'd seen him with at Tate Britain?

Suddenly Kat remembers to inhale.

8

Uplifting birdsong fills the air and the sun casts intricate, dappled patterns across the walled garden as it filters through the branches and blooms of the magnolia. Having enjoyed an *al fresco* breakfast, Kat nurses a cup of coffee as Tara reads the local newspaper.

'We're off now,' announces Niles from the open French doors. 'See you ladies later.'

His wife glances up. 'What time do you expect to be back?'

'Doubt it'll be much before three.'

'OK. See you then.'

Standing behind his dad, Gulliver waves.

From inside the kitchen, Tyler calls out, 'Bye, Mum. Bye, Auntie Kat.'

'Have fun!' responds Kat, as Niles and his sons disappear inside the cottage

'Right. I fancy some good old-fashioned girl time,' Tara says, folding the newspaper and placing it on the patio table. 'What do you say to us checking out the shops? I've got my eye on a lovely top I saw in Crew Clothing's window. Thought it would go perfectly with my red trousers.'

Kat smiles. As far back as she can recall Tara has been into clothes. 'Sure, and then what about lunch at The Ferry Inn?'

'That's a great idea. If we get there early enough we can grab a table on the terrace. We might even catch a glimpse of the boys and Niles messing about in the dinghy.'

Quickly finishing her coffee, Kat rises from the table. 'I'll get my purse and then we can hit the town!'

* * *

Two hours later, having deposited their purchases back at the cottage, Kat and Tara walk along Cliff Road towards The Ferry Inn. Salcombe is awash with Easter tourists and the shopping expedition has proved a bit of a trial, although Tara successfully purchased the coveted designer top. Turning down a flight of steep steps, they approach the entrance to the pub.

'Love this place,' comments Tara. 'They put on great events. You should come down for New Year's Eve. It's a riot!' She pushes open the door.

The pub is already busy and a cacophony of chatter assaults them as they make their way over to the bar.

'Don't suppose there's a free table on the terrace for lunch?' Tara asks a barman.

'For how many?'

'Just two very slim, attractive women,' Tara responds with a flirty smile.

The young man grins. 'I think you're in luck. Not many people have filtered out there yet. If you get your orders in quick I'm sure we can squeeze you in.'

Kat and Tara do as advised and as soon as their drinks are poured, they carry the glasses out to the terrace. The barman was right; it is surprisingly empty, considering the throng of people inside. Weaving their way through a small cluster of holidaymakers enjoying the surprisingly pleasant weather, they approach an empty wooden table in the far corner next to the water.

'Well, isn't this nice?' Tara says, hooking a leg over the fixed bench and sitting down.

'Certainly is!' Kat sits opposite and gazes out at the sandy beaches on the other side of the estuary. 'It's a beautiful area.'

'You can see the attraction, can't you? As you know, we take any opportunity to escape the confines of the city.'

The river is deep blue and crystal clear and a holiday atmosphere lingers in the air. Kat's gaze shifts to the nearby Jubilee Ferry Pier, where an open-topped, clinker-built motorboat waits patiently for people to board. They'd used its service yesterday to cross over to Small's Cove. Her mind strays to her conversation with Hugo about his cousin, Stella.

Fowey is only sixty or so miles further along the south coast. Maybe this is what it's like there. How lovely to live in such a location . . .

Perhaps she *should* accept Stella's offer?

'Who ordered the homemade black bean chilli?' asks a waiter, suddenly arriving at their table.

'That would be me,' Tara says with a smile.

He places the bowl in front of her. 'So yours must be the Moroccan falafel burger,' the young man says to Kat.

She nods.

'Wow! My powers of deduction never fail to amaze me!' He grins and passes over the plate. 'Is there anything else you two ladies require?'

'All good here,' says Tara.

'Just shout if you need anything,' he says, with a flirtatious sparkle in his eyes.

Tara's gaze follows the waiter as he makes his way back to the pub. Kat raises an eyebrow.

'What? It's only window shopping!' Tara says, giving her an impish grin.

Kat laughs. 'OK, window shopper, I believe you.' Picking up a chip, she pops it into her mouth.

'So,' Tara says, loading her fork with chilli. 'Tell me about this opportunity you've been presented with.'

Still unsure, Kat takes a deep breath. 'My boss's cousin, Stella, is a Professor of History at Harvard. She's writing a book about the West Country's landed gentry through the ages and wants accompanying images to go with the text. Hugo suggested I produce the illustrations.'

'Sounds good so far,' says Tara.

Taking a bite of falafel burger, Kat mulls over the implications of accepting the job. 'It would mean taking a six-month sabbatical, probably unpaid, but the fee more than compensates for that.'

'So, what's stopping you?'
'She wants me to draw the venues *in situ*.'
'Six months away from London!' Tara states. 'I ask again . . . what's stopping you?'

Kat gazes across the table at her friend. She's always been blessed with the gift of confidence. But, then, so has Kat, mostly. It's only her lousy romantic track record that has knocked her off balance and made her second guess everything, and discovering Colin's ultimate deception hasn't helped. She's still reeling from that revelation.

'I know this next piece of information will make you think I'm nuts not to jump at the chance.'

'Go on,' Tara encourages.

'Stella has a house in Fowey. She says I can stay there while I complete the assignment.'

'Hmm . . . What's that going to cost? Fowey's not cheap.'

'Nothing. It's part of the deal.'

Putting down her fork, Tara sits up straight and stares at her friend. 'Yep, you're right. Absolutely nuts.'

Kat sighs. 'But what do I do with my flat? Mothball it for six months?'

'I'll keep an eye on it for you. Or you could rent it out and earn some additional dosh.'

Yes, she could do that.

'Let's face it,' continues Tara, 'what's keeping you in London? That fella you've just extricated yourself from isn't going to suddenly grow a backbone.'

Kat pulls a face. 'I've yet to speak to HR but other colleagues have taken sabbaticals and gone off travelling for a year. As employers, Bryanston Publishing is pretty enlightened.'

'Probably why you've been so loyal to them for the past six years,' Tara says. Suddenly her voice takes on a serious edge. 'Listen, Kat. A change is as good as a rest, and you have no idea what doors may open from this job.'

Kat nods. 'I can't deny it's kind of tempting. Hugo says

it's good to take risks and experience new things, otherwise life has a habit of passing you by.'

'Your boss sounds very wise.'

'He's an old soul.'

'Then you should seriously consider what he suggests,' Tara advises. '*Old souls* have been around the block a few times and they know a thing or two.'

9

It's pleasant sitting out in the sunshine, cocooned by the general hubbub of fellow diners and the hypnotic noise of water lapping against the wall of the riverside terrace. Neither Kat nor Tara is in a hurry to bring their ladies' lunch to an end and they prolong the occasion by ordering desserts and coffee.

From out of the corner of her eye, Kat notices several people enter through the gate that accesses the pier for the ferry. Immediately, her attention snaps to the person at the rear of the group. As yesterday, he looks relaxed and at ease, dressed in light-coloured chinos and an indigo-blue T-shirt that shows off his tanned, muscular arms to perfection.

What are the chances of that? London AND Salcombe!

Amongst his party are the dark-haired woman and the teenagers who were with him on the yacht. The woman is slim, attractive and classy, and as she turns to say something to him, Kat notices the man lightly catch hold of her elbow.

Is this his family? Who, then, was the woman at Tate Britain?

With his swarthy looks, Kat wouldn't put it past him being one of those men with a woman in every port . . .

As much as she tries, she finds it impossible to tear her gaze away from the small gathering.

'What's grabbed your attention, Kat? I've been talking to you for the past five minutes!' Tara swivels in her seat and follows her friend's gaze. 'They look like the yachting type. No doubt they have some incredible craft moored in the estuary and are probably just stopping off for a bite to eat and a lazy afternoon before sailing off into the sunset.'

'We saw them sailing by yesterday . . . from Small's Cove.'
'Not that beautiful yacht?'
'Yes. The dark-haired guy in the blue T-shirt was on board, as was the woman beside him and those two teenagers.'

Tara studies the group with interest.

'I've seen him before,' Kat says quietly.

Tara turns back to her friend. 'You mean before yesterday?'

Kat nods. 'In London.'

'Well . . . London folk do have a habit of migrating to the South Hams!'

'I've seen him twice before, in fact,' Kat continues.

Why does her voice sound so far away?

Tara's eyes widen. 'Well, he's memorable, that's for sure. Where did you see him?'

Kat sighs. 'I first spotted him from my office window, when I was having that awful conversation with Colin's sister-in-law. I happened to glance out at the street and he was hailing a taxi. Then, incredibly, when I visited Tate Britain that lunchtime, he was *there* . . .' She colours at the memory. 'With a woman. No one in this group, though.'

'Goodness! That's kind of coincidental.' Tara chuckles. 'So tell me, who's stalking whom?'

Kat snorts.

'One indulgent Eton mess,' the young waiter announces as he arrives at their table. 'And one delicious chocolate torte with ice cream.'

'Thanks.' Tara smiles beguilingly. 'Place them anywhere you like. We're sharing.'

'Very cosy,' he remarks. 'Would you like coffee now or after?'

Tara glances at Kat. 'With?'

Kat nods.

'Right you are. At your service.'

Once again, Tara's gaze follows the young man as he makes his way through the tables towards the pub.

'Tara, you're incorrigible!'

'*Puh-lease* . . . Cut this old shackled woman some slack! It's not often I have the chance to revisit my former self.'

Kat laughs, but her laughter peters out as the man's party heads towards the table with the open sunshade next to theirs. As the group approach, their easy banter reaches her ears. It's obvious they're all old friends, although she's surprised to see the attractive, dark-haired woman and the teenagers sit at the opposite end of the table to the man.

'Kat . . .' Tara's voice is a harsh whisper.

'Hmm . . .' She half-turns back to her friend.

'You're staring!'

Kat shakes her head, as if trying to free herself of some enchantment. Picking up a spoon, she plunges it into the Eton Mess and forces herself to ignore the neighbouring party. In compensation, however, her hearing heightens and she listens to the man's deep, mellow voice as he joshes with the others around the table. It doesn't surprise her that he displays a keen intellect – witty without being sharp – and the sound of his laughter is as delicious as the desserts she shares with Tara. Oh, how she wishes she could meet someone like him . . .

The young waiter is at their table again, holding aloft a tray. 'Two coffees with cream.'

Rising to her feet, Kat indicates to Tara she's going inside to the ladies' loos. As she passes the man's table, she avoids looking in his direction and keeps her eyes on the building in front of her, but a wry smile lifts the corners of her mouth as she scuttles by. Once safely inside, Kat makes her way to the washroom and stares in the mirror. She hardly recognises herself. Strange emotions besiege her and her cheeks are flushed. Running the cold tap, she splashes water onto her face before, once again, meeting her eyes in the mirror.

He's just a good-looking man, who she's happened to come across a few times. *Enjoy it for what it is!*

But that little niggle insistently taps on her shoulder.

You may never see him again . . .

'And so be it,' she says firmly to her reflection.

Straightening up, she takes a deep breath and heads towards the door.

Stepping back out into the bright, afternoon sunshine, Kat walks purposefully across the terrace towards Tara in the far corner. She smiles to herself when she sees that her friend is chatting with the young waiter again. Tara is popular – there's a reason she's one badass marketing manager – and she connects with people from all walks of life, steadily increasing her network. Maybe Kat should take a leaf out of her book.

As she passes the man's table again, Kat can't help but notice a woman who was not with the group earlier now sitting beside him, his arm casually around her shoulders. Rejoining Tara, she sits down, and the young waiter takes a step away from the table.

'I'd better get back to work, now that your friend's back.' He smiles at Tara and nods to Kat.

'What an interesting lad,' says Tara. 'He's just returned from a year-long trip around the world. Doesn't have a penny to his name but says his wealth far exceeds that.'

'Very philosophical.'

'True, though. Life experience can't be measured in pound signs.'

'OK, Tara. I get the message.'

'At last!' Tara exclaims, clapping her hands together.

At that very moment Kat glances over at the neighbouring table and finds the man looking directly at her. He stares for a long moment, a small frown creasing his brow, and then suddenly surprise registers. Should she acknowledge his reaction, smile as if they know each other, or say a cheery '*Hi*'?

Dropping her gaze, she turns away.

Tara checks her watch. 'Well, as much as this has been an absolute dream, it's fast coming to that time when the boys will be home.' She glances at Kat and then over at the adjacent table. 'Goodness! Oh, to have someone look at me like that! How deliciously sexy.'

Looking up at her friend, Kat follows her gaze.

The man's arm is still draped around the woman's shoulder, but he is also still staring at Kat, this time with a new intensity, as if he can't quite believe what he sees and is unable to avert his eyes. Once again, as at Tate Britain, Kat feels a calm, delicious stillness wrap around her, brought on by the weight of his deeply penetrating gaze.

10

'Here you go, Tyler.' Niles holds out a fishing net to his son. 'Hang on to this while I sort out the crab lines.'

Tyler places the bucket on the ground that he and his brother filled earlier with seawater, pebbles and seaweed, and takes the net from his dad.

'That's a good temporary home for the crabs,' says Kat, peering over the top.

The young boy smiles.

All too soon, the final day of the Easter break has arrived and having spent an enjoyable morning kayaking around the coves, they are now at Victoria Quay for a spot of crabbing. Kat looks along the harbour wall at the line of children and adults with the same idea and sees Tara and her eldest son approaching.

'Pooh, this stinks!' exclaims Gulliver, holding out a bag at arm's length.

'We asked the fishmonger for stinky bait,' Tara explains with a laugh.

'What did he give you?' Kat asks.

'Pongy sardines and sludgy mackerel heads,' Gulliver says with glee.

'Yuck!' cries Tyler.

'Particularly odious-smelling bait is like ice cream to crabs!' says Niles. 'They have an incredible sense of smell and detect odours via their antennae.'

Kat smiles at the boys' enraptured faces as they listen attentively.

'Good, it's an incoming tide,' Niles continues, observing

the river. 'Crabs like to hide in the mud on the ebbing tide and it's reckoned they're more active during spring tides.'

'Three guesses how Niles spent his childhood!' Tara teases, winking at Kat.

'What's a spring tide?' asks Tyler.

'A tide that occurs just after a new or full moon, when there's the greatest difference between high and low water,' his dad explains.

'Why does it do that?' the boy asks.

His parents' eyes meet. Explaining the complexities of gravitational forces to a six-year-old would no doubt confuse the lad and more than likely result in further questions, which could possibly go on for hours.

'The tides are affected by the moon, son,' Niles says. Diverting the boy's attention, he adds, 'Come on, Tyler. Let's get these lines baited up. You and Gul put some fish scraps in the bags and then we can tie them on.'

Kat turns to gaze out over the harbour, enjoying the warmth of the afternoon sun on her face. It's perfect weather for their last day in Salcombe. The river is alive with activity. Yachts, catamarans, motorboats, kayaks and paddle boards jostle for space on the water, and a number of dinghies bob alongside the pontoon as they react to the wake of a passing speedboat. How she will miss this when she's back in her flat. The only *jostling* she'll be doing in London is with fellow commuters on the Tube as she navigates her way to and from the office.

'Penny for them,' Tara says, slipping an arm around her friend's waist.

Kat pulls a resigned face. 'Oh, just contemplating the daily grind.'

'Hey, don't go depressing yourself.' Tara gives her a squeeze. 'Anyway, don't forget you hold a "get-out-of-jail-free" card.'

It's true, she does . . . If she's bold enough to use it.

Turning her head, Kat spots the elegant dark-blue-hulled yacht moored in the deeper channel along with several others. It really is a stunning boat, possibly fifty feet long. As she scans the vessel, appreciating its beauty, she notices movement on board. A woman emerges from below deck, closely followed by the dark-haired man. At this distance she can't see who his companion is, but she has the same brown hair as the woman who had joined him late at The Ferry Inn. Kat watches as they climb down a ladder into a RIB sitting quietly alongside in the water.

Such a different way of life!

As she compares it to her own, suddenly Kat feels claustrophobic.

'Is that your man again?' Tara asks, as she watches the tender skimming across the water towards the quay.

Kat snorts. 'He's not *my* man, Tara! But, yes, it's him. Anyway, I've given up men.'

Tara gives her a disbelieving look.

'I have,' Kat says defensively. 'I've decided to embrace the future free from the encumbrance of the opposite sex.'

'If you say so,' Tara says, humouring her friend.

'I do.'

'Dad, something's tugging my line!' Tyler calls out anxiously.

'Slowly draw the bait bag to the surface and see if any crabs have hitched a ride with their pincers,' Niles says. 'That's good, Tyler. Not too fast.'

'I can see three,' Gulliver says, glancing over from where he's sitting, with his legs and line dangling over the harbour wall.

'Steadily land your haul,' Niles instructs his youngest son, 'and then use the catch net to transfer them to the bucket.'

As Tyler draws in his line, one of the crabs suddenly releases its grip and plops back into the river.

'I've lost one!' the boy wails.

'Don't be disheartened, Tyler. It's all part of the fun,' his mother encourages.

As soon as the bait bag is brought onto the quay, Niles takes the line.

'Here you go.' Tara hands her son the fishing net.

Carefully, the young boy lowers the bait bag into the net and once the crabs are safely deposited in their temporary home, he kneels and peers through the sides of the see-through bucket.

'There's a tiny one and a big one. Is it a dad and his son?' he asks enthusiastically.

Kat smiles.

'It could be,' says Tara, studying his catch.

'Hey, I've got something, too!' shouts Gulliver, drawing his line up the side of the harbour wall. Four crabs cling to the bait bag and the boy carefully manoeuvres it over the bucket. Shaking it gently, he dislodges the crustaceans into the water to join the others.

'That's quite a catch you've got there.'

Kat stills. The deep timbre of his voice is unmistakable.

'We'd like to say it's skill but actually it's beginners' luck,' Tara says, conversationally.

'We've all got to start somewhere,' says a female voice with a light Devon burr.

Kat turns. His companion *is* the woman who had joined him at the pub yesterday.

That's a novelty – the same one two days in a row!

Up close, the man is even more glorious and the hazel eyes that meet hers are full of hidden depths. If she's not careful she could drown.

Swim away . . . fast!

He smiles at Kat.

Even, white teeth.

'Are you here on holiday?' he asks.

Is she? She can't recall!

Tara glances at her friend in amusement. 'Niles and I have a cottage here. We try to use it as often as possible. Sadly, though, we all head back to London tomorrow.'

'That's a shame. London has its attractions . . .' the man's eyes flicker to Kat again, 'but there's nothing quite like the joys of the sea.'

Oddly, all of a sudden the sun feels exceptionally warm.

'I'm with you on that!' agrees Tara.

There's a subtext going on here and Kat desperately tries to unscramble her brains to follow it.

'But Kat, here,' continues Tara, indicating her friend, 'has the opportunity to stay in Fowey for six months.'

Kat's eyes open wide. She can't believe it! What does Tara think she's doing?

The man observes her with interest. '*Cat* . . . that's an unusual name.'

She's lost the power of speech, for pity's sake! Cat got your tongue?

'Katherine,' she manages to croak.

'Aha!' He smiles.

Dazzled, Kat lowers her gaze.

The man turns his attention to the boys. 'Did you know there are more than four thousand species of crab in the world?'

They shake their heads.

'They were sidling around the seabed during the Jurassic period, two hundred million years ago.'

'Cool!' exclaims Gulliver. 'Do they have special names?'

'Yes. The world's smallest crab is the pea crab. It spans less than half an inch. The largest is the mighty Japanese spider crab, and those can measure three metres and more between pincer tips.'

'There's a pea crab in my bucket!' shouts Tyler.

Peering into it now, the man carefully moves a frond of seaweed aside with his index finger.

'How long do crabs live?' Gulliver asks.

'I know that one,' Niles says, joining the conversation. 'Most have a life span of between three and four years.'

'That's not very long.' The boy pulls a sad face.

'It's a lifetime in crab years,' Tara says, ruffling her son's hair.

'Come on boys, I think it's time we put them back in the water,' their dad suggests. 'Let's go down to the pontoon and release them there. We can drain the bucket and watch them scurry back into the water, as we don't want to drop them from a height.'

Picking up the bucket, Niles and his sons make their way along the quay towards the slipway.

The man turns to Kat and Tara. 'Well, it was good meeting you both. I hope the traffic isn't too heavy on your journey back to London.' His gaze settles on Kat. 'There's a great community in Fowey and the river is very special. I'd say that opportunity is worth considering.'

'So I keep telling her,' says Tara with a laugh.

The man's eyes linger on Kat for a moment longer before turning away.

As he and his companion walk along the quayside towards the town, Kat notices the woman reach for his hand.

She will never see him again . . .

She forces herself to take a breath.

'So, we've finally met the mystery man!' says Tara. 'His friend didn't say much.'

The couple are fast disappearing, but before they turn onto the high street and are swallowed up by the crowd, the man looks back and a smile tugs at his mouth as he sees Kat watching. Raising a hand, in slow motion he salutes her.

'Well, well, well . . .' Tara titters. 'What was that about giving up men?'

'I have,' Kat says in a small voice.

'Don't give me that. You two could hardly take your eyes off each other!'

Kat snorts. But perhaps her boss and Tara are right: life is for living. Suddenly she knows exactly what to do. For the first time in years, Katherine Maddox is about to take a huge leap of faith.

11

At around eleven the next morning, Gulliver and Tyler stand in the kitchen doorway watching Tara and Kat busily emptying cupboards.

'Mum, can we have an ice cream?' the older boy asks.

Tara looks up from loading food into a box on the table. 'Now? Honestly, Gul, your timing is way out. We've got the cottage to close up before heading home!'

'Please,' begs Tyler.

Kat straightens up from cleaning the fridge. 'I can take them into town for ice creams, if you like.'

'That would be very helpful, thank you.' Distractedly sweeping a hand across her forehead, Tara says to her sons, 'You do realise that you two are very lucky boys having such a great auntie.'

Gulliver grins. Turning on his heels, he heads towards the front door.

'Come on, Tyler,' Kat says, holding out her hand to the younger boy. 'Let's go and track down some treats for you and your brother.'

As they make their way down the hill towards the main part of town, Tyler skips alongside Kat. She smiles to herself. Niles and Tara's children are a joy to hang out with. They're so sunny-natured and she's always been a part of their lives, having a keen affinity with both boys. And what she said to Tyler on the beach is true. If she did ever have children, she would want them to be just like these two.

Approaching the newsagent, her footsteps falter. Displayed on the pavement in front of the shop is an array of items for sale, and studying a rack of postcards is none other than *the man*. Consumed by conflicting emotions, Kat glances along the street for another ice-cream parlour, but Gulliver is already disappearing into the interior of the store.

'Come on, Auntie Kat,' Tyler says, tugging at her hand.

With her anxiety levels increasing, Kat reluctantly allows herself to be dragged ever closer. He's only feet away now and he's bound to see her, but the man concentrates on the card in his hand and she enters the shop without drawing his attention. Gulliver is already at the cabinet peering through the glass at the array of ice cream on display. There's plenty of choice; twenty thrilling colours and as many tempting flavours. Dropping Kat's hand, Tyler runs to join his brother.

'So, what do you fancy?' Kat says, approaching at a more leisurely pace. She smiles at the young girl behind the counter wearing a red-and-white striped apron.

Gulliver reads aloud the labels on the tubs. 'Clotted Cream Vanilla, Chocolate Flake, Mint Tea, Raspberry, Strawberries and Cream, Bubblegum . . .'

'Bubblegum for me!' shouts Tyler.

'What's that brown-coloured one?' Kat asks, pointing to a tub in the back row.

'Salcombe Mud,' Gulliver replies. 'Yuck.'

'I'm sure it's not actual mud,' she says, turning to look out at the street. The man is still studying the postcards and she watches as he removes one from the rack and considers it. Behind her, she hears Gulliver's conversation with the shop assistant.

'What's in it?' the boy asks.

'Black cocoa powder and gluten-free chocolate shortbread,' replies the girl. 'It's a perfect colour match to the famous mud in the Salcombe estuary. Just don't go mixing the two up!'

He grins and says, 'I'll have that one, please.'

Something about the man is so compelling and Kat wonders what that is. Suddenly he moves aside to allow another customer access to the rack and she blinks in surprise. Beside him is a young boy whom she hadn't noticed before. His features are remarkably similar to the man's and his thick dark hair also curls onto his shoulders.

'Which one are you having, Auntie Kat?' Gulliver's voice rings out.

She turns back to the cabinet. 'Spoilt for choice, Gul, but I think I'll have the Stem Ginger.'

As the girl places three cones in a rack and picks up a metal scoop, dipping it into one of the tubs, Kat turns back to the doorway.

The man has entered the shop and spots her immediately. He hesitates for a second before smiling. 'We meet again,' he says softly. 'How are you today?'

'Good, thanks.' Awkwardness siezes her, and she flounders for something to say.

'Hello,' says Gulliver, turning to him with a filled cone in his hand.

'Hello, young man. I think you've chosen my son's favourite flavour, if I'm not mistaken. Salcombe Mud?'

'Yes!'

Kat looks around for the boy she'd seen with him, but he's not in the shop. She looks through the front window, but she can't see him in the street, either. Perhaps the woman who was with the man yesterday is his wife and she's somewhere outside and the boy is with her now. She frowns.

'I've got Bubblegum,' Tyler says, holding out his cone.

'Great colour,' says the man.

Kat moves to the counter and pays for the ice creams.

'Would you boys help me decide on these two postcards?' the man asks. 'My son's about your age and I like to send him a card from wherever I'm working. Which of these do you like the most?'

Kat frowns again. *So who was the boy with him in the street?* She turns towards him. 'Is your son not here with you?'

As his gaze meets hers, she's suddenly gripped by an overwhelming surge of sadness.

'Unfortunately not.'

Numerous emotions flicker in his eyes and she tries to grasp their meaning, but before she has a chance to decipher them he blinks and the moment passes.

'I like that one,' says Tyler, pointing to a boat in full sail.

'Thank you. I do, too.' The man smiles down at the lad. Stepping up to the counter, he pays for the card.

'Come on, boys, we should be getting back,' Kat says.

As the man follows her out, she's acutely aware of his close proximity.

'It was good seeing you again,' she says, turning to him.

'And you,' he replies, holding her gaze. 'I'm Mac, by the way.'

She smiles and nods, as baffled thoughts tumble through her mind, and she's thankful when Gulliver and Tyler exit the shop and provide a distraction. As the brothers start walking up the hill, licking their ice creams, she calls out after them. 'Watch out for passing traffic, boys.'

'You have two fine sons,' Mac comments.

'Oh, they're not mine,' she says, suddenly feeling unaccountably flustered. 'They're my friends' boys.'

'I thought they were yours,' he says in surprise. 'You're so natural with them.'

'I've known both of them since they were born, so I suppose we're used to each other.' Her eyes meet his again. She's still confused by that vision of the boy. 'It's a shame your son's not here with you.'

Again, she picks up on sadness.

'Unfortunately, it's not possible for him to be with me while I'm away working, but he's OK in London with family.'

Strange. She could have sworn the boy standing beside him was his son. They looked so alike.

Realising she's staring, she hurriedly says, 'I'd better catch up with the boys.'

'Have a good journey home,' he says.

'Thanks.' She gives him a brief smile before heading up the hill in the direction of the cottage.

'Don't forget about that opportunity in Fowey,' Mac calls out after her.

She turns back.

'You won't be disappointed,' he adds with a smile.

Swiftly, she catches up with the boys. All at once, a feeling comes over her – one she can't explain – and she turns and looks back down the street.

Mac is still standing outside the shop, watching her. Raising a hand, slowly he smiles.

He looks so devastatingly attractive. She sighs.

How typical that another man with children has caught her attention. It's definitely the right thing to give up men.

But as these thoughts lodge in her brain, Kat is surprised by the tingling sensation coursing through her body.

12

Nestled on the south Cornish coast between Plymouth and Falmouth is the small and inviting, vibrant waterside town of Fowey (pronounced 'Foy'). Stretching for a mile or so along the western banks of the River Fowey, the town is steeped in history and has been in existence since well before the Norman invasion. The local church was first established during the seventh century.

Set within an Area of Outstanding Natural Beauty, the estuary of the River Fowey forms a large, natural harbour that is a magnet for sailing enthusiasts. The harbour has always been an important maritime access point and enabled the town to become a significant trading centre. Privateers also made use of the sheltered harbourage, and the Lostwithiel and Fowey Railway brought China clay here for export. Fishing and other water sports are also popular and the harbour and its surrounds are great places to explore by foot, car or boat.

Literary buffs will be familiar with Fowey; synonymous as it is with Daphne du Maurier. The author – famous for novels including Rebecca *and* Jamaica Inn *– moved to the town with her family at the age of 20. She soon began writing short stories, and a few years later her first novel was published. Inspired by Fowey and the surrounding Cornish landscape, she continued as a successful writer into her sixties.*

Fowey: a magnet for sailing enthusiasts? No wonder Mac was so positive about the place. It suits him right down to the slightest wind in his sails.

'Have you finished?' a female voice asks.

The question brings Kat back to the present and she looks up from the page she'd been reading.

'Yes, thanks.'

As the waitress takes away her empty plate, Kat glances out over the lake at the Canada geese, swans and ducks paddling in the shallows. She checks her phone. Damn! Her escape to a different place has flown by and her lunchbreak is over. Stuffing the guide book into her bag, she quickly rises to her feet. Morning meetings at Bryanston Publishing, at which production schedules and tight deadlines for the forthcoming year are discussed, have always made her yearn for wide open spaces. Today, Hyde Park and The Serpentine have somewhat fulfilled that need, but now she must get back to the office in double-quick time. Exiting the café, she walks swiftly along Serpentine Road and threads her way through the London streets back to her desk.

'Do you have a moment?' Hugo asks from the doorway of her office.

'Of course.'

Coming in, he closes the door behind him and approaches her desk. 'How was your Easter jaunt?'

'Good, thanks. Salcombe was packed but we managed to escape most of the crowds by hiring boats and kayaks and finding less populated beaches.' Kat smiles at her boss. 'How was yours?'

'North Norfolk was empty, thankfully!' Hugo perches on the edge of her desk. 'I just wondered if you'd given any further consideration to my cousin's offer.'

'I have. I'm going to accept.'

He smiles at her. 'I'm so pleased. Stella emailed yesterday evening asking if you'd made up your mind. Apparently, someone else has shown interest. I'll email her straight away and give her the good news.'

'Please will you tell her I'd like to schedule a call for this evening, if that's convenient?'

'Will do. You won't regret it, Kat. You deserve a break and Stella's property in Fowey is quite something. Perhaps this is fate knocking!'

Getting up from the desk, Hugo walks towards the door, which suddenly flies open. He jumps back – not quickly enough to avoid colliding with Gemma, who is looking down at her phone.

'Careful!' he says good-naturedly.

'Sorry, Hugo. Didn't see you.'

'No damage done.'

'God, it just gets worse!' Gemma groans, collapsing into her chair. 'The sodding letting agency refuses to let me pay in instalments. HR say they've given me too many loans already, and Mum says she's having trouble paying her own mortgage, let alone funding her daughter's rent as well. At this rate I'll be dossing in some grotty hostel.'

'I'll catch you later,' Hugo says to Kat, retreating swiftly.

She gives him a nod before turning her attention to her colleague. 'Actually, I think I may have a solution to your problem, Gem.'

'Really?'

'Yes, *really*.' Kat smiles encouragingly.

'Always open to suggestions. Spill.'

'It's not common knowledge yet, but I plan to leave London for a while. How about renting my flat? I don't want to leave it unoccupied and you'd be doing me a favour.'

'Wow!' Gemma grins. 'That would be fantastic. In one fell swoop you've sorted out my life. Thanks, Kat!'

'You're welcome,' Kat says, almost envious of this practical solution to Gemma's problems.

If only she could sort hers so easily.

13

Two weeks later, having driven non-stop from London, Kat arrives in Fowey one late afternoon. Her mind and body fizz; it feels not unlike jetlag. The sat nav tells her to take a steep hill down towards the town and she hopes it's correct because, if not, making a U-turn in the narrow road could prove tricky. She's almost at the bottom when a lane to the right displays the name of the street she's looking for – Esplanade. Breathing a sigh of relief, she indicates right, and after a short distance pulls into a parking bay and switches off the engine. With her hands still on the steering wheel, she takes a long, steadying breath before turning her head. On the opposite side of the narrow street, she observes Stella's property.

Accessed from a thin sliver of pavement, the double-fronted terraced house is painted a cheery yellow with white, wooden sash windows and a smart, navy-blue front door sporting a brass dolphin knocker. She wonders why Hugo had referred to his cousin's property as *quite something,* because at first glance it's not obvious. Sure, the paintwork looks fresh, but the house is a standard two-storey; one a child would draw, giving it a friendly face.

Kat rolls her shoulders, relieving the tension brought on by driving for five hours, and summons the energy to unload the car. She hasn't brought much with her – just enough to fill two suitcases – but there's the easel to set up, and all the associated drawing equipment to unpack. Opening the driver's door, she gets out and waits for a lone car to pass by before crossing the street.

On her last day in the office Hugo had presented her with a key to the house. Extracting it now from the depths of her handbag, she inserts it into the lock and opens the front door to a bright and spacious entrance hall with black-and-white chequered mosaic floor tiles. She steps over the threshold, and through an open doorway to her right she catches a glimpse of a tidy, well-equipped kitchen with cream-coloured Shaker units. She continues on towards two doors on opposite sides of the hallway. One leads into a dining room, the other to a large sitting room. Kat enters the latter.

'Oh, my goodness!'

For a brief moment she wonders if she's in the right house. Light floods in through a large bay window and Kat immediately crosses over to it. The views are stunning! Neither Stella nor Hugo had thought to mention its exact location, and when she'd turned the car onto the Esplanade there was nothing to differentiate the road from any other in the town. But the house is frontline to the river, which is busy with watercraft, and on the opposite bank a huddle of slate-roofed properties spill down a hillside to the water's edge.

That must be Polruan.

She'd noticed the village on a map of the area she'd examined a while ago, when she was planning her sabbatical.

Kat looks to her right, where a small balcony houses a patio table and two chairs. Her gaze travels to the neighbouring properties and beyond, to the mouth of the river and the open sea. Turning in the opposite direction, she sees a natural, woodland-flanked estuary with a number of boats and yachts on mooring lines. Instantly, she feels the tension in her shoulders release. Glancing down, she's surprised to find a lower level where a large, wooden table and six chairs nestle on a paved terrace, and built into the far wall is a stone-built barbeque. At once, she imagines enjoying *al fresco* meals whilst being entertained by the comings and goings on the river.

Deciding to check out the rest of the house before unpacking the car, she descends the stairs to a lower hall, where she finds a stained-glass door opening out to the paved terrace. To her left is a large room set up as an office/family room, and to her right is a utility/laundry area with a separate cloakroom. On the first floor she discovers two, double bedrooms with the same panoramic view as the main reception rooms, while a stylish bathroom overlooks the street. Lastly, nestled in the eaves on the top floor are two further bedrooms with dormer windows overlooking the river, and a shower room.

Kat smiles. If nothing else, she'll get fit staying here!

She checks her mobile phone and sees it's close to five, but she may be in luck and find a shop that's still open. Why hadn't she thought to bring basic provisions with her? Quickly making her way downstairs, Kat leaves the front door open and crosses the road to her car. It's very quiet and there's hardly anyone around – though further along the street a couple stroll hand-in-hand – but the place is bound to get busier during the summer months.

Swiftly, she unloads the car, depositing the suitcases at the bottom of the stairs to take up later. As she enters the dining room, which is also bathed in light from a large, bay window, she realises it's a perfect space for her studio, and propping the easel against a wall, she places her box of artist's materials on the table. Then, grabbing her bag and checking she has the key, she steps out into the street and closes the door behind her.

Instantly, tantalising aromas waft across the road from a small tapas bar and Kat's tummy rumbles, reminding her she's had nothing to eat since breakfast. A number of tables and chairs set up on the pavement invite diners to enjoy the bar's laid-back feel, and displayed on an outside wall is a menu. She crosses over to it and stops to read, drooling over such dishes as *albondigas*, *chorizo picante*, spider crab and saffron *croquetas*, and *calamares*. Lively voices sound from within, and Kat suspects she will become a frequent visitor to this little restaurant that brings a taste of Spain to Cornwall. For now, she turns and walks in the direction of the town.

The houses fronting the river are the same age and design as Stella's and all appear well cared for, their owners obviously priding themselves on the period listings. The properties on the opposite side of the street, though of a similar age, are mostly three- or four-storeys and set back from the thoroughfare in elevated positions. Several have pretty, ornate, cast-iron balconies that take advantage of river views over rooftops, and many have tiered gardens Mediterranean in style, full of exotic sub-tropical plants and palm trees, highlighting that Cornwall, on the eastern edge of the Gulf Stream, enjoys a mild maritime climate.

Kat continues on and soon comes to a combined off-licence and grocery shop, which is still open.

How convenient! Less than a minute from the house.

Stepping into the shop's cool interior, she picks up a basket and works her way around the stacked shelves. The place is impressively well stocked with a large variety of handcrafted and more mainstream spirits, and along with the daily essentials she's already put in her basket, Kat adds a bottle of Fowey Valley's Foy Gin. As the man behind the counter waxes lyrical on its subtleties and velvety rich flavour, she listens with interest.

'A juniper-heavy gin made with a selection of six botanicals,' he says, as she pays for her purchases. 'While juniper sits at the fore, you can still easily pick out brilliantly light floral notes, making it an excellent choice to pair with elderflower tonic.'

Thanking him for the suggestion, Kat exits the store and retraces her steps to the house. Tomorrow she will explore the town and stock up on further groceries, but tonight she will email Stella to confirm that she's arrived and all is well with the property. She will also message Tara and let her know she hasn't suffered any mishaps on the journey to Cornwall. She must also formulate a work plan from the list of properties she's been asked to illustrate.

14

Kat wakes early to pale yellow light shimmering through the bedroom curtains, hinting at the promise of a fine spring day. As soon as her head touched the pillow the previous night she had fallen into a deep, uninterrupted sleep, but now, refreshed, she's eager to embrace the day. The sound of an outboard motor and the sudden raucous screech of a seagull remind her she's no longer in London. Throwing back the duvet, she gets out of bed and crosses over to the window. As she draws back the curtains to a pale-blue sky laced with thin, wispy clouds, sunlight reflects off the deep-blue river, dusting its surface with tiny crystals. She watches as a yacht glides by heading towards the mouth of the river, its crew busy on deck with ropes and sails, and a smile spreads across her face.

Turning away, Kat quickly dresses and descends the stairs to the kitchen. Coffee and toast will do. She busies herself making breakfast and carries it out to the balcony, sitting down at the small patio table. A brisk breeze whips around her and she rubs her arms.

Is it too early in the year to sit outside?

Her eye is drawn to an open-topped, bright orange boat powering across the water from the opposite bank. Behind its covered cabin are two stacks of matching coloured lifebuoys. It reminds Kat of a child's bath toy, earnestly tackling the river like one of the *big boys*, and she chuckles to herself. As the boat draws nearer before turning into the main channel, black letters adorning the front of the cabin are clearly visible – *Polruan Ferry*.

'Hello there.'

She turns towards the voice. A man stands on the neighbouring balcony, his jumper at stretching point across a large, round belly as the breeze snatches at greying hair, revealing a bald patch.

'You're hardy,' he comments.

'I wondered if I was being rash.'

'A tad on the fresh side, I'd say.' He eyes her curiously. 'I'm Jerry, by the way.'

'Nice to meet you. I'm Kat.'

'On holiday?'

'Sadly not, I'm working. Although I can think of worse places to do that!'

'Yes. My wife, Sandy, and I moved here last year from the Midlands. Early retirees, don't you know. Can't say we've looked back.'

'I thought I detected a Brummie accent.' Kat smiles politely. 'That's the Polruan Ferry, isn't it?' She indicates the little tug chugging through the water. 'Where does it go to?'

'It connects Fowey with Polruan, and vice versa,' he says, glancing at the boat. 'At this time of year it goes to Town Quay, but come May it will pick up passengers from Whitehouse slipway.' He points to a stone quay jutting out into the water to the right of the row of houses.

'That's convenient,' Kat says, thinking how well situated Stella's house is. 'How often does it run?'

'Daily, except for Christmas day. About every ten to fifteen minutes. Have you been over to Polruan?'

'No, but it's on my "to do" list.'

'You must. It's quaint. And then there's the Hall Walk, which is also a must!' He laughs, the sound bellowing across the divide between the balconies. 'It's a circular walk through woodland and along creeks and it has stunning views of the Harbour. You have to take two ferry rides, from here to Polruan and from Bodinnick to Fowey.'

'I'll add that to the list as well,' Kat says with a smile.

'Well, I must be getting on.' He turns away and then pauses. 'Are you here on your own?'

Surprised at the direct question, Kat's left eyebrow twitches. 'Yes.'

'Well, if there's anything you need, or if you want to know what to do in the area, just give us a shout. Neither Sandy or I bite!'

She gives a small laugh. 'Thank you, that's kind.'

'Not at all. That's what neighbours are for.' He winks and turns back inside his house.

Kat gazes out at the river again. It's a world away from the life she's known. How sad Colin isn't here to share it with her. They could have visited Polruan and hiked the Hall Walk together. She picks up her mobile. Still no message. At this time he'd be away from his family and on his way to work. A moment of weakness makes her consider contacting him and, briefly, her finger hovers over his name before she places the phone firmly back on the table.

Another cool breeze gusts up the river. Perhaps she should give it another few weeks before eating outside. Quickly finishing her coffee, Kat decides to explore the town and see what Fowey has to offer.

There are many more people about than on the previous afternoon, no doubt because it's a Saturday. Reaching the end of the Esplanade, Kat turns right and heads down the hill towards the main part of town, pausing to look in an art gallery's window before continuing on past a couple of cafés, a gift shop and a pub. She can't help but laugh at the irony of brewery men unloading beer barrels from a van parked outside Fowey's parish church, St Fimbarrus. Still, they will have moved on by the time the church-going fraternity flock to Sunday services.

It's sheltered in the ever-narrowing lanes away from the river and Kat tilts her face up to the sun, revelling in its warmth. Strings of bunting flutter in the breeze, connecting one building to another across the street, and a sense of festivity pervades the air. Resuming her exploration of the town, she discovers a number of small, independent shops selling unusual gifts, artwork and clothing, and a selection of bistros, cafés and restaurants. Medieval and Georgian buildings cast shadows over their neighbours as they jostle with each other, and Kat senses a vibrant, maritime history hidden in their stonework. She wonders if Stella would like her to draw some of Fowey's older buildings. She must remember to ask.

Making her way along Fore Street, she has to weave through an increasing number of visitors to the town. As the road starts to rise, her eye is drawn to an elegant, eighteenth-century house that exudes an important air with its three dormer windows gazing proudly over the main street. Above the front door is a curved canopy, its underside moulded in the shape of a large scallop shell and she wonders if this is simply for decorative purposes or whether it nods to the property's past. Intriguingly, on street level, a small clock face has been inserted into one of the panes of a sash window by the front door. Although the house is clearly a private residence, Kat considers its history, located as it is on Custom House Hill. There is so much to discover about the town. Perhaps she should join a guided tour. That way, she could winkle out buildings that might be of interest to illustrate.

She continues on, passing an alleyway between the house and its neighbour, where a metal A-frame displays a Sunday lunch menu and information on forthcoming sailing events taking place at Gallants Sailing Club. Kat walks up the hill and around the corner, following a narrow lane running parallel to the river and hemmed in by properties opening directly onto the road. The street is barely wide enough for a car to comfortably navigate, even without pavements, and she is forced to stand in narrow doorways to allow vehicles to pass. The shops are fewer here, with only the occasional interesting piece of *objet d'art* in a window suggesting the door beside it leads to a shop or gallery. Intriguingly, a number of properties have steps leading down to curiously low doors and she assumes these are entrances to basements.

Continuing on, she passes a stepped alleyway leading between two cottages that offers a tantalising glimpse of water, and presently she arrives at a small car park directly fronting the river. A lifeboat is moored alongside a pontoon, and on board a group of people are obviously enjoying a tour. At the entrance to the car park, a mobile unit sells the day's catch from one of Fowey's fishing boats – mussels, local crab, mackerel, prawns and tuna. If Kat hadn't recently had breakfast she'd be tempted to buy a punnet or two.

She crosses over to the wall fronting the river. Further upstream, on the opposite bank, a characterful property basks in the midday sun, its blue-painted window frames and shutters standing out smartly against pale cream render. Alongside is a road, and a line of cars inches its way towards a waiting car ferry. Shielding her eyes, she watches as the ferryman waits until the last vehicle boards the vessel before closing the gates.

That must be the second water crossing on the Hall Walk that Jerry had mentioned.

As the drive-on ferry starts making its way across the racing tide, Kat decides she will definitely do the circuitous walk. Viewing Fowey from the other side of the river will present a different perspective of the town and she may discover historic buildings not immediately visible from street level.

15

On her way back to Stella's house, Kat stops at the bookshop on the corner opposite the church. Its bright-blue brickwork makes it an obvious landmark. On an exterior wall next to the window is a poster depicting Fowey's deep-river valley, highlighting various points of interest in and around the town. St Catherine's Castle looks intriguing and walking distance from Stella's house, too; she decides to check it out that afternoon.

A jaunty blue-and-white striped awning shades the window and her gaze shifts to the books displayed on the shelf within. Someone has creatively arranged an eclectic mix of contemporary novels and antiquarian books written by both local and more mainstream authors; the majority referencing Cornwall. The Daphne du Maurier novels are a certain temptation for holidaymakers seeking a good read, as is a selection of Winston Graham's *Poldark* novels, their up-to-date covers depicting the attractive stars of the most recent TV series. How could anyone ignore them?

All at once shadows cloud the glass and Kat refocuses on the reflections of a group of people walking by, but it's the person quietly observing her from across the street who makes her catch her breath. Dark-haired and tanned; his looks are unmistakable.

Mac?

She turns but there's no one there. Frowning, she looks in both directions, but there's no sign of him anywhere. Turning back to the window, Kat studies the reflections again but the space Mac had inhabited is now empty, and she dismisses it as mind games and pure association. Fowey reminds her of Salcombe. But she can't deny the level of disappointment consuming her.

Forget him. It's pointless to think about him. She will never see him again.

'Passing ships in the night,' she says under her breath.

However, the unexpected vision has disturbed her and feeling unsettled, Kat walks down a side street towards Town Quay. It, too, is festooned with bunting, giving the area a celebratory, party-like feel, albeit with strangers. A loud burst of laughter erupts from the open windows of the King of Prussia pub and she glances in its direction. On the steps leading up to the entrance, a group of men stand with pint glasses in their hands and openly appraise her. Quickly, she averts her gaze. To one side of the quay is an obviously popular restaurant with very few empty seats on its terrace. She looks towards the river where a group of people lean over iron railings, observing the busy comings and goings on the water. It's impossible to miss the large sculpture of a bird clutching a book and, crossing over to it, Kat reads the plaque installed below the artwork.

> *'Rook with a Book' celebrates the author Daphne du Maurier's legacy, inspiration and love of Fowey where she lived. She is famous for writing many wonderful books including* The Birds, *which was adapted for Alfred Hitchcock's film of the same name in 1963.*

The detailing to the bird's feathers and the scales on its legs and feet are superb, and the sculptors have done a brilliant job in conveying an ominous air with the rook's blank eye and sharp beak.

'It's impressive, isn't it?'

Kat turns. Beside her stands a smartly dressed, older lady wearing a twin-set and skirt, unlike the majority of tourists wandering the streets in T-shirts, shorts and sandals, pretending it's already midsummer.

'It is.'

'Of course, Daphne is only *one* of the town's famous past residents. Sir Arthur Quiller-Couch lived here, as did, until recently, Dawn French. And Kenneth Grahame holidayed at Fowey Hall Hotel, which is understood to have been the inspiration for Toad Hall in *The Wind in the Willows*.'

'I can understand the attraction,' Kat says.

'The temptation is rather hard to resist,' the informative lady agrees. 'I've been fortunate to live here for the past ten years.'

'You're very lucky. I've just arrived – staying for a few months.'

'Ah, you have a lot to discover. See that house over there?' The woman points to the waterside property with the blue shutters on the opposite side of the river. 'That's Ferryside, the du Maurier family's second home. Daphne wrote her first novel there, *The Loving Spirit*. Of course, she later lived at Menabilly, which she remodelled as the atmospheric and doom-laden house, Manderley, in her marvellous novel, *Rebecca*.'

Kat smiles. 'It looks a wonderful property, but I suspect it didn't start life as a house.'

Keen eyes observe her. 'Well spotted! It was originally a boatyard, built in the early 1800s. When the du Mauriers bought it they turned the original quay into a garden, the sail loft into bedrooms and a bathroom, and the former boat store into the family's sitting room.'

Kat observes the woman with interest. 'Have you seen inside?'

'No, but there's a wealth of information in the museum. If you haven't already visited you must, although it's closed today. My daughter, Lisa, works there on Mondays and Thursdays.'

Kat turns back to Ferryside and imagines a young Daphne working on the manuscript of her first novel. Which room had she written it in? Did she have a desk in one of the windows overlooking the river? That view would certainly provide inspiration. She notices the ferry making its way across the river once again and thinks the property is well named.

'Is that the Bodinnick ferry?' she asks.

'Correct. There's been one in operation between Bodinnick and Fowey since the thirteenth century.' The woman glances at her watch. 'Well, I mustn't be late. My daughter is preparing a family lunch.'

'Thank you for all the interesting information,' Kat says sincerely.

'You're very welcome, dear. It's a lovely town with a rich history. As I said, you'll learn a lot from a visit to the museum.'

As the woman bids her farewell and walks away, Kat looks around the quay. Forming a neat queue at a kiosk selling boat trips, a family eats ice creams. They appear oblivious to the seagulls overhead who screech their mournful cries, while keeping a speculative eye out for the next impromptu meal. Kat heads towards the steps leading down to the water, where several children dangle lines over the edge in the hope of catching a crab or two. She smiles. It wasn't so long ago that she and Tara's family were in Salcombe doing just that.

Suddenly a strong breeze snatches at her long hair and holding it out of her face, she peers across the water to the many yachts straining their moorings. The river is a beautiful, dark teal today and a number of boats and inflatable craft pass within inches of paddle boarders and canoeists. Kat lifts her gaze to the wooded hillside on the opposite bank and then turns to observe the town, wondering how it appears from the air. Was it Fowey she'd been dreaming about when Hugo found her slumped on her desk? She has never visited the area before. How strange that would be if it was! Checking the time on her mobile, Kat leaves the quay and starts making her way back to Stella's house.

* * *

Later that afternoon, having briefly checked online and googled St Catherine's Castle, Kat stows her drawing equipment in a shoulder bag and sets out along the Esplanade under a high sun that's surprisingly warm for the time of year. Within minutes, she comes to the quay serving the Polruan Ferry during the summer months. Turning off the street, she walks down a steep approach and stands gazing up at the 'red rocket', which a display board conveniently informs her is a navigational aid guiding sailors into the harbour, and which on clear days is visible from eight miles away. Following a path to the right, Kat arrives at a natural paddling pool carved out of the rocks; its water obviously refreshed each tide. Beyond this is a small, secluded beach and a few yards offshore is a rocky outcrop of an island. A beach... Within seconds of Stella's house! It's so well hidden that Kat doubts many people are aware of its existence. At once, she imagines spending summer evenings there after the more adventurous and inquisitive visitors have departed its sands.

Retracing her steps to the road, she continues on towards Readymoney Cove and presently comes to the Italianate-style property known as Point Neptune. As she peers through its impressive iron gates, she recalls from her research that the house had been built in the mid-nineteenth century as the family beach house for William Rashleigh, of nearby Menabilly.

Some beach house!

It looks fascinating, perched on the rocks at the entrance to the river and it must surely have a rich and interesting history. She's surprised Stella hasn't included it in the list of properties to sketch, but perhaps the professor has had to ruthlessly select the houses to feature in her book.

Following the lane down into the valley and passing a 'Saints Way' marker, Kat skirts a small, gently sloping beach surrounded by high cliffs. She pauses to observe an attractive dwelling, once the stables and carriage house to

Point Neptune and converted to residential use in the 1930s. She'd read that this was where Daphne du Maurier had written *Hungry Hill* while renting the property for a short time during the Second World War.

Shouts and laughter from the beach make Kat turn and she notices several holidaymakers in the sheltered, sandy cove. A few hardy souls have even braved the cold water and children squeal as they dive from a platform moored not far from the shore. Continuing on past a cluster of cottages, she reaches a track signed 'Coast Path' and heads up the steep wooded valley, stopping once to catch her breath. At a fork in the trail, she takes the path leading towards the headland and it's not long before she reaches the castle ruins.

Above unguarded, precipitous drops to the sea, Kat listens to the waves crashing on the rocks below as she takes in the superb, panoramic view. There's a strong breeze, and she watches a number of small sailing boats jostle for position at the mouth of the Fowey Estuary. It's a spectacular sight and as they head out into the bay, the wind fills their white sails causing the boats to lean alarmingly. There are so many that she wonders if it's a race. A few minutes later, a dozen smaller dinghies approach the entrance, their cheerful, multi-coloured mainsails and jibs sporting the insignia 'FR'.

How exhilarating!

But she has work to do and tearing her eyes away from the scene, Kat looks around her surroundings. Thanks to her earlier research, she knows St Catherine's Castle was an artillery blockhouse built in the 1530s on the orders of King Henry VIII, as a defence against invasion. It was one of the first fortifications constructed as a result of his break with the Roman Catholic Church and England's subsequent isolation from Catholic Europe.

She considers where the best place is to sit and sketch. It's not immediately obvious. Steep slopes fall away from the D-shaped two-storey castle ruins, and walls extend to meet the cliffs on either side. Carefully descending an open-sided flight of stone steps, Kat sits on a wall and removes the bag from her shoulder.

Good, there's no one about.

Extracting her drawing equipment, she opens the sketchpad to a clean page and it's not long before she has lost all sense of time.

16

The next morning, Kat rises early. Eager to continue working on her sketches of the castle ruins, she enters the dining room and sets up her easel in the bay window to maximise on the light. Sipping her first cup of coffee of the day, she studies the drawings in her sketchpad and compares them to the photos she's taken. Unsurprisingly, there are a number of differences. Experience has taught her she can only create a *true* likeness from photographs, because when she's on site – once her pens make contact with paper – the life of the buildings takes over. She gives a wry smile. It's the only way she's been able to circumnavigate her particular *gift*.

Kat glances out of the window. The weather is changeable today and there's a threat of rain in the air. Grey clouds tumble over each other and sweep across the landscape as Greek god, Zephyrus, blows in from the west. The river is demonstrating it's an unpredictable beast and boats are tossed about in its choppy waters as if mere matchsticks. This hasn't, however, deterred two intrepid kayakers paddling by a few yards out from the near bank. Perhaps they imagine they are white water rafting! She watches the Polruan Ferry valiantly tackling the swell as it heads towards Town Quay. No doubt the ferrymen have formidable sea legs, but she wouldn't want to be out there today.

Turning back to her mobile, Kat examines the image on the screen; St Catherine's Castle looking out from the edge of the headland. She checks it against her written notes. Both lengths of rampart terminate in sheer cliffs, effectively cutting off a near semi-circular area at the end of the promontory, while on a lower level, two rows of gunports cover the approaches to the estuary and the harbour itself.

When Kat had explored the castle the previous afternoon, she'd been surprised at the thickness of the tower's walls – possibly four feet or more. On the ground floor there were three gunports and a tall, narrow fireplace, and on first-floor level were two further gunports and five thin musketry slits. In one corner stood the remains of a spiral staircase that would have accessed the upper floor and roof. Curiously, there were no signs of domestic quarters and she'd wondered where the soldiers had lived, or had they been billeted in the town? Venturing outside, she'd come across a series of square, granite plaques intriguingly marked 'WD 1855'. What did those refer to? Were they a mark recording the refurbishments carried out at that time?

Kat places her mobile on the easel. Keeping the image open, she picks up a pen and is soon immersed in her work. Oblivious to time passing, when she next checks her phone she's shocked to find that four hours have flown by. Stepping back from the easel and rotating her shoulders, she critically assesses her work. Three different illustrations portray the castle ruins as they appear today.

'Not bad,' she says aloud.

When she'd returned from her visit, Kat had immediately checked online and searched for further information on St Catherine's Castle. The results confirmed that her sketches drawn *in situ* portrayed the site as it would have appeared during the Second World War, when the Tudor castle had acted as an observation post controlling a submarine minefield laid across Fowey harbour. Kat stares now at the illustrations in her sketchbook that portray an intact castle and a much-enlarged fort spreading over the headland, exactly as described.

'The past is but a whisper away,' she murmurs.

She decides to continue work on the sketches after lunch and once fully satisfied with the illustrations, she will photograph each, including her historical drawings of the fort, and email them all to Stella. It will be good to receive feedback.

Turning away from her easel, Kat heads towards the kitchen in search of a second cup of coffee of the day.

17

The following morning, Kat leaves the house and walks along the Esplanade towards the town with the intention of visiting the museum. Within minutes she arrives at the Ship Inn. Turning to her right, she heads down a narrow street towards a charming stone building next to the Aquarium. A short flight of steps leads up to an open entrance door, and as she enters the building a middle-aged woman sitting behind the reception desk looks up.

'Hello,' Kat says. 'I'd like a ticket please.'

'Just the one?'

She cringes. Is it always going to be like this, having to confirm it's *just the one*?

'Yes.'

The woman issues a ticket and smiles, and immediately Kat sees the likeness to the impromptu town guide she'd met at the statue of the rook.

'Are you Lisa?' Kat asks, handing over some coins.

The woman's eyes widen. 'Yes. How did you know?'

'I met your mother a couple of days ago. She mentioned you worked here and suggested I visit.'

Lisa laughs. 'Good old Mum! Since she moved to Fowey she's become the museum's unpaid PR.'

'She did a grand job filling me in on the town's famous inhabitants,' Kat says with a smile. 'She left me wanting to find out more.'

'Well, you've come to the right place. There's a rich and varied history attached to this harbour town and its inhabitants, and although it may only be one room, the museum is packed full of interesting artefacts.'

Kat glances around. 'The building looks very old.'

'Yes. It's one of the oldest in town and dates back to the fifteenth century.' The woman picks up a leaflet and offers it to her. 'Wander at your leisure and if there's anything you want to know, just ask.'

Taking the pamphlet, Kat enters the room and walks around, peering into various display cabinets. Among the many interesting curiosities recording the town's history are Mayoral Regalia: costumes, old photographs, postcards, models of old sailing ships, boat-building tools from the days of sail, and the cape worn by Garibaldi during his Italian campaign. The finds from the Fowey area are fascinating, even the display that includes the contents of a medieval garde-robe.

Turning her attention to a cabinet filled with Daphne du Maurier memorabilia, Kat studies several photographs of the author, various early editions of her works, a shirt reputedly worn by her, and a charming ceramic model of Ferryside.

'One of our most famous residents,' Lisa says, joining her. 'Reference to her work can be found everywhere in and around the town. If you haven't already read her novels, the bookshop opposite the church stocks many of her titles.'

'I noticed several of her books in their window, and I'm sure I haven't read all her novels. I'll pay them a visit.' Kat smiles at the woman. 'The church looks interesting.'

Lisa nods. 'It's generally open to visitors during the day. It's dedicated to St Finn Barr, the first Bishop of Cork. He made a detour here during his pilgrimage to Rome in the seventh century and built a little church there. The present church, however, dates from 1328, although vicars are noted from as far back as the early 1260s.'

'Interesting,' remarks Kat.

'Did you know Fowey was a base for pirates during much of its history?' the woman asks.

'No, but I can imagine pirate ships making their way stealthily upriver under the cover of darkness.'

Lisa chuckles. 'The town has attracted a lot of attention over the years. In 1457 it was attacked by French marauders who destroyed the church. However, it was restored three years later with the help of the Earl of Warwick, and his badge can still be seen on the outside of the tower.'

'A fount of knowledge! What an interesting job you have, Lisa.'

'Well, I enjoy it, and my husband says it keeps me out of mischief!' The woman turns curious eyes on Kat. 'But, tell me. What do you do?'

'I'm an illustrator.'

'That sounds like fun.'

'It can be.' Kat smiles. 'I'm currently illustrating a book about the West Country's ruins.'

Lisa bursts out laughing. 'Well, there are certainly a few to be found hereabouts, and I don't just mean of the building kind!'

Kat grins.

'I remember now,' the woman continues. 'Mum mentioned she'd met you. She said you're here for a few months.'

'That's right. I am.'

'In town?'

'Yes.'

'On your own?'

Kat grimaces. There it is again . . . that reference to her single status.

'Sorry,' says Lisa, suddenly colouring. 'How rude of me! I don't mean to pry and you don't have to answer. It's none of my business.'

Kat gives a half-smile. 'Yes, I'm on my own.'

'In that case, if you'd like some company, you must come to Sunday lunch at Gallants. It has a great atmosphere and you'd be very welcome as my guest. Derek, dear husband, helps out behind the bar at weekends. Here, let me give you my number.'

Kat follows the woman to the reception desk and waits while she jots down a telephone number on the pamphlet. They chat for a while longer, until more customers arrive, and promising to give Lisa a ring, Kat leaves the museum and heads towards the parish church.

Later, as she opens the front door to the house, a strident ringing sound echoes along the hallway. Hurrying to the sitting room, Kat snatches up the phone.

'Hello. It's Stella. I hope I'm not interrupting.'

'Hi, Stella.' Kat sinks into one of the overstuffed armchairs. 'No, you're not interrupting anything. I've just had an educational visit to the museum and the parish church.'

'Good idea to immerse yourself in the town's history. It will give you a strong sense of place. I hope you're settling in well.'

'Oh, yes. The house is very comfortable,' Kat assures the professor. 'Thank you for making it available to me.'

'There's no point in it sitting empty all summer. Have you discovered our jetty yet?'

'No.'

'We own a set of steps down to the foreshore as well as the stone jetty. It's useful when you want to approach the property from the water. The immediate neighbouring houses have a right of access but they hardly ever use it.'

'I've met the neighbours on the right . . .' Kat says. 'Or rather, Jerry. I've still to meet Sandy.'

'Ah, I thought it wouldn't take him long to make himself acquainted! A very helpful, jovial sort of chap.'

Kat gives a laugh. 'He told me that neither he nor his wife bites!'

Stella chuckles. 'I've only met them a handful of times and on each occasion they've been very friendly.'

Kat gazes out of the bay window at a passing yacht; its hull painted dark blue.

'Now, I wish to discuss the illustrations you emailed to me yesterday.'

Kat's attention snaps back to Stella and she settles more deeply into the comfortable chair.

'They're exactly what I'm looking for. Hugo was so clever to recommend you. Your style is realistic but also romantic without being overly whimsical. It will certainly enhance the book. However, I'm intrigued by a few illustrations that don't correlate with the others and I wondered what they were.'

Kat bites her lip. How best to describe her *gift* to the professor?

'It's how the site would have looked during the Second World War.'

'So the sketches are your interpretations?' Stella queries.

'Yes. By the end of the nineteenth century the fort had been abandoned, but from June 1940 it formed part of a more extensive battery and observation post. The anti-aircraft gun I've drawn was positioned on one of the earlier gun emplacements.'

'To make sure I understand correctly, the drawings are your imaginative assumptions based on researched findings.'

Kat knows they're accurate, but how can she possibly explain?

'Yes,' she says simply.

'Well, I love them. They add another dimension to the castle and I would like you to provide similar illustrations for all the properties on the list. Obviously, if my descriptions are insufficient to go by, you will have to do further research and I understand it may not be possible if nothing remarkable comes to light. However, with those properties that enjoy a plethora of recorded historical information, I'd like you to sketch your interpretations as to how they may have appeared in the past.'

Kat smiles, knowing she won't have to do any further research to uncover the various histories of the buildings.

'It will be a pleasure to create historical illustrations,' she says.

'Wonderful! Now, which property have you chosen to visit first?'

'I thought I'd continue with the castle theme and visit Restormel.'

'Good choice,' Stella says. 'It's a remarkable place and one of the oldest and best preserved Norman motte-and-bailey castles in Cornwall. I think you'll enjoy the time spent there.'

'I should have illustrations ready by the weekend.'

'Well, I look forward to receiving them. Now I must away. I have a lecture to deliver. But please don't hesitate to let me know if anything is unclear.'

Kat says goodbye and replaces the handset. This should be fun. She will be able to flex her creative muscles and produce illustrations that come naturally to her.

Swiftly exiting the room, she hurries along the hallway to the door opening to the small balcony and steps outside. Leaning over the wall, she peers upstream in the direction of the town, just in time to catch sight of the tail-end of the dark-blue-hulled yacht as it disappears around a bend in the river.

18

On the far outskirts of the medieval town of Lostwithiel, Kat indicates left and follows the sign for Restormel Castle. To one side of the road, driveways lead off to a number of individual properties while on the opposite side, an attractive stone wall borders a tranquil cemetery. Soon the houses are left behind and she drives along a lane lined with high hedges and colourful wildflowers that glisten in the morning sun.

Travelling deeper into the wooded countryside, Kat passes the town's bowling club before coming to the entrance to Restormel Farm. Ignoring this, she follows the road around to the left that wends its way uphill, and it's not long before the trees thin out to reveal a pale-blue sky threaded with wispy clouds, heralding another fair day. A smile spreads across Kat's face as she reaches the car park.

Good. Only two other vehicles.

She'd made a concerted effort to arrive early in the hope there wouldn't be too many people around as she'd like to work unhindered. Although experience has taught her that whenever she brings out her sketchbooks people have a habit of appearing and approaching for a chat.

Parking in a spot not far from the entrance, she switches off the engine and reaches for her art bag on the back seat. Some minutes later, having entered the grounds through a wooden gate, she follows a post and rail-bounded track leading up through a wooded area, and as she emerges from the copse into a clearing, the castle suddenly appears. The circular ruins are remarkable. As Kat approaches, her senses heighten and she's aware of the familiar onset of tingling in her fingers and blood coursing through her veins; sure signs the castle's history will reveal itself and demand to be drawn. She stands for a moment on the far side of a dry moat crossed by a wooden bridge, and stares up in awe at the high, stone walls.

The previous evening she'd re-read Stella's summary of Restormel Castle.

> *It is one of the most remarkable castles in Britain. The present circular structure, built in the late 13th century, was a luxurious retreat for its medieval owners. In the 14th century the Black Prince, Edward III's son, stayed there twice. At this time Restormel, and nearby Lostwithiel, was a centre for the highly lucrative tin industry, from which the Duchy of Cornwall drew much of its wealth. The castle has been ruined since the 16th century.*

Kat looks up at artificial embankments rising as high as the first floor of the castle walls. Built as a powerful deterrent to raiders, its defences were necessary only once over the course of its long history, in the summer of 1644 during the English Civil War. All at once, carrying on a breeze that has sprung from nowhere, Kat detects the strong smell of hot, sweaty horses and she's sure she can hear men shouting and the sounds of fighting.

Turning, she gazes out over the beautiful, far-reaching views across the valley of the River Fowey. A family with two young children sit at a picnic table, one of half a dozen and strategically positioned to enjoy the panoramic vista. Kat takes in the immediate grounds. If she'd visited a month earlier the area would have been covered in primroses and daffodils. Instead, swathes of bluebells now take centre stage, whilst a supporting cast of mature rhododendron bushes covered in bud are on the cusp of displaying their vibrant colours.

Laughter echoes from within the ruins as Kat walks across the wooden bridge, knowing that in the past this was the location of the drawbridge. Pausing at the entrance, she takes a deep breath, clears her mind, and invites the castle's atmosphere to guide her. It's a ritual that allows her to become *open* to whatever buildings wish to convey. Here, whispers from the ancient walls suggest that where she stands was once the gate house. Kat searches for clues that might reveal the past grandeur of the castle, and it's not long before the ruined remains give her a sense of their once-opulent surroundings. She can easily envisage large fireplaces, high windows and the Great Hall used for gatherings.

Suddenly, from out of the corner of her eye she sees a flash of red and glances up. High on a wooden walkway circling the inner walls, a young man dressed in a brightly coloured jacket holds out his hand to a slim, blonde woman. Pulling her into his arms, the couple stand locked together gazing out at the view. Uninvited, a vision of Colin pops into Kat's head. She sighs and wonders what he's doing right now.

Probably grappling with nappies and sleepless nights!

But there's no point in revisiting that time. It's over . . .

She heads towards a wooden staircase and climbing to the top of the castle wall, she walks around the inside of the keep. The tingling sensation in her body increases as noises and shadowy movements in the courtyard below replay memories of a bustling castle from centuries ago. All is energy, and she watches in fascination as the scene unfolds.

A loud clattering of hooves across the drawbridge announces the arrival of several men on horseback and a servant swiftly appears from out of the shadows. He hurries towards the first horse, just as its rider athletically leaps from the saddle and strides across the yard towards a set of stone steps leading up to a closed door. What is this man's story? Why does he bound up the steps in a hurry? Does he have important and urgent news to impart? From what period is the scene? Could she be witnessing a time when the Parliamentarian army under Lord Essex briefly garrisoned the castle before being driven out by Charles I's forces? However, the next minute she's distracted by a friendly *hello* as the young couple approach along the walkway, and the visions swiftly dissolve into thin air as she's unceremoniously jolted back into the twenty-first century.

Smiling politely, Kat returns the acknowledgement and turns to gaze out across the landscape. The views over the valley from the top of the castle walls are even more magnificent than from the plateau below. The castle's grounds were once a deer park and she imagines herds of beasts roaming the landscape, blissfully unaware of the next, inevitable, hunting party. Closing her eyes, Kat turns her face to the sun and breathes in the Cornish spring air. It's so pure and unpolluted; her lungs must surely thank her for the respite from breathing in London's fumes.

Completing the circuit of the inner keep, she descends a set of stone and wooden steps and stands in the centre of the courtyard slowly turning around, visualising how the castle would have appeared in its heyday. As she gazes at the ruins, undefined layers of previous time blur her vision before a porter's lodge, guard houses, cellars and a kitchen emerge out of the fog. She sees a well cut into the bedrock, and on either side of the courtyard a set of wooden staircases lead up to the first floor where Kat senses the Great Hall, an inner hall, a Chapel and a Great Chamber are.

On the far side of the courtyard, at the entrance to one of the cellars, is a low section of wall. It looks just the right height for a seat and crossing over to it, she places her art bag on the ground, removes her jacket and lays it over the stones. Sitting down on it, she opens the flap of her bag and extracts her sketchpad and pencil case. Heat radiates in waves from her hands and a tingling sensation pulsates through her fingers. Impatient to start drawing, Kat selects a pencil and places its point lightly on the paper. As soon as the lead makes contact, her hand sweeps across the page in a series of strokes, as if possessed with a life of its own.

19

'How's it going?' Tara asks.

It's Thursday evening and Kat is in the kitchen preparing supper. Wedging the phone between her shoulder and ear, she adds a cup of white wine to the risotto simmering in the pan and pours herself a glass . . . for good measure.

'Great! I'm on track. The sketches are coming along nicely, and Stella's happy with the ones I've produced so far.'

'That's good to hear. And how is Fowey? Living up to your expectations?'

'The town is lovely. There seems to be plenty happening.'

'Have you put yourself out and about?'

'A bit.' Kat changes the phone to her other ear. 'I've met a couple of interesting people – a woman who works in the museum and her mother. They've asked me to join them for lunch this Sunday at the sailing club.'

'Ooh, la, la. Very swish!'

Kat tosses a handful of mushrooms into the pan and gives them a stir. 'I don't think it is. The *yacht* club has 'Royal' in its name!'

'It's a good way to meet people.' Tara pauses. 'I do miss you, Kat. London wine bars just aren't the same without you.'

Kat laughs. 'I miss you too. Perhaps we can meet up when you're next in Salcombe. It's not too far.'

'Good idea. I'll let you know when we're heading that way. So, tell me, what's Stella's property like?'

'Brilliant! There's even a cleaner twice a month.'

As she describes the house to her friend, Kat extracts a bowl from a kitchen cupboard and spoons the contents of the pan into it. Grabbing a fork from a drawer, she carries her meal and glass of wine through to the sitting room.

'... And steps lead directly from the property to a private jetty.'

'Wow! Some people have all the luck,' says Tara. 'You realise you'll have to take up sailing.'

Kat sinks onto the couch. 'I'll let you know once I've lunched at Gallants and checked out the instructors.'

Tara laughs. 'Yeah, you do that!' The next minute, her voice takes on a serious edge. 'Kat, I met Colin earlier in the week outside South Ken station. He was coming around the corner pushing a buggy.'

The unexpected change in subject causes Kat's stomach muscles to spasm. 'How was he?'

'To be honest he didn't look so good – pale and drawn.'

'Not surprising really, what with a new baby and two toddlers. He's probably not getting much sleep.'

'I'm so sorry he turned out to be such a cad. I can't believe he did that to you.'

'Me neither, Tara, but it is what it is. He's a lying, scheming toad and I'm well rid of him... even if it doesn't feel like it.'

'Oh, Kat, I wish I was with you right now. I'd give you a huge hug and top up that wine glass.'

Kat snorts. 'You know me so well.'

'I do. And one day you'll meet someone who wants to know you that well, too.'

'Well, they'd better hurry up. Forty beckons...'

'Don't even go there! But you're one of the lucky ones. You will always look youthful, what with your gorgeous autumnal locks and emerald-green eyes. I'll have you know, people kill for half of what God dished out to you.'

Kat smiles. Even at a very young age Tara had her back, and her friend has the knack of raising her spirits even when she's unaware they need lifting.

'Enough of me, Tara. How's that lovely family of yours?'

A while later, phone call over, Kat rises from the couch and crosses the room to gaze out over the river. It's still active with watercraft, and the setting sun casts a soft, golden glow over Polruan's rooftops tumbling down the hillside on the opposite bank. She'd like to capture this view with the warming light in a watercolour, but she has work to complete before the weekend. However, she will paint it once the illustrations are out of the way. Taking her mobile from her pocket, she takes several photos of the scene.

Turning away from the window, she walks out of the room and crosses the hallway into her studio. On the easel sits an unfinished illustration of Restormel Castle. She's worked on several drawings since her visit earlier in the week, but this one has eluded her. As the sun bathes the room in its glorious, fading light, Kat wonders whether the illustration will come true this evening. Picking up a pen, she approaches the large sketch and closes her eyes, recalling the scene that had presented itself, *in situ*. Immediately her hand starts to move and when she opens her eyes again, emerging on the paper are shapes recording an earlier life of the castle.

Some while later, Kat checks the time on her phone and decides to sketch for a further hour. Crossing the room, she switches on the light, and immediately half a dozen, recessed ceiling downlights illuminate the space. She examines the illustration, some sixth sense telling her it's a true reconstruction of the Great Hall as it was in the fourteenth century. She's drawn the sketch in a cutaway fashion, revealing a large area beneath the floor of the Hall that provides storage for a number of wooden crates and barrels. Two men wearing caps remove a lid from a wooden keg while a scullery maid searches through one of the crates. Above, in the main hall, a man dressed in a tunic and stockings stands at a trestle table; beside him, a woman in a long dress and wearing a simple head covering, kneads bread. A Coat of Arms adorns an imposing fireplace, in front of which stands a servant with a pair of bellows encouraging a fire in the hearth. Two large, arched windows with elaborate glazing and open shutters look down the valley in the direction of Lostwithiel. In one, a nursemaid sits in a window seat while keeping an eye on a young boy peering out.

Those windows would have been vulnerable to attack. Surely it's more likely the castle was built as a symbol of power rather than a defensible fortress?

The walls of the window alcoves are decorated in vividly coloured murals depicting brave knights. Kat looks down in surprise at the red watercolour brush in her hand. She has no recollection of discarding her pen and replacing it with this. An impressive timber roof arcs over the Great Hall, and at the far end she has sketched intricately carved, wooden panelling spanning the full width of the room. Above this is another colourful mural portraying a fierce battle, with a heroic leader at its centre and a dozen horses in full charge.

'Goodness!' Kat steps back in astonishment.

Many pieces of her artwork are spread over the dining table and, crossing over to it now, she rifles through the papers and selects one. Walking back to the easel, she holds up the drawing alongside the illustration she is currently working on.

'So, what are you doing here?' she asks incredulously.

As she compares her drawing of the man standing in the bow of the boat to that of the soldier commanding the battle, her cheeks redden. Each has glorious, dark, wild hair curling at the nape of the neck and a pair of twinkling hazel eyes, full of hidden depths. In fact, they are one and the same . . .

20

Seagulls shriek discordantly from the rooftops as Kat makes her way along the narrow street, dodging the many early May Bank Holiday visitors swelling the town's population. It's another bright day and she's glad she's remembered her sunglasses. As the lane starts to rise, Kat looks up at the house with the scallop shell canopy above its front door. It's such a handsome building; she must remember to ask Lisa about its history. Turning down the alleyway between it and the neighbouring property, she follows the sounds of a party in full swing. The door to the sailing club stands open and as she enters, a vibrant, joyful atmosphere enfolds her.

'There she is!' a woman's voice calls out over the general hubbub. 'Kat, come and join us. We've saved a seat for you!'

She turns. Sitting at a window table that has stunning views over the river are a group of people, among them Lisa and her mother. She makes her way through the crowd, smiling as men move aside for her, and laughs at their various compliments. Arriving at the table, she slides into an empty seat.

'Hello,' she says to the assembled gathering.

'We're so pleased you've joined us,' Lisa says with a smile. 'Here, let me introduce you. You've already met my mum, Jean.'

Kat turns to the older lady, who once again is elegantly dressed. 'Hello, Jean.'

'Hello, my dear. I hope you're settling in well.'

'I am, thank you.'

'And these, here, are my two reprobates,' says Lisa, pulling a young lad sitting next to her into an affectionate, rough hug.

'Mum!' the boy exclaims, squirming to escape his mother's grasp.

'This is Steven,' she says, ruffling his unruly, blond thatch of hair, 'and next to him is my daughter, Jenny.'

Kat smiles at the teenagers. 'Hi. Are you both keen sailors?'

'Yes, although I'm better at it than Jen,' says the boy proudly.

As his mother releases her hold, Steven quickly smooths down his hair and self-consciously glances at Kat.

She hides a smile. He must be all of thirteen.

'Not so,' says Jenny.

'I am!' Steven retorts.

'Come on, you two, don't squabble,' their mother reprimands.

Kat is introduced to the other people at the table: a local solicitor and his estate agent wife; the owner of an art gallery and his male partner; a librarian and her husband; and a dapper, older gentleman sitting next to Jean.

'That's Stan,' says Lisa, lowering her voice to a whisper. 'He's a former headmaster and has designs on Mum.'

Kat grins.

A slim, middle-aged man with a familiar thatch of blond hair suddenly arrives at the table.

'Everything OK here?' he asks.

'This is the artist I was telling you about,' Lisa says. 'Kat, this is my husband, Derek.'

'So you're the lady that visited the museum earlier this week. Welcome to Fowey! Are you having the Sunday roast?'

Kat nods. 'Please.'

'And what would you like to drink?'

She orders a glass of red wine.

'Does anyone else need a top-up?' Derek glances around the rest of the table and a few minutes later, having taken their orders, he returns to the bar.

'Be a couple of loves,' Lisa says to her children, 'go and help Dad with the drinks.'

Jenny groans. 'Gawd, it's his job!'

'I know, but look how busy he is.'

The girl sighs dramatically. 'Fiiiiiine! Come on, Stevie, give us a hand.' Reluctantly she gets to her feet and heads towards the bar.

'Growing pains . . . Sixteen's a difficult age,' explains Lisa to Kat. 'But underneath all that teenage irritability lurks a really sweet girl.'

'And I'm a really sweet boy, too,' says Steven, getting up from his chair and giving Kat a disarmingly cheeky grin.

'I guess you'll do,' says Lisa, winking at her son.

Kat glances around. There's a variety of people and a wide range of ages in the sailing club. All are dressed casually – mainly striped sweatshirts, cotton trousers and deck shoes – apart from Jean and Stan who are in their Sunday best. Laughter reverberates around the room and the snatches of conversation Kat catches are generally of a nautical theme. A waitress approaches carrying plates of roast beef, closely followed by Jenny and Steven, armed with drinks.

'Does anyone want anything else?' the waitress asks, placing the last plate down on the table.

'Don't think so,' says, Lisa, checking the range of accompaniments. 'Looks like we've got everything we need here, thanks.'

Kat loads her fork with roast beef.

'What is it that you do?' asks Stan, leaning forward and addressing her across the table.

She hesitates and then places the fork down on her plate. 'I'm an illustrator, working on a book for a historian.'

'That sounds interesting. Anyone I'd know?'

'Possibly. The writer has a holiday home here. Professor Stella Marsh.'

The man purses his lips. 'The name rings a bell but I can't quite place her. What is she writing?'

'An account of the West Country's landed gentry through

the ages. I've been commissioned to illustrate various properties.'

'And what have you illustrated thus far?'

Kat glances down at her roast lunch. At this rate it will be cold by the time she gets to it.

'I visited Restormel Castle this week and found it fascinating. Penhallam Manor is also on my list, which I believe was owned by a previous owner of Restormel.'

'Ah yes, the Cardinhams. A rum lot.'

'Stan.' Jean places a hand on the man's arm. 'Why don't you let Kat enjoy her lunch in peace? You can quiz her after she's finished her meal.'

'Oh yes, I'm so sorry, young lady,' says Stan, suddenly flustered. 'Pray continue. We'll catch up later.'

Kat gives the man a smile. Picking up her fork again, she adds a portion of roast potato and a dollop of horseradish to the beef already skewered on it and takes a mouthful. All at once a shout sounds out from over by the bar, swiftly followed by laughter. Chewing, she turns towards the commotion and almost chokes, her eyes opening wide as her stomach involuntarily tightens.

No way! This cannot be happening . . .

Entering the sailing club, with a slim blonde in tow, is none other than Mac. He looks *so* good, relaxed and carefree, and Kat is unable to drag her eyes away from him. As he walks towards the bar acknowledging various groups of people, she notices how guys tend to slap him on the back and shake his hand, while women hug and kiss him on the cheek. Her gaze slides to his companion. Unlike the women she's seen him with in London and Salcombe, this one looks more outdoorsy.

Yet another woman in a different port! What is it with him? He must be exhausted, juggling so many.

Silently, Kat gives a derisive snort. Her attention wanders back to Mac, who is now standing at the bar, and watches as his companion cosies up to him and puts her arm familiarly around his waist. She recalls his pretty companion in Salcombe had reached for his hand as they walked along the quay. Obviously, he's used to women making all the advances. And there's still no sign of his son. She frowns. A small group of people have gathered around the couple, eager to buy them drinks.

Popular! But then, with his looks people probably fall over themselves to befriend him. Little wonder he has no trouble picking up women.

Her internal chatter fills Kat with sadness and disappointment. But how ridiculous; she doesn't even know him. Why should the way he conduct his life concern her? She certainly shouldn't have any opinions about him. Get a grip . . . Refocussing on the people at the table, she turns to Steven and asks about the history of the Scallop Shell House.

'It used to be the Post Office until a couple of years ago,' the boy says eagerly, delighted at the attention.

'Is that so?' says Kat. 'That would explain the clock in the window.'

He nods. 'There used to be a slot beneath the clock where you posted letters and also a telephone box outside,' he explains, as if imparting some earth-shattering news.

Jenny grimaces at her brother. 'Steady, Steve. *So* obvs!'

Blushing to the roots of his hair, the lad shoots Kat a look of acute embarrassment. She makes sure her expression remains impassive.

'The house is Georgian and marks the site of a medieval resting place for pilgrims,' explains Lisa. 'In the early fifteenth century, seven Fowey shippers were granted licences to carry pilgrims and it's recorded as the point where hundreds embarked on the vessel, the *Camino de Santiago,* on their journey to the shrine of St James of Compostela in Spain.'

Leaning forward, Stan adds to the story. 'The canopy above the door is in the shape of a large scallop shell because that has long been the symbol of the *Camino de Santiago*.

The shells also served a practical purpose for the pilgrims on board, being the right size for gathering water to drink, or as a makeshift bowl to eat from.'

Lisa nods. 'Legend has it that after St James died, his disciples shipped his body to the Iberian Peninsula so he could be buried in what is now Santiago. However, during the journey, a heavy storm hit the ship and his body was lost overboard, though it washed ashore some time later, undamaged, and covered in scallops.'

'That's quite a story,' says Kat.

'It is,' Stan agrees.

Steven nods sagely, the colour in his cheeks remaining high.

21

'Good afternoon, folks.'

His voice is deep and resonant and she looks up into twinkling, hazel eyes.

Oh, no, you don't...

'Hey, you're back!' cries Steven.

'When did you arrive?' asks Lisa.

Obviously he's well-known to these people, too.

'Yesterday lunchtime.'

'Are you here for long?' asks Jenny in a soft, silky voice.

Kat glances at the girl. Gone is the stroppy attitude and the sulky face, and in their place are shining eyes and rosy cheeks.

For God's sake, even teenage girls!

'I'm here for the summer, offering yacht charters aboard *Windsong*.'

'Oh, great!' says Steven. 'Can we go sailing?'

'Steve, don't be so pushy,' Lisa reprimands.

'That's OK,' Mac says. 'I'm pleased Steve's so enthusiastic. Yes, of course.'

'Yes!' The boy punches the air.

Kat frowns. *If he's here for the summer, why didn't he mention that when he discussed Fowey with her?*

As the man's gaze flicks back to Kat, Lisa exclaims, 'Oh what am I thinking? Kat, this is Mac.'

'Cat? That's an unusual name,' he says quietly, his eyes teasing her.

'As is yours,' she says, and he smiles warmly.

'James MacNamara, but everyone calls me Mac.'

Her mouth stretches to a brief smile.

Suddenly strong, practical fingers appear at his waist and he tenses as the blonde woman peers around his torso, his expression turning to one of irritation.

'Have you abandoned me, Mac?' she says, gazing up at him.

He stands to one side, making room for her.

'Hi, Sarah,' says Lisa. 'I guess you've got something to smile about now.'

The young woman grins, her grip tightening on his waist. 'Just a bit!'

Lisa laughs.

Feeling detached, yet strangely involved, Kat watches the scene play out in front of her. Why does it seem like Sarah makes Mac uncomfortable? She looks up and is shocked to find him watching her. Emotion flickers in his eyes.

What?

If she didn't know better she'd think it was almost an apology.

'Hello, James,' says Jean. 'It's good to see you again. The town is definitely not the same when you're away.'

He turns to the older woman. 'Hello, Jean, and thank you. I do miss Fowey, that's true, but I intend to make the most of my months here.'

'Well, I hope we'll see a lot of you.' Jean's face lights up with a smile. 'In fact, Stan, why don't we throw a party in that wonderful garden of yours? We could have a barbeque.'

'That's a good idea,' her admirer says. 'We'll arrange a day.'

'Love a barbeque,' says Sarah, nestling under Mac's arm.

Kat watches with interest, as Mac holds his arm rigid, as if trying not to touch Sarah. Surely she can feel that? But the young woman seems oblivious to his aloofness with her.

'Hey, Mac,' the solicitor calls from the far end of the table. 'Are you in the market for a property? Tamsin has some terrific houses coming on.'

Taking the opportunity to extract himself from his companion's embrace, Mac moves away. Sitting in an empty chair, he immediately enters into a lively conversation with the solicitor and his estate agent wife.

As Kat finishes her meal, she joins in with the general chatter around the table and fights the temptation to glance in Mac's direction. When a group of young women enter the clubroom, Sarah excuses herself and moves away to join them, and Kat notices Mac visibly relax. She frowns.

'Are you all right?' Jean asks, her voice registering concern.

Kat smiles at Lisa's mother. 'I was just thinking about all the work I've still to do on my illustrations so they're ready to send tonight,' she lies.

'It must be wonderful to make a living from your creativity,' Jean says.

'It is, although I admit there are times when I wonder if it would have been wiser to take an easier, more lucrative route.'

'Money isn't everything,' Stan interjects, joining in their conversation.

'No, but it pays the bills,' Kat responds.

'Where is home?' Jean asks.

'North London. A work colleague has rented my flat while I'm in Fowey.'

'A lovely breather by the sea,' comments Stan.

'It certainly is! I'm staying in Stella's property in the Esplanade. It's on the waterfront.'

'Very nice,' remarks Jean.

'Stella Marsh, you say?' Stan considers the name. 'I still can't place her. I'll have to look up her body of work.'

Suddenly Lisa gets to her feet. 'Sorry to be a killjoy but I've just noticed the time and I have to get back to let the dog out.'

Kat glances at her phone. It's past four. She should make tracks, too.

'I'm so pleased you joined us, Kat,' Lisa says, turning to her.

'Thanks for inviting me. It's been fun.'

'We often come here for Sunday lunch and you're welcome to join us any time.'

'Thanks.' Kat smiles at the woman. 'I guess I should be on my way too.'

Leaning down, she retrieves her bag and pushes back her chair. As she takes her leave of the people around the table she's aware of Mac's scrutiny. Uncharacteristically, it makes her hot under the collar and when she says goodbye to Steven, a vivid blush creeps up his neck and her sympathies go out to the boy.

'It's been great meeting you,' he says in a rush.

His sister shoots him a withering look.

'And you, too, Steve. And Jen.'

The girl smiles. She really is rather pretty when she ditches the scowl.

As Kat walks away from the table she hears Jenny mimicking her brother in an exaggerated voice: *'It's been great meeting you . . .* Honestly, Steve, you made a right twit of yourself.'

Kat pays for her meal at the bar.

'Hope to see you in here again sometime,' says Derek, as he processes her payment. 'The sailing club has a full social calendar and we often have live music nights.'

'That sounds great. I'm sure I'll be back.'

'Look forward to it.' He hands over her credit card and receipt.

Kat gives Lisa's husband a smile and turns for the door. She's halfway down the alleyway when she hears someone calling to her.

'Kat.'

Mac. Steeling herself, she turns. *Dear God! Why does he have to be so good-looking?*

'I'm pleased we bumped into each other,' he says, approaching her.

He sounds genuine enough, but then so had Colin. She won't fall for the tricks of men again.

'Why?' she asks bluntly.

'Because . . .' His voice falters and his forehead creases.

'It's a small town,' she continues flippantly. 'If you're here for the summer I guess our paths are bound to cross.'

He takes another step towards her but Kat springs back. His frown deepens and the look in his eyes turns to confusion . . . and something else.

An uncomfortable silence stretches between them.

'I have to go.' Kat waves her hand in the direction of the street.

He doesn't move, just continues to assess her.

A sudden flurry of movement behind him announces Sarah's arrival as she bursts in on their awkwardness.

'Oh, there you are, Mac! I wondered where you'd got to.' She glances inquisitively at Kat. 'Are you leaving? It was good meeting you.'

Kat's lips twitch into a courteous smile. 'You too.'

Giving Mac one last glance, she puts on her sunglasses and walks out of the alleyway into the warmth of the afternoon sun.

22

That night, sleep evades Kat. Increasingly restless and unable to get comfortable, she eventually gives up trying to chase its restorative powers. With a sigh, she throws back the covers and stumbles downstairs to the kitchen. Like an automaton, she goes through the motions of making a mug of tea before carrying it through to the sitting room.

Opening the blinds, she sits in the armchair with her knees drawn up to her chest and watches the eastern sky soften to the milky, uncertain light of dawn. But as the sun rises above the rooftops of Polruan, all at once the river sparkles, as if someone has switched on a thousand fairy lights and cast them across its surface. In contemplative mood she sips her tea. *Mac* has already found his way into her head, and all night long she's tossed and turned, waking to fragments of broken dreams, in which images of her lying ex morphed into visions of Mac. Fleetingly, she'd believed she was still with Colin, or at least a rose-tinted version of him; one free of the reality of a heavily pregnant wife and young family. She had felt complete, and warmth had entered her heart, only for it to turn stone cold again as soon as she'd opened her eyes.

She takes another sip of tea.

Why had Colin deceived her? What had he thought to gain from the deception? He couldn't maintain a dual life forever. There was obviously no way forward for them as a couple. He wouldn't abandon his young family and, anyway, would she have wanted him if he had? Doesn't that show the true nature of a man?

Kat shudders with humiliation, but also sadness that Colin's deceit has affected her to the extent she now wants nothing more to do with the opposite sex. She lets out a deep sigh. *No one* is going to take advantage of her like that, ever again. And certainly not that man, Mac, regardless of how devastatingly attractive and personable he may be. No, her eyes are finally wide open!

Walking to the kitchen, Kat places the empty mug in the sink and hurries upstairs. Entering the bathroom, she scowls at herself in the mirror. Dark circles smudge beneath her eyes.

'You sure look hot this morning . . . *not!*' she tells her reflection.

With only a couple of hours' sleep, she is too spaced out to concentrate on illustrating. Instead, she decides to take the ferry across to Polruan and explore the Hall Walk. Rushing through her ablutions, she weaves her long locks into a thick plait and grabs a small rucksack from the wardrobe, stuffing her packaway waterproof jacket into it – though the beautiful dawn promises a good day ahead, she knows the Cornish weather can be unpredictable. Returning to the kitchen, she adds a bottle of water and some fruit to the rucksack before checking the ferry timetable.

'OK. What have I forgotten?'

She glances around the room and her gaze alights on her sunglasses. Picking them up from the counter, she checks her mobile is fully charged and exits the house.

A harsh rattling from the other side of the street announces the roller shutters of the tapas bar opening.

'Morning!' says a young woman, her strong Cornish accent evident, as she emerges from beneath the shutters to set up tables on the pavement. She glances skywards. 'Looks like we're in for a good day.'

'It does,' responds Kat, pulling the front door to.

'I've seen you around. Maybe you'll pay us a visit sometime?' The woman smiles at her.

Kat smiles back. 'I intend to. I love Spanish food.'

The woman nods and moves to the next table. 'Well, have a good day.'

'You too.'

Putting on her sunglasses, Kat walks along the Esplanade towards the town and wonders if the bar does takeaways. Sternly, she tells herself not to be such a wuss. There's nothing wrong with a woman dining at a restaurant on her own. What kind of spineless individual has she turned into?

A short while later, Kat arrives at Town Quay. A surprising number of people are out and about, and the outside seating area to the restaurant is heaving. Blue and green bunting flutters in the breeze and a plethora of watercraft moored in the estuary patiently await the forthcoming day's adventures. Picture perfect!

As she approaches the ticket office and joins a small queue, she spies the little orange ferry chugging its way across the water towards the quay. Five minutes later, she embarks, along with six other passengers, and as the boat powers out into mid-channel a fair breeze whips up the river. Thankfully, she's wearing a T-shirt under her sweatshirt. Kat glances back at the town, surprised to see a large, castellated stone property located above the dominant spire of St Fimbarrus Church. She hadn't noticed it from street level.

The crossing is short and in no time at all the ferry pulls up alongside Polruan Quay. After disembarking, Kat checks the information board. A map of the walk is displayed and she takes a photo of it before following the sign pointing uphill to the South West Coast Path. Some way ahead are two fellow passengers from the ferry and she wonders if they, too, are doing the Hall Walk. If so, she'll be able to follow them and avoid wandering off the trail. However, they're obviously seasoned walkers and it's not long before she's left behind. After a while she comes to a fork in the path, each track running either side of a wire fence. She checks the map on her phone, but it's not obvious which route she should take.

'This one, I guess.' She observes the lower track's wooden decking boards. 'Looks more official.'

Kat squints up at the sky. It's not even midday and the sun is already hot! Rifling through the rucksack, she finds her baseball cap and puts it on, then sets off once again.

As she follows the lower path that hugs the contours of the cliff edge, the views are breathtaking and she stops at a wooden bench to watch the seagulls swooping on thermals above two perfectly curved, horseshoe bays.

'Lantic Bay,' she says to herself, checking the map.

The rhythmic movement of the waves as the sands are washed clean is hypnotic, and opening her arms wide Kat fills her lungs with the salt-laden air. After a while, feeling invigorated, she continues on and soon arrives at a set of steps leading down to a wooden gate. Here, too, there are choices: either head down to the bay or remain on the coastal path. Guided by the map, she walks a little further until she reaches another wooden bench, where a public footpath turns inland across a field. She takes this path, and on the opposite boundary she climbs over a stile onto a road. It seems strange to be walking on tarmac. But after a short distance, she takes the first right and soon joins the Hall Walk to Pont Pill.

High above the River Fowey, Kat walks a shaded trail through ancient woodland. The area is awash with wildflowers and carpets of white, starry blooms secrete the smell of wild garlic. Walking towards her is a man with a dog, and she stands back to allow him to pass on the narrow path. Presently, the trail emerges from the woods at a point where the river narrows and she lingers for a while, taking in the view towards the estuary, before continuing her descent through the woodland.

23

There's no one around when Kat reaches the hamlet of Pont Pill situated on the wooded banks of the river, and she stands for a long moment, enjoying the peace and tranquillity. She gazes around at the cluster of cottages nestled in the hidden tidal creek, just metres away from the water, imagining how pleasant it would be to while away a few hours reading a book on the riverbank, or launching a kayak or boat at high tide and hopping across to Fowey. Somewhere close by, a bird suddenly calls, and two ducks busily inspect the reeds at the water's edge. But apart from that all is silent.

A stone cottage with a row of pigeonholes below its slate roof hints at a former agricultural building, perhaps a stable with loft above, and positioned immediately in front of this is a characterful, honey-coloured farmhouse. A plaque displayed on the wall catches her attention and she approaches. It's the original 1894 notice for shipping dues. Immediately to the right of the farmhouse is a stone building with an open archway, leading to what looks like an old lime kiln, and Kat snaps a few photos on her mobile before walking beneath the arch and into the lichen-covered building. The interior is cool and dank, and she remains only a short while before stepping out of the musty building and into the fresh air once again.

Wandering over to the stone quay, she listens to the water slapping against a couple of moored rowing boats and wonders how the hamlet might have been in the past. She can sense the bustling and vibrant, former life it once had and she's conscious of shadowy images lining up; barges waiting to come alongside to discharge their cargoes. All at once, a gentle breeze springs up and she hears the muffled shouts of men busy working on the quayside.

Yet again, Kat's *gift* reminds her the past is never far away.

Taking a last look around at the cluster of cottages, she crosses a wooden footbridge spanning the river and heads up a track on the opposite hillside. Halfway up she stops, her calf muscles burning. If nothing else, this hike must be doing her fitness levels a world of good. Kat gazes back down the path, but she's still alone on the Walk and continuing on, nearing the top, she turns to take in the views of the Fowey Estuary.

'Spectacular!'

Without taking her eyes off the breathtaking vista, she removes the water bottle from her rucksack and raises it to her mouth, savouring the cool liquid. Suddenly, she notices a dark-blue-hulled yacht coming into view. Lowering the bottle, Kat pushes her sunglasses on top of her head and squints, sharpening her vision. But it's no good. The yacht is too far out in mid-channel. Rummaging in the rucksack once again, she extracts a pair of binoculars and focuses them on the yacht, and its name becomes legible: *Windsong*.

Such a stunning boat!

Slowly, she scans the deck. Standing at the wheel, facing into the wind, is Sarah, the young woman from Gallants. Her blonde hair is tied back in a ponytail and she looks every inch the competent sailor as she steers the boat towards the mouth of the river. Kat trails the binoculars along the length of the yacht and comes to an abrupt halt. Mac expertly unfurls sails and she watches as he glances back at Sarah at the helm, says something and roars with laughter. Swinging the binoculars in Sarah's direction again, Kat catches the broad grin on her face. Despite his discomfort at the sailing club, it's obvious they're at ease with each other. Once again, she trains the binoculars on Mac. Despite her conflicted feelings towards him, she has to admit that there's something so free about him. He seems to be in exactly the right place, doing what he loves. She can't deny how attractive that is. It was her first impression of him, when she'd initially spied him from her office window in the busy London street, that this is the sort of life he leads. Something about him had made her think of vast oceans and then, later, when he'd entered the art gallery, she'd heard the cry of gulls, the snap of a sail caught by a gust of wind, and the sound of rigging lines slapping against a mast.

She watches as the yacht sails downstream and only when it's out in the open sea does she continue her journey. As she leaves the track and steps onto the headland, ahead of her is a memorial stone with a large 'Q' carved into the top and a plaque displayed below. She stops to read the inscription and discovers the stone was erected in memory of the great Cornishman, writer and scholar, Sir Arthur Quiller-Couch, who was a resident of Fowey for over fifty years.

Turning, she takes in the mesmerising view again. Laid out before her is the ancient village of Polruan, the mouth of the River Fowey, and on the opposite headland, St Catherine's Castle. From this viewpoint, it's obvious why two blockhouses had been built on either side of the river during the fifteenth century. With a boom chain strung between them, they would have provided effective protection for the harbour town against invasion from the sea. The blockhouse on the Fowey side, however, is now in ruins and simply a feature within a private garden.

Kat turns away. Setting off down the incline towards Bodinnick Quay, it's not long before she passes the pub and arrives at the river crossing, where half a dozen stationary cars wait for the ferry approaching from the other side. She gazes up at Ferryside, the du Mauriers' home, and wonders what it must have been like to live there, as the young Daphne had. Fifteen minutes later, the ferry deposits her at Caffa Mill Car Park – a reclaimed area of land that was originally a creek – and with aching feet she walks through the town. Calling into the bookshop, she treats herself to another guide book on Fowey before making her way back to Stella's and the promise of a long, hot soak in the bath.

24

Three days later, Kat turns off the main road and drives along a thickly canopied lane with trees showing late-spring growth. Turning right at a T-junction, her car soon emerges into open countryside and she looks towards the next property on her list. Across a pastoral landscape of gently sloping parkland dotted with trees and peacefully grazing sheep, an impressive country house stands perched on the hillside. Stella emailed her to say the property was on the market and that the owners had arranged for the agent to show her around.

Bringing the car to a stop, Kat gazes through the windscreen at impressive Palladian pillars adorning a south-facing elevation, which is bathed in late morning sunlight. Her trained artist's eye appreciates the symmetrically pleasing proportions of the majestic house, and even at this distance she can sense its fascinating history. Kat puts the car into gear and continues along the lane, and within a short distance a discreet sign announces the entrance to the property. Turning the car onto a broad, sweeping driveway bordered by black-metal estate fencing enclosing pristine meadows, she rounds a bend on the final approach to the Grade II listed house, just as a smart Bentley driven by a middle-aged man heads towards her. A stylish woman in the passenger seat beside him scrutinises Kat with an unsmiling stare as they pass by.

Standing at the top of a short flight of steps in front of an open entrance door is a balding man dressed in a tweed jacket, Tattersall checked shirt, mustard-coloured tie, moleskin trousers and shiny leather brogues. Kat swallows her smile. If there was ever a caricature of a country-house estate agent, he is it! Swiftly, she parks next to a smart, dark-green Land Rover Estate and gets out of her car.

'Ms Maddox,' the man greets her in a plummy voice. 'Gerald Carrington, Carrington and Partners.'

'Good morning.' She climbs the steps and shakes the well-manicured hand. 'Thank you for agreeing to show me over the house. I believe it's empty.'

'Indeed. The owners live abroad.'

'That will make my job a lot easier,' she says with a smile.

'I'm only here because I've just completed a tour of the property with an interested party,' he informs her. 'My colleague, Annabel, is due to arrive shortly and she will show you around. I understand Professor Marsh wishes to feature the mansion in a book. That will certainly add to the property's full and interesting history and I'm sure any new owner would be only too pleased to obtain a copy.' He looks down the driveway and then at his watch. 'Now, how would you like to proceed while we wait for my assistant to arrive?'

Glancing through the open doorway behind him, Kat suggests, 'Perhaps I could have a quick tour of a few rooms, so I can get an idea of what to sketch.'

'Indeed,' he says, turning smartly.

Kat follows him into a grand entrance hall with an impressive, ornately balustraded staircase and extensive oak flooring.

'A highly desirable, family home with flexible accommodation,' Gerald announces, before giving a small, embarrassed laugh. 'But, of course, that's not why you're here.'

'Sadly not.'

He picks up a brochure from a mahogany side table and hands it to her. 'This may assist you.'

'Thank you.'

'We'll start here.' He opens a wide door to the right.

The room is spacious with a large, open fireplace set in a marble surround and tall sash windows overlook the wooded landscape. Kat glances up at the high ceiling and observes the intricate cornicing.

'Egg and dart,' the agent comments.

'May I take photographs as I walk around?' she asks.

The man nods. Standing side by side, they gaze out of the windows at a formal terraced garden.

'At one time, this impressive Cornish mansion stood at the centre of a large 4,500-acre estate,' the man says. 'Today, it comes with just four.'

'It's sad that so many historic properties have had their land sold off,' Kat comments.

'Fluctuating prosperity and acts of necessity through the centuries, as much as anything.' He turns away from the view. 'This is one of two principal drawing rooms, although in its heyday the house had four.'

'I suppose previous owners entertained a lot.'

'Indeed. Royalty and more . . .'

She gives him a sideways glance.

'As I say, the property has a fascinating history,' he adds.

'That's what I'm interested in,' she says. 'I want to get a feel for the house, so that my illustrations do it justice.'

The sound of tyres crunching across gravel makes them both turn to the window again. A silver Range Rover pulls up and a smartly dressed, middle-aged woman in a tweed skirt-suit steps out. Looking up at the house and seeing them standing at the window, she waves and heads towards the steps.

'Good! Annabel has arrived. I'll leave you in her capable hands,' the agent says, striding from the room.

Kat smiles after him. 'Thank you.'

Gerald's assistant turns out to be far less pompous than her boss, and Kat enjoys a pleasant afternoon exploring the house and grounds with Annabel. Over the next three hours she learns that the original manor house dates back to a time before the Norman Conquest and was listed in the Domesday Book, as well as having connections with Cornish national and international events throughout the ages.

'From the mid-fifteenth century,' Annabel explains, 'for almost four hundred years it was occupied by one family, who distinguished themselves as mine owners, royal commissioners, sheriffs and MPs. They were also owners of other significant property interests, including a local estate, which is now in the ownership of the National Trust and a jewel in their crown.'

They enter one of the main reception rooms.

'In 1819, a fire swept through the house destroying one of the great libraries of the South West.' Annabel indicates the ceiling. 'That plaster cast is a copy of a medal awarded to the distinguished Major-General who purchased and restored the property in 1833. In time, he became a Baron and his family held the house until the Second World War. You'll see several different plaster-cast medals in the other main reception rooms.'

'It's a lot to take in,' Kat says, as she photographs the ceiling decoration.

Annabel smiles. 'I can assure you it's a lot to remember, too!'

Kat laughs.

'During the war, the property became a secret naval station and was visited by Lady Mountbatten. It was also machine gunned by a German plane.'

'It's survived a great deal,' Kat remarks.

'Yes. Many historic properties in the county have.'

As Annabel continues the tour of the house, she points out a number of intriguing features that would have gone unnoticed if Kat had been left to her own devices, such as the vaulted ceiling dating from an earlier dwelling in the old bakery, and the Prayer Hall, complete with a staircase, balcony and cupola. Stepping outside, Annabel draws Kat's attention to the bells on the main house, as well as a bowl from the old larder, now acting as a fountain on the main lawn, and a Celtic cross – discovered in an estate cottage where it had been used as a fireplace mantle.

The weather remains good throughout the afternoon, and after checking out a handsome Coach House that's ripe for conversion, the women find a shady spot for Kat beneath the boughs of a magnificent, three-hundred-year-old oak tree. While Kat sketches the house from a distance, including the remains of an orangery intriguingly left as a folly, Annabel keeps her company, telling her how she had moved from Berkshire to Cornwall a decade earlier. By the time the two women bid each other farewell, a friendship has been struck, telephone numbers exchanged and a future catch-up for drinks suggested.

25

Satisfied that her sketches of the house are useful for reference material, Kat returns to Fowey. As she drives along the Esplanade and pulls into the allocated parking bay for Stella's house, she's aware of a number of people sitting at tables outside the tapas bar. How she'd kill for a drink . . . And some tapas would go down well, too. Gathering up her art bag, she climbs out of the car and glances again towards the bar, and her heart skips a beat as she recognises Mac sitting at one of the tables with a woman who isn't Sarah. This one has silver hair cut fashionably short.

Spotting Kat, Mac's eyes open wide and he raises a hand in greeting. Involuntarily, Kat clenches her teeth, determinedly ignoring his friendly gesture. Instead, she locks the car and swiftly crosses the street, acutely aware of his gaze on her, and refusing to look in his direction, she inserts the key smartly into the lock.

But she's not quick enough.

'Kat,' he calls out, striding towards her. 'Wait . . .'

Bracing herself, she turns and is dismayed at the fierce attraction she has to him. She's always found him good-looking, but in the early evening light he appears even more so.

'Mac,' she manages to say in an even voice.

'Are you staying here?' he asks, glancing up at the property. 'Fantastic position, right on the waterfront.'

What can she say but yes? She's got the key in the door.

'Indeed.' Inwardly, Kat groans.

Now she sounds like the estate agent!

'Listen, Kat . . .' Mac says, not appearing to have noticed her aloof tone. His eyes sparkle at her. 'Do you like to sail?'

Despite herself, she's disarmed. 'I think so. I haven't done much . . . but the idea appeals.'

He smiles and warm, golden hues light his inquisitive hazel eyes. 'Then . . . we should put the idea to the test.'

Straight nose, gorgeous lips, even white teeth. Kat frowns. 'Oh, I don't have the time.'

Disappointment registers in his face. 'Not even at weekends?'

'Not usually, with my workload.'

'What do you do?' Mac glances down at the bag in her hand.

'I'm an illustrator,' she answers curtly. 'Look, I don't mean to be rude but I have a hundred and one things to do this evening, and I'm sure your date isn't happy with you talking to me.'

His look turns to one of confusion. 'Date?'

Kat nods in the direction of the woman sitting patiently at the table. She has a lively face and killer cheekbones, and is watching them intently.

Mac glances over towards his companion, courteously nodding at her, before turning back to Kat. 'She's not a date. She's a client.'

Conquest, more like . . .

If she is *just* a client, Kat wonders whether she should tell Mac that the woman is sending her very clear warning signals that she intends to be much more than that.

'OK,' she says, 'client, then.'

'Jane really doesn't mind.'

Kat begs to differ, but it's not her business. 'As I said, I have to go.'

Disappointment again registers in his eyes, but this time Kat is firmer with herself, and without a further word, she turns the key in the lock and steps into the safety of Stella's hallway. As she closes the door, ensuring she doesn't look at him, she waits for a minute until she hears Mac step away. She frowns. He's little more than a stranger but it's curious how she feels *involved* in some way, and she definitely hates being so frosty towards him. It's not her usual style.

Ruffled, Kat walks along the hall to the sitting room. Depositing her art bag on the couch, she immediately crosses over to the drinks cabinet and pours herself a large measure of gin and elderflower tonic water. The man from the off-licence was right, it is an excellent choice to pair with the Foy Gin. With glass in hand, she walks over to the bay window and gazes out across the river to Polruan, bathed as it is in the mellow rays of a setting sun. She smiles. It's such a beautiful view. How lucky is she to have secured this assignment? A contented glow now envelops her. She has plenty of photographs and a few useful sketches from today's visit, and meeting Annabel has increased her circle of local friends. Yes, it's been a good day, on the whole. She swallows a large mouthful of gin. But still there's that niggle and she finds herself frowning once again. She really shouldn't have been so dismissive and rude to Mac. Oh well, the damage is done. There's nothing she can do about it now.

Sitting on the couch, Kat delves into her bag for her phone and flicks through the photographs, discarding the most obvious rejects. The country house has such a strong image and she's tempted to start work immediately on the final illustrations, but they can wait until tomorrow.

She wonders what to have for supper. Obviously tapas is out of the question! She's about to get up and go to the kitchen in search of inspiration when her phone rings. Glancing at the screen, a nervous panic consumes her as Colin's name displays. She can't believe he's trying to make contact after all this time. Maybe bumping into Tara jogged his memory and made him think of her.

Kat's thumb hovers over the accept button as she contemplates what to do, but before she can make a decision the mobile falls silent. Good! She throws the phone down on the couch, but almost immediately it rings again. Is it her imagination or does the ringtone have an urgent and angry edge to it? Biting her lip, she picks up the mobile again. Should she answer? God, no! What is she thinking? He's been a complete and utter bastard. How dare he treat her like that? Kat firmly presses the decline button, and blocks his number – something she should have done long before. She's finished moping over Colin.

Knocking back the last drop of gin, she rises to her feet and heads towards the kitchen in search of supper.

26

Over the next four days, Kat concentrates on producing a number of illustrations. It's important she gives Stella a selection spanning the Palladian mansion's history but she's finding it a challenge to differentiate between past and present, even when sketching from the photographs. Usually, she can block out what's gone before by using this method, but not this time; there's so much information channelling through. Standing back from the easel, she critically scrutinises her large drawing, which presents the house at an angle, best displaying the impressive two-storey columns that grace its south-facing elevation and the flight of stone steps leading down to a terraced lawn. Beyond this, the orangery is intact. To the eastern side she's portrayed the formal gardens leading to the entrance porch with its shorter Palladian columns, but dominating the illustration – and hard to ignore – is the Second World War German bomber flying low overhead. This is an important part of the mansion's history, and Kat believes it should feature in Stella's book, but it's up to the professor to decide what to include.

Kat puts down her pen, satisfied she can add no more to the piece, and checking her mobile phone, she's surprised to find it's already lunchtime. Time takes on a different dimension when she's lost in her work. It could be any season, any year. She glances out of the window. A quiet, grey day hangs over the river and hardly a ripple disturbs the surface of the water. A large gull standing on the wall of the balcony eyes her. Suddenly it lets out a cry and launches into the air. Kat rolls her shoulders. Having concentrated intensely on the illustration all morning, her body is full of tension. What she needs is a walk. Making her way to the front door, she grabs a jacket from the coat hooks and shrugs it on, and ensuring she has her purse and the front-door key, she lets herself out of the house.

The tapas bar opposite is busy with diners and, involuntarily, Kat finds herself glancing across the street to check if *he* is there. Irritation fizzes as she wonders why she has the need to do this, followed the next minute by disappointment when she realises he's not there. She sets off purposefully in the direction of town. As she rounds the corner at the bottom of the hill and passes the parish church, Jean and Stan emerge from the bookshop.

'Hello, you two,' she says, coming up behind them.

Jean spins around. 'Kat! How delightful. How are you getting on?'

'Good, thanks. I visited a wonderful property last week, which I've since been working on. I thought it would be a sensible idea to stretch my legs and get some fresh air.'

'Yes, you don't want to overdo it,' agrees Stan.

Kat smiles at the couple. 'Have you bought anything interesting?'

'We enquired if they had any of your history professor's books,' Jean says.

'They didn't, but I've ordered a copy of her most recent publication,' adds Stan, '*Tudor Britain*.'

'That's entertaining bedtime reading!' Kat comments wryly.

'You'd be surprised what he reads at bedtime,' says Jean.

'My dear,' says Stan, eyes twinkling, 'I fear you've rather let the cat out of the bag.'

Realising what she's said, Jean becomes flustered. Kat chuckles.

'What are you doing now?' Stan asks. 'Would you like to join us for a spot of lunch?'

'I was going to walk through the town, but joining you

for lunch would be very pleasant, if you're sure three won't be a crowd.'

'Not at all,' Jean says in a no-nonsense voice, having quickly regained her composure. 'We're far too advanced in years to worry about such things.'

'I'll have you know,' says Stan with a wicked grin, 'there's life in this old dog yet!'

Kat falls into step with the couple, and a few minutes later they enter a hotel on Fowey's main street. The restaurant is a pleasant, modern dining space – relaxed and unstuffy – with French doors opening onto a charming waterside terrace where a family sit at one of the tables. After a brief discussion, Kat and her companions agree it's too cool to eat outside and select a table in the dining room overlooking the river.

'We're fortunate to have found a table without a reservation,' comments Jean, as she makes herself comfortable in the chair next to Kat.

'Now let's see what's available today,' says Stan, sitting down opposite her and handing out menus.

'I can thoroughly recommend the seafood dishes,' advises Jean.

'I'm a meat and two veg man, myself!'

It's not long before a waiter appears with notepad in hand and they place their orders. Cornish mackerel for Jean, a sirloin steak for Stan. Kat decides on herb-crusted hake – with crushed new potatoes, confit fennel and courgettes, accompanied by a dill velouté.

'Would you like any drinks?' the waiter enquires.

As Stan orders a bottle of Chenin Blanc, Kat glances around at their fellow diners. It's obviously a lunch venue that appeals to all ages.

'So,' says Jean, turning to face her. 'You say you visited a property last week. Was it interesting?'

'Oh yes,' Kat enthuses. 'A lovely Palladian-style house – with wonderful, dressed stone elevations and tall sash windows. It has such a mellow appearance,' she smiles, 'and it's privately situated at the end of a long drive. There's a glorious outlook, too – over a beautiful wooded valley.'

'Sounds rather intriguing,' comments Stan.

Kat nods. 'It has a remarkable history. The estate agent said that a number of its early overlords had influence with Kings Henry II and Edward I, as well as Queen Elizabeth I.'

'That's quite something,' Jean says.

The waiter arrives with the wine. Pouring a taster into Stan's glass, he stands back from the table.

'Very acceptable,' Stan confirms.

The man smiles politely and fills their glasses.

Stan turns his attention back to Kat. 'Is it one of those old estates with acres of land?'

'It used to have over four thousand acres, but it's for sale with considerably less . . . four, in total.' Picking up her glass, Kat takes a sip. 'But the terraced gardens that the house stands in the centre of are quite something – there's a wealth of mature shrubs and trees and also some rather fine rhododendrons.'

'Gracious living of yesteryear,' remarks Jean wistfully. 'I wonder who will buy it.'

'Hopefully someone who will treat it as a home,' says Stan. 'Not some institute or major business with plans to convert to offices.'

'It's so important for these old houses to be loved,' agrees Jean. 'It's far too easy for them to become run-down and lose their splendour.'

'My dear,' exclaims Stan, 'you could be describing me before I met you!'

Jean's eyes dance merrily at the man sitting opposite her.

Kat smiles to herself. Giving the couple a private moment, her gaze wanders to the bar, and alights on a man sitting with his back to her. Her pulse quickens. Even from behind there is no mistaking him. Battling the surge of adrenaline hitting her, Kat tries to push away the feeling that fate is somehow working its magic, and that she and Mac seem destined to collide wherever she goes.

As if aware of her gaze, Mac turns and his eyes find hers, and though they widen at first in surprise, even pleasure, they very quickly take on a hard edge.

Kat turns away at the snub. Who can blame him, after the other day when she was so rude to him. Still, his reaction burns. She wonders about making her excuses and leaving, but Jean has already spotted Mac.

'Oh look, there's James,' she says, waving. 'Mac, do come and join us.'

Kat tenses, and glances across the restaurant again. Mac's body language is hesitant and awkward, and he speaks to the barman before approaching their table.

'Jean, Stan,' he says, smiling respectfully at the couple, before turning to her. 'Kat.' The smile fades. 'Found time to break away from your work, I see.'

His tone is polite but the edge is unmistakable and something inside Kat turns.

What has she done? It's not his fault she's anti-men.

'Hello, Mac,' she says, gifting him a charming smile.

His eyes widen and then soften slightly, though there is a hint of confusion in them.

Jean observes them both with interest. 'So, Mac, are you meeting someone for lunch?'

He shifts his gaze to the older woman, and Kat wonders if he's thankful the couple are present and that he's not alone with her.

'No. I'm just picking up some booze for tomorrow's boat trip.'

'How's that going?' asks Stan.

'Good. *Windsong* is booked well into the summer.'

'I hope you make room for some downtime this year,' says Jean. 'Remember, Mac, it's so important to have fun while you can.'

Kat watches the hazel colour of his eyes deepen, as unreadable emotions cloud his gaze.

He nods. 'That's sound advice, Jean.'

The touch of sadness in his response makes Kat's heart squeeze. She takes a deep breath.

'Good man,' says Jean with a genuine smile.

Kat tries to decipher the unspoken conversion taking place here.

'Talking of fun,' Jean adds lightly, 'I hope you'll come to our barbeque at the end of May – the Bank Holiday Monday, Mac?' She turns to Kat. 'And of course you must come, dear!'

'That's very kind of you,' Kat says. 'I'd love to.'

But Mac shakes his head. 'Apologies. *Windsong* is chartered to the Scillies for a few days. We're not returning until later in the week.'

'Oh, that's such a shame.' Jean pulls a sad face. 'Well, then, no excuses, you will just have to come to supper once you've returned.'

'Thank you, Jean. I promise,' he says, stepping back as the waiter approaches with their food order. 'I'll leave you in peace to enjoy your lunch.'

He gives Kat a final glance before heading back to the bar, briefly disappearing behind it before re-emerging a couple of minutes later holding a crate of champagne. Kat tries not to stare, but the sight of his straining, tanned biceps as they take the weight is too much, and a twinge of desire stabs at her. She can't deny the attraction any longer. And as Mac heads towards the exit without looking back again in her direction, disappointment sticks in her throat.

'He's such a lovely man, don't you think, Kat?' Jean says in an innocent voice.

'Yes. And judging by the number of women I've seen him with, he's very much in demand,' Kat says, before she can stop herself, or the judgement in her tone.

Jean fixes her with a penetrating stare. 'But *of course* there are a lot of women interested in him. He's a charming and handsome man!'

She can't argue with that.

'He's married . . . with a son, isn't he? ' Kat says.

Jean shifts in her seat, and briefly exchanges a look with Stan before replying. 'He . . . was married, yes. We've never met his son, but I know he's a doting father. Always thinking of the boy and sending him little gifts.'

'Perhaps you should get to know him better,' Stan suggests to Kat. 'Then you will understand what Jean means. Take it from us; James MacNamara is a good man, through and through.'

27

After lunch, Kat bids the couple farewell, watching them as they set off towards Jean's house, which is located in one of the quaint backstreets of town. Then, feeling strangely wrong-footed and not yet ready to return to work, she continues along Fore Street and turns into Albert Quay car park, and from there makes her way towards the river.

The air holds a quiet stillness, but jostling for position at the pontoon are a variety of tenders, dinghies and rowing boats. Kat's gaze extends to the outer jetty where a dark-blue-hulled yacht is secured alongside. Immediately her eyes are drawn to its name: *Windsong*. A strange energy takes hold and she nervously looks around, unsure of what she'd say if Mac were to suddenly materialise.

The car park and pontoon are busy but there's no sign of him, and for a while she stands in the shadow of the Harbour Office watching the comings and goings on the sheltered, deep-waters of the Fowey Estuary. A group of kayakers paddle by, and a large cargo ship, accompanied by a pilot boat, makes its way upriver against the beautiful backdrop of the steep-sided, tree-lined valley.

There's movement on board *Windsong* and she observes Sarah emerging from below deck. As the young woman shields her eyes and scans the car park, instinctively Kat shrinks back, although she's not sure why. Sarah turns away and busies herself on deck. No doubt, Mac and she are preparing to sail off into the sunset. Thank God she hasn't bumped into him! What was she thinking? And what would she have said to him anyway?

Kat stands watching Sarah for a while longer. Slim and natural, dressed in white trousers and a blue striped sweatshirt, she appears completely at home as she moves around the boat sorting things out. Every inch the yachtswoman.

So, which one is his preference? The stylish woman he was with at Tate Britain, the classy dark-haired woman with the two teenagers in Salcombe, or the pretty brown-haired one . . . Or outdoorsy Sarah? Or is the *client* with the killer cheekbones now more than a client to him? Kat shakes her head despairingly. What's it to do with her anyway?

Turning, she makes her way onto the street and then stops dead. Mac is walking towards the car park carrying three heavily laden bags. Kat's in plain sight, and panic grips her – she even considers ducking behind a car – but he's already spotted her. He slows, taking a few tentative steps towards her and her face flushes.

'Kat . . .' he says, then hesitates before adding, 'I trust you enjoyed your lunch?'

'Yes . . . thanks,' she mumbles, almost shyly. She has no idea what to say.

Putting the bags down on the pavement, Mac regards her. His eyes no longer hold the hard edge as they had in the restaurant, but are instead curious. 'So what are you up to now?'

'Just taking a walk before getting back to work,' she says.

'Ah, work.' He nods. 'Work is clearly important to you, Kat?'

There's something about his tone, again. Is he having a dig at her? She bristles, aware that her cheeks have turned crimson.

'As yours is to you, I gather.'

'It's seen me through,' he says evenly.

What does that mean?

Another uncomfortable silence threatens, and Kat finds herself keen to dissolve the atmosphere.

'I see your yacht is tied up at the jetty,' she says, aiming for a friendly tone.

He makes a sound in the back of his throat. 'Pleased to hear she's still there, and Sarah hasn't sailed off without me.'

'No, that wouldn't do.'

His lips twitch in amusement, and she can't take her eyes off his mouth. It's so beautifully shaped and inviting . . .

'So, Kat,' he says, with mock-seriousness, 'have you changed your mind, about the idea of sailing?'

She can't hide her smile. 'Well, what do they say about all work and no play?'

'It seems we're both guilty of that,' he says.

She meets his soft, hazel eyes.

'Jean was quite insistent, wasn't she?' Kat lifts an eyebrow.

'Jean's a wonderful woman. She keeps me on track.'

Puzzled, Kat frowns.

Everyone talks in riddles, as if she should know what's going on.

A man suddenly approaches from the other side of the street. 'Hey, Mac, fancy a game of snooker?' he asks in a thick Cornish accent.

Obviously worse for drink, he puts an arm around Mac's shoulders and roughly mock-wrestles him.

Mac shakes himself free with a laugh. 'Sorry, Jim. No can do today.'

The man's rheumy eyes shift to Kat. He reeks of booze and some other sour odour and she tries not to gag.

'Yeah, matey boy!' Jim's gaze scans the full length of her body. 'Understand why you turn me down with this on offer.'

'That's enough, Jim,' Mac says, but in a non-threatening voice. 'Go home and sleep it off.' Gently taking hold of the man's shoulders, he guides him in the opposite direction.

Jim staggers a few steps before turning back. Blatantly, he again ogles Kat. Wiping spittle from his mouth with his sleeve, he calls out, 'Special, is she?'

'Just go home, Jim,' Mac says evenly. 'We'll have that game another time.'

Mumbling to himself, the inebriated man finally shuffles off down the street.

'Sorry about that,' says Mac, picking up the bags.

She smiles, and considers this man in front of her. What was it Stan said at lunch? James MacNamara is a good man, through and through. She thinks she may have just witnessed that.

'That was nicely handled, Mac,' she says softly.

He glances at her in surprise. 'Ah, Jim's OK. Just a slave to demon alcohol.' He hesitates. 'Would you like to come aboard? We're not sailing until the tide turns.'

Briefly – exhilaratingly – she considers saying *yes*, but then remembers Sarah. Three would definitely be a crowd on the yacht.

'Thank you, but I really do have to get back to work.'

He nods. 'OK, but you can't accuse me of not trying.'

She laughs. 'No, I can't accuse you of that!'

'I'll risk asking one more time,' he says with a faint smile. 'Would you allow me to take you out sailing one day, see if it appeals to you?'

'I'd like that.'

'At last!' he says triumphantly.

Just as their eyes lock in a sweet ceasefire, a voice rings out.

'Mac! What the hell are you doing?' Sarah calls loudly, as she approaches across the car park. We're on a tight schedule.'

Without breaking eye contact with Kat, Mac calls over his shoulder, 'Just coming.'

'Oh, it's you again,' Sarah says, appearing beside him.

'It is!' Kat says, supressing a smile.

Mac discreetly grins. 'Come on, Sarah, make yourself useful.' Picking up a bag, he holds it out to her.

'OK. No need to bully me. I've been waiting *ages*!'

Mac rolls his eyes good-naturedly. 'Nice to bump into you, again,' he says to Kat.

And with that, he and Sarah turn and make their way over to the pontoon. As Kat watches them go, she wills him to turn back. And as Sarah sets off down the gangway, he does.

'I'll be in touch,' he calls out, his eyes lingering on her for a long heartbeat.

She nods and waits until he disappears from sight.

That look he gave her was the same as the one he'd given her when she'd first seen him at Tate Britain, and it's having the same effect on her now as it had then.

Just breathe . . .

28

'Hi, Gem. How are things?' Looking out of the bedroom window, Kat holds the mobile to her ear.

Across the water, Polruan is painted gold by the late afternoon sun and she casually watches a sailing dinghy tack close to the western shore. On board is a teenager, who is obviously receiving instruction from his companion, a middle-aged man. His dad, she assumes, and her thoughts briefly flit to Mac and his son. She wonders what kind of father Mac is.

'Three things,' Gemma is saying. 'First, everybody sends their love and hopes you're having a great time.'

'Well, yes, but I'm also working hard, Gem.'

'Yeah, sure, with all those beefy sailing types around to distract you!'

Kat laughs. 'So, what's up?'

'Second, the boiler's buggered.'

'Oh, dear.' Kat turns away from the window. Walking over to the bed, she sits down heavily on it.

'Yeah. Luckily, the weather's not too bad so I haven't had to put the heating on, but cold showers take a bit of getting used to.'

Kat groans. 'How long have you been without hot water?'

'Two days. I hoped the thermostat might kick in again, but it hasn't.'

'I'll phone the plumber now. I'll also text you his number so you can explain what's happened. Hell! Hope it's not too expensive.'

'Sorry.'

'Oh, it's not your fault, Gem. These things happen. I was just thinking aloud.'

'You realise that's a stone's throw away from the first sign of madness!'

'Yeah, well.' Kat rakes a hand through her hair, still damp from the shower . . . a hot one. 'And the third thing? Don't tell me it's another emergency.'

'Depends how you look at it.'

Kat's stomach churns.

'You had a visitor last night,' Gemma says mysteriously. 'Or rather, I did.'

'What? Who?'

'That ex-fella of yours.'

Kat's heart races. 'Colin? What did he want?'

Gemma laughs. 'You! He was pretty insistent, kept banging on the door. I was surprised he came round so late. It was way past ten. Must have been desperate or something . . .'

'Oh, God.' Kat shivers, then hears Gemma take a deep breath.

'I told him you weren't here. He didn't believe me at first, but I explained you'd gone away. Don't worry, I didn't say where.'

'Thanks, Gem.'

'No probs. Anyway, he kept looking over my shoulder, as if I was lying and you were hiding. I told him I couldn't let him in as I didn't know him and the flat wasn't mine to invite any old stranger in.' Gemma pauses. 'He'd definitely been drinking and seemed pretty cut-up, Kat.'

Good. Serves him right . . .

'Kept saying he'd made a terrible mistake.'

Kat closes her eyes.

'He asked when you'd be back,' Gemma continues. 'I said I wasn't sure but it wouldn't be anytime soon. Hope that was OK?'

'Thanks, Gem, and I'm sorry he turned up and harassed

you like that. He's actually pretty harmless . . .' Kat pauses, because Colin hadn't been exactly harmless when he was cheating on his wife with her. 'But if you have any further trouble, let me know and I'll put him straight.'

'Don't worry about me, Kat,' Gemma says. 'He seemed OK, apart from being a bit drunk and oversentimental. I thought if he got pushy I'd be well able to outmanoeuvre him with a few of my killer kickboxing moves.' She laughs.

'Well . . .' Kat is about to say it's what Colin deserves, but she doesn't want to drag Gemma into the whole sordid mess. 'I wouldn't have blamed you if you did,' she says instead.

They chat for a while longer and Kat catches up on what's been happening at Bryanston Publishing. Then she phones the plumber, but there's no reply. She leaves a message.

So, Colin had turned up at her place! It had taken him a while and by all accounts, with his tail between his legs. What did he think she'd do? Welcome him back with a pat on the head and tell him he'd been a naughty boy for deceiving her? A few weeks ago, maybe she'd have given in. But now . . . She has to admit she's changed, a little, at least.

Kat gets off the bed. Walking over to the chest of drawers, she pulls out a clean T-shirt and pair of jeans, and no sooner has she changed when she hears a knock at the front door. She glances at her mobile – quarter to seven. Who could that be?

Running downstairs, she opens the door and swallows her gasp.

Mac stands on the pavement looking across the road at the tapas bar, but as she opens the door wider he turns and smiles. He's sporting a pair of sunglasses and wearing jeans and a crisp white, cotton shirt that accentuates his tan.

Good God! Is it possible for this man to get any better looking?

'Kat . . .' he says, removing his glasses. 'I wondered, on the offchance, if you fancied grabbing a bite to eat . . . Or, maybe you have other plans this evening?'

She catches her breath. She should probably play it cool, say she's not free . . . But to hell with that. She's wasted too much time being frosty towards him.

'That sounds like fun,' she says, keeping her voice casual.

He smiles, and visibly relaxes. 'I thought we could go over the road. The tapas is superb. If you like Spanish cuisine.'

She glances over his shoulder. The place is filling up quickly, but there are a couple of empty tables on the pavement.

'Sure. Give me a moment to find some shoes. I've just jumped out of the shower.'

He glances down at her bare feet but not before she catches his left eyebrow twitching at this revelation. She laughs.

'I'll go grab us a table then,' he says.

Kat closes the front door and rushes upstairs to the bedroom, excitement nipping at her heels. It's just tapas, she tells herself sternly, and she's certainly not about to jump into the fire and become yet another one of his women. Absolutely not! But spending time alone with Mac is too good an opportunity to miss. She's intrigued to find out for herself whether James MacNamara is what other people believe him to be.

Scrabbling under the bed for her trainers, she exchanges her T-shirt for a more feminine top, then extracts her debit card from her purse and stuffs it in the pocket of her jeans before dashing into the bathroom and applying a coat of mascara. Taking a deep breath, she stares at her reflection in the mirror. Her hair has dried naturally and curls tumble uncontrollably over her shoulders. Too bad she doesn't have time to do more with it, but there it is . . .

'It's just tapas, Kat!' she says out loud.

If Gemma could hear her now, she would definitely think she'd slipped into madness.

Turning away from the mirror, Kat rushes downstairs, takes a moment behind the closed front door to compose herself and then coolly steps out into the street.

29

Sitting at a table on the pavement reading a menu, Mac is caught in a shaft of light as the sun works its way across the sky. It won't be long before it slips behind the rooftops of Fowey and eventually disappears over the far western horizon, but for now it's glorious. Kat observes the golden rays that accentuate the planes of Mac's masculine face. He appears comfortable and at ease, as if he's on holiday in a little European town, somewhere far more exotic than the south coast of Cornwall. She's always had the impression he belongs somewhere else; the deep, early tan and dark, wild hair curling so beguilingly, hinting at foreign shores. Kat thinks she has never seen anyone more beautiful. He's a work of art, all right.

As she crosses the street towards him, Mac looks up and watches her for a long moment before getting to his feet and pulling out a chair.

That's nice. Gentlemanly...

When he smiles at her, Kat smiles right back.

'I was thinking, you've probably eaten here before,' he says, taking his seat again.

She shakes her head. 'I've been meaning to. It always looks such fun and the aromas that waft across the street are heavenly!'

He nods. 'I like to eat here because it reminds me of the bars in Spain. The laid-back feel and outside tables bring a little taste of that country to Cornwall and – always an added bonus – no reservations necessary. It also has the best sherries.'

'Have you spent much time in Spain?' she asks.

'Yes, a fair amount, but in other parts of the Med, too.'

A waitress approaches and Kat recognises her as the young woman she'd spoken to when she'd set out on the Hall Walk.

'Well, hello,' she says to Kat. 'So you've decided to give us the opportunity to impress.'

Kat laughs. 'You've already done that. I've been tempted ever since I arrived in Fowey.'

'I'm glad you've finally given into temptation. Are you ready to order or would you like a few minutes more?'

Kat hurriedly picks up the menu.

'Perhaps a few more minutes, Mel,' Mac suggests, then raises a questioning eyebrow at Kat. 'How about we order a plate of sourdough and aioli while we decide?'

'That's a good idea.'

'Would you like wine . . . Or something else?' he asks.

'Wine is great.' She flashes him a smile.

'We have a full selection, from a mouth-watering Manzanilla to a rich Rioja,' the waitress states. 'If you're going to have the *Jamón Ibérico*, arguably the greatest food in the world, I would recommend the chilled, salty Manzanilla from Sanlúcar de Barrameda in Cadiz. The two together are a match made in Spanish heaven!'

They agree on a bottle of the Manzanilla and Mel retreats inside.

'What takes your fancy?' Mac asks, scrutinising the menu.

Kat almost chokes. *Is he serious? How can he ask her that?*

'It all sounds wonderful,' she says, straight-faced. 'Do *you* have a preference?'

By the time the waitress returns with their wine and starters, they have made a decision and place their order.

'How's your work coming along?' Mac asks, pouring wine into Kat's glass.

'Proceeding according to schedule, thanks.' She picks up a piece of sourdough and dips it into the bowl of aioli.

'So, you are an illustrator?'

'Yes,' she says, pleased that he's remembered. 'I've been commissioned to illustrate a history book.' She pops the appetiser into her mouth.

'What kind of illustrations?'

Kat swallows. 'Mainly houses and castle ruins. The book is about the West Country's landed gentry through the ages.'

'Sounds interesting.'

'The places I've visited so far have been.'

The waitress reappears carrying a tray loaded with an array of plates and dishes. As she sets them down on the table, she explains a little about each of the tapas they've selected. Kat wonders if the bar staff are expected to do this all the time. If so, Mac will have heard it all before. She glances across the table. He seems as interested in what Mel has to say as she is.

As Kat spoons tapas onto her plate she suddenly realises her inner voice is unusually quiet. Surprisingly, it's not offering an opinion or querying what she thinks she's doing spending time with this beautiful man, and the corners of her mouth lift in the faintest of smiles.

'Something amused you?'

Her eyes widen with surprise. The smile had been extremely subtle. With Colin, she would have had to spell it out before he noticed anything. But she can't possibly tell Mac what she was thinking, but neither can she remain silent. She has to say something . . .

'I was just thinking of a conversation I had earlier this evening with my colleague back in London.'

'Colleague?' He helps himself to a spider crab and saffron *croqueta*.

'Yes. She's renting my flat while I'm here and she rang to tell me the boiler has packed up. She says the cold showers are something else, poor girl.'

'It's healthy, and good for the system, especially cold water swimming.'

'Do you do that?' she asks.

'It has been known, although I prefer warmer seas.' He smiles.

'Don't we all?' She gives a small laugh. 'However, when the sun shines in this country I can't think of anywhere I'd rather be.'

The look in his eyes softens and she watches, mesmerised, as flecks of green and gold mingle with the rich hazel. She notices each iris is ringed by a dark brown line and that his eyelashes are luxuriously thick and black. What she'd do to have such a set! Suddenly aware that she's staring deep into his unflinching gaze, she lowers her gaze.

'I've spent a lot of time abroad,' he says.

She glances up again, her interest piqued. 'Doing what?'

'This and that. Mainly what I'm doing now, skippering yacht charters. I also deliver boats around the world. I've tried shore-based jobs, but they didn't suit me.'

'It sounds such an adventure.'

'It can be,' he says. 'It can also be miserably uncomfortable when facing weeks of bad weather and mountainous seas.'

'I suppose there's yin and yang in all things.'

All at once, unreadable emotions shadow his eyes. 'Yes, there's no escaping the light and shade in our lives.'

As she helps herself to a spoonful of *calamares*, Kat wonders what feelings their conversation has stirred. It's time to lighten things up.

'It's odd how our paths keep crossing,' she says conversationally.

'I don't think it's odd, Kat,' he says, holding her gaze. 'I see it as a gift.'

'I don't mean *odd* in that sense . . .' she trails off, suddenly flustered.

'I know what you mean,' he says, smiling warmly at her. And once again she's dazzled. How can one man be *so* perfect?

'But what are the chances of seeing each other at Tate Britain, Salcombe and now here?'

'Ah, the Tate Britain. You were definitely in the right place amongst all those paintings,' he gently teases.

Warmth courses through her veins and reaches for her heart. Instantly, Kat halts its progress.

'If you'd been around in their time,' Mac continues, 'those Pre-Raphaelite painters would have been falling over themselves to have you as their muse.'

'I guess I do have that look,' she says in what she hopes is a nonchalant tone, although she feels anything but.

'A masterpiece,' he says softly.

She glances at him, her eyes narrowing slightly.

No wonder he has women falling at his feet. He's so subtle and skilled at massaging the ego.

Ah, there it is; her inner monologue. She knew it wouldn't be too far away.

'I mean that your colouring is very striking,' he continues. 'It's not often you find flame-haired women with emerald-green eyes.'

She doesn't know what to say. Half of her wants to enjoy the compliment, but the other half is wary. She's been seduced by sweet talk before and the cynic in her warns her to back away, build that brick wall and reclaim her protective shield. But Mac is just so charming, and charismatic, even a little humble in a strange way. Reminding herself that all the other women she's seen him with have no doubt fallen under this exact spell, Kat errs on the side of caution after all.

'I prefer to fly under the radar,' she says evenly. 'And I don't like to trade on my looks.'

His eyes widen. 'Why not? They're something to celebrate in my opinion!'

Fingers of heat breach her defences and encircle her heart.

Be gone!

'Well, thank you, but I've had my fair share of attention in that regard over the years. It's all turned out to be pretty superficial in the end, and it's taken me a while to grow a thick skin.'

'That's a great shame,' he says, gazing at her with compassion. 'The world can be a tough place and to survive we all have to find a set of armour that fits. But it's just wrong that such beauty should be hidden away.'

Kat stares at him in astonishment.

Where has this Prince Charming come from?

'I doubt that you've had to find a set of armour,' she says, managing not to blush.

For a long moment, Mac doesn't say anything and she begins to think he's not going to respond.

'Yes, I have, Kat,' he says quietly.

She frowns.

'People make assumptions all the time. About one's appearance, to how one's life *seems* on the surface . . . and all the different shades in between. It's all about perception and from even the little you've told me about yourself, I think you know that.'

She considers him. 'I got the impression that you live life on your own terms,' she says. 'A free spirit, doing exactly what you want, when you want.'

He lets out a sad sort of laugh. 'My life has its challenges – and situations that aren't perfect,' he says. 'I have a son whom I don't see as often as I would like. He lives in London and I have to live wherever the work takes me.'

'That must be tough,' she says, more softly. 'Does he ever visit you on the boat?'

'He does and he loves it. He's at the stage when he wants to be a pirate when he grows up!'

Kat smiles. 'When I saw you in Salcombe, you mentioned he lives with *family* in London.'

'Yes.'

'With his mother?'

Hesitating, Mac frowns. 'No. With his aunt and uncle.'

He offers no further explanation and Kat has the strong impression the subject is closed. There's so much more she wants to ask, but she doesn't want to pry. She recalls Jean mentioning he had been married.

If Mac and his wife are divorced, that would explain all the women she's seen him with, but not why his son lives with an aunt and uncle when he's not with his father. Perhaps his ex-wife doesn't want anything to do with the child?

Kat can't imagine any mother behaving so callously.

Maybe the poor woman has mental health issues?

From the corner of her eye she notices the waitress working her way over to their table.

'Everything to your satisfaction?' Mel asks.

'Great, thanks,' replies Kat, looking down at the dessert menu.

'Just perfect,' says Mac.

Kat looks up to see Mac's eyes locked on her. Despite her resolve, her heart misses a beat and her stomach flutters.

This is so unfair! How is she supposed to protect herself?

'Is there anything else I can get you?'

'I'm OK,' Mac replies, 'but would you like anything, Kat?'

She shakes her head.

'Just the bill please, Mel,' he says.

When it arrives, Kat attempts to pay half, but Mac refuses.

'It's my treat,' he says, handing over his credit card before she has a chance to produce hers.

'That's so kind of you. Thank you.' Kat checks her mobile. It's still early – not long past nine. 'Would you like to come back for coffee? I could show you some of my work.' When he doesn't immediately respond, she adds, 'Unless you'd rather get back to *Windsong*?'

'No . . . that sounds wonderful,' Mac says with a smile.

30

She thought she'd be a bundle of nerves inviting him back, but as Kat inserts the front door key into the lock she feels remarkably calm.

It's a polite thing to do, inviting a dinner date back for coffee in the privacy of one's own home . . . well, Stella's home. Anyway, he's only come to see her artwork. Nothing else!

'This is nice,' Mac says, glancing around the hallway and taking in the period features and the striking, Victorian, black-and-white chequered floor tiles.

'Isn't it,' Kat says, entering the kitchen. 'It's the owner's holiday home and she's offered it to me for the duration of the assignment.'

'Very generous!'

'It is,' Kat agrees. 'It's wonderful to have the house to myself, and such a treat to work without interruption.'

Surprise registers on Mac's face. 'Don't you find it lonely?' His look is genuine and not at all pitying.

'No. I'm used to being independent.' Unflinchingly, she meets his gaze.

'Independent. Yes.' He smiles. 'Someone who knows her own mind.'

'Oh I don't know about that!' She gives a small, self-deprecating laugh. 'I've recently been involved in a relationship that ended messily, and I want some time to myself, I guess.'

The look in his eyes turns to compassion and the air turns heavy with something that feels like expectation. She can tell he has more questions but he remains silent. Perhaps he's being polite, or there's some other reason he doesn't probe further.

'What would you like to drink?' she says, dispelling the moment. 'There's coffee, tea, juice, or would you prefer something stronger?'

'Coffee's fine. White, no sugar, thanks.'

Extracting mugs from a cupboard, she glances at him as he stands in the doorway.

'The studio's down the hallway on the right. I'll bring the drinks through.'

He nods and turns away.

Five minutes later, Kat carries two mugs of coffee into the studio. Mac sits at the table, an open sketchbook in his hand.

Shit! She'd forgotten the sketchbook was on the table.

Mac looks up. 'When did you do this?' He turns the illustration towards her.

Dear God! It was the very first day she'd seen him . . . at Tate Britain.

'I'm not sure, I was just doodling one day,' she says, making sure her voice sounds casual.

'You've caught my likeness very well and also *Windsong*'s. You should add her name.'

'I didn't know the name of your yacht when I drew it.'

His eyes narrow.

'It caught my eye in Salcombe,' she hurriedly carries on. 'I was messing about one afternoon and that's what came out on the page.'

Stop blabbering!

'Well, for a *doodle*, this is terrific. But having seen your other artwork I'm not surprised.' He gestures towards the easel and the large illustration of the Palladian mansion. 'The detail is astounding.'

'Thanks,' she says, now feeling a flush of pleasure at his appreciation. She places a mug in front of him and sits down in a chair on the opposite side of the table.

Mac continues to flip through the pages of the sketchbook. 'These are tremendous,' he says, as he arrives at the set of Rossetti drawings.

She cranes her neck and peers at the sketch. He's probably guessed the chronological order of illustrations but, if not, it won't take him long to realise she did the one of him aboard *Windsong* at around the same time.

'Where is this?' He points to her drawing of the securely chained, massive iron gate.

'Highgate Cemetery.'

Surprise registers and Mac's eyes widen. 'The detail is first-class and that padlock . . . it's as if I'd be able to insert a key and open it . . . And as for the weight of that chain . . . I can practically feel it.'

'Thank you,' Kat says again, nerves and happiness swirling in her. She can't deny how much it means, for Mac to admire her for something other than her Titian looks.

He flips the page to the next illustration. 'And who's this young woman holding a parasol?'

She glances at it. 'Ah, that's Fanny Cornforth, a model Dante Gabriel Rossetti liked to feature in his paintings.'

'Lovely.' Turning to yet another sketch, Mac lets out a low whistle. 'Well here's trouble in triplicate, that's for sure! I assume these are all of a Rossetti theme?' He glances up inquisitively.

She nods. 'Dante and his friends, William Holman Hunt and John Millais, enjoying a picnic by the River Thames.'

He gives a slight shake of the head. 'Did you draw these after I saw you at the Pre-Raphaelite exhibition?'

'I guess around that time,' she says vaguely.

'Your imagination is wild!' He turns the page to the next illustration.

The compilation is the dreamlike, Rossetti-style vignettes of Colin. Partly framed by unkempt floppy locks, his mischievous eyes gaze out from the page. The next sketch shows them filled with desire and a promise of things to come, while the next is a full-length illustration of him wearing a Victorian painting smock and frowning as he paints a canvas propped on the easel.

Mac's eyes meet hers. 'Who's this?'

She colours. 'Someone I used to know, drawn in the style of Rossetti.'

Curiosity lurks within his gaze as he observes her.

'Looking at you now, with your hair falling over your shoulders in a mass of untamed curls . . .' he smiles, 'well, Rossetti wouldn't have stood a chance. He'd have been blindsided. Not only would you have swept him off his feet, he'd have been envious of your talent.'

Self-consciously, Kat's fingers fly to her trailing locks.

Mac flips the page again, to the sketch of him aboard *Windsong*. Kat cringes. There's no way the sequence of illustrations can have escaped him, but if he has made the connection he makes no comment. Instead, a smile plays on his lips as he closes the sketchpad and looks across the table. 'You are one very talented artist,' he says softly.

'That's very kind of you to say,' she says modestly, letting out a long silent breath, only then realising she'd been holding it. 'Do you like art, Mac?'

He considers her question. 'I appreciate a good painting but I'm no aficionado.'

So, why was he at Tate Britain? Was it simply because the stylish woman had asked him to accompany her, or was he trying to impress?

'Enough to visit a London art gallery though,' she ventures.

'Yes. That was a lovely respite in an otherwise busy day,' he says easily. His expression gives nothing away.

'And, of course, it's always good to do that with a pleasant companion,' she says, making sure her voice is light.

'Well, I always prefer to spend time with a pleasant companion rather than an unpleasant one . . . don't you?' he teases.

'Absolutely. If you can find one of those these days.' She

gives a half laugh. 'Although *you* don't seem to suffer from the same drought as the rest of us!'

He laughs, then finishes his coffee and glances at his watch, which she notices is appropriately macho with a large, round face and titanium strap.

'As much as I'd like to prolong this evening, sadly I have an early start tomorrow,' he says apologetically, getting to his feet with his empty coffee mug in one hand. 'I'll just put this in your kitchen.'

'Don't worry about that,' she says, impressed by his manners – Colin would never have been so helpful. 'I'll sort it later.'

He follows her to the front door and suddenly Kat feels shy and awkward. How do they say goodbye? A hug? A kiss on the cheek? A formal handshake? What?

'Thank you, Kat, for a thoroughly enjoyable evening spent in such *pleasant* company.'

She meets his teasing eyes and the blood rushes to her cheeks.

'And . . .' he pauses, 'maybe you'll contemplate repeating the experience.'

'Yes, in case this was just a fluke,' she says, more blithely than she feels.

He gives a half laugh. 'Well, I must away.'

Kat opens the door and for a moment they linger in the close confines of the hallway.

'Until next time,' Mac says, reaching out and giving her arm a gentle squeeze.

31

The narrow streets of Fowey are quiet as Mac walks through the town in contemplative mood. It's way past chucking out time and only a few stragglers loiter. Two men call out and he acknowledges them with a wave and a brief exchange. The moon rides high in a starless sky, peering out from behind banks of ominous cloud, and he senses a change in the weather. It wouldn't surprise him if sailing proved challenging over the next few days. Hopefully his clients possess good sea legs.

Turning onto Albert Quay, he makes his way across the empty car park towards the gangway. There's not a soul around. Away from the protection of the town's huddle of buildings, a keen breeze whips up the river and little waves slap noisily against the sides of the small boats tethered to the floating pontoons. Mac walks to his tender. Loosening the cleat hitch and maintaining tension in the painter, he steps agilely aboard. Making his way to the stern, he presses a switch and the outboard tilts into the water. As he starts the engine, the sudden noise is a rude assault to the senses and he quickly reverses, slipping the throttle into forward and navigating out of the visitor pontoon. Feeling the pull of the current and guided by the light of the full moon – the *sailor's friend* – he sets off across the illuminated river towards the inlet where *Windsong* is moored.

It's peaceful out on the water and that's how he likes it. The thrum of the outboard is the only sound. He can party like the rest of them, but his natural habitat is out here... out on the water and in the elements. This is where he feels released from his responsibilities and at peace with his conscience. These periods of freedom are what keep him going, even though he knows it's only a moment's relief from the concerns that haunt him and the decisions he has to make. Mac's brow furrows. Discussing his son with Kat this evening makes him realise the situation is unsustainable.

As the dark bulk of Fowey's waterside buildings retreat, Mac gazes downriver. The properties along the Esplanade are all in darkness, except for one, where a light shines from an upstairs window. He tries to work out if that's Kat's house, and a smile tugs at his lips as he thinks back over the evening they've just spent together. She's like a breath of fresh air; with that luxurious chestnut-red hair and her lovely green eyes. And what a talent she possesses. Her sketches have the lightest touch, but also depth – sensitively hinting at what lies beneath and leaving the viewer wanting more. A sudden rush of pride takes him by surprise and he carefully considers his reaction.

As the tender enters Pont Pill Creek, out of the darkness a number of quietly moored yachts take shape. *Windsong*'s interior lights glow in welcome and he steers towards her. She's a stunning yacht, and though she was expensive to purchase, it was money well spent. He had bought the seaworthy vessel a few years before, from a broker in the Hamble, and under his ownership she's spent most of her life in the Mediterranean, with a couple of seasons in the Caribbean. However, this summer they are calling the waters of the Fowey Estuary *home*.

Drawing smoothly alongside *Windsong*, Mac cuts the engine and secures the lines, then climbs the boarding ladder and steps onto the deck. In the shelter of the inlet the breeze has dropped, but still the boat rocks gently beneath his feet as she responds to the ebb and flow of the current. On the night air, the haunting call of a curlew sounds and Mac listens intently, breathing in the atmosphere. For a moment he allows a memory of another time and a different place to gather momentum, but before it has a chance to consume him, he simply acknowledges the feelings it evokes before tenderly placing them aside. Taking a last walk around the deck, checking all is in order, he steps into the cockpit and crosses over to the hatchway.

A warm glow emanates from below as he opens the hatch. Holding onto the rim, Mac swings down the stairs with familiar ease and glances around. All seems in place. He knows he should go to bed – there's a shedload of work to do tomorrow – but he's wired and sleep seems a million light years away. Entering the galley, he pours himself a whisky nightcap hoping it will take the edge off. Raising the glass to his lips, he takes a large mouthful and swallows, savouring the drink's mellow taste. He checks the label on the bottle and agrees with the distiller's description: '*Waves of honey and vanilla fudge, dotted with raisin, almond and cinnamon spiciness*'. Moving into the saloon, he sits down and stretches out his legs. Leaning back, he rests his head against the wood panelled surround and with the glass dangling between fingers and thumb, closes his eyes. It's not long before he hears the door to the main cabin open.

'Hi,' Sarah says. 'It's late. Where have you been?'

He prolongs the moment a while longer before opening his eyes and turning to her. Standing in the doorway, wearing nothing more than a T-shirt, Sarah looks dishevelled, as if she's just woken up, but he suspects she's been clockwatching for some time.

'I had some business to attend to.'

Keen eyes survey him.

He takes another large swig of whisky, enjoying the warming sensation of the amber liquid working its way to his stomach.

'Do you want a wee dram?' he asks, allowing his once-strong Scottish accent to come to the fore.

'I wouldn't say no.'

Rising to his feet, he walks to the galley and takes down a glass. 'Everything OK here?' he asks, pouring her a shot.

'Yes, all arranged.' Sarah steps from the doorway into the main saloon. 'I thought I'd move us into the forward cabin tomorrow morning while you're collecting the clients.'

She plonks herself down next to where he'd been sitting.

Mac hesitates. Is it his imagination or are *Windsong*'s walls closing in?

Exiting the galley, he approaches Sarah and holds out the glass to her. 'The plan was to pick you up in the morning from Albert Quay along with the Murrays,' he says, sitting down next to her.

'I know, but I thought it made more sense to stay over tonight,' she explains, avoiding his level gaze. 'That way, I'll be organised and ready as soon as they arrive tomorrow.'

He gives her a long look. 'How did you get here? I didn't see your boat.'

'Water taxi.' She takes a sip of whisky.

Mac frowns. He doesn't like this manipulation. It's something he's noticed creeping into their *arrangement* more and more. Holding back a sigh, he glances at his watch. Only six hours before he has to be up. There's no point dropping her back to the jetty now; by the time he returns to the yacht it will be five hours. Draining the remaining whisky, he gets to his feet and places the tumbler on the table.

'OK, Sarah. Seeing as you've made yourself at home you may as well stay,' he says in a voice more aligned to chiding a naughty child.

A blush spreads across her cheeks, and he wonders if it's because she feels guilt at her cunning . . . or some other emotion.

She rises and meets his gaze. 'You won't regret it.'

His mouth twitches into a semblance of a smile. '*Sleep*,' he says, accentuating the word. 'That's what I need.'

Her eyes gleam. 'Oh, don't you worry, Cap'n. What I've got planned will make you sleep like a baby!' She flashes him a wicked grin and turns away.

Mac's eyes take in the exaggerated, sexy swagger as she heads towards the main cabin. Inwardly he groans. The sight of Sarah in just a T-shirt – *his*, he realises – no longer has the same hold over him. Since setting out across the water earlier that evening his world has shifted on its axis and the horizon, now altered, holds a promise of something altogether new and invigorating. But how should he handle this? He doesn't want to offend her and he certainly doesn't want an atmosphere clouding the imminent charter.

Suddenly, *Windsong* rocks on her moorings as she responds to the swell surging up the main river only a few yards away. Mac frowns.

'Sarah, I'm sure what you have in mind is highly pleasurable, but I'm shattered, and judging by the change in weather I'll need to have my wits about me over the next few days.'

She freezes in the doorway before slowly turning back to him, her jaw set.

'I'll grab some shut-eye in the single cabin,' Mac says, turning away before she can voice her objections.

32

'So Gemma's already phoned you. That's good.'

Standing in the bay window with her phone to her ear, Kat watches rain-filled clouds chase each other across the sky. Since arriving in Cornwall the changeable weather has surprised her. She assumes it must be because the county is governed by the vagaries of being *almost* at sea.

'Please let me know the cost before you do any work,' she says to the plumber.

Having received his assurance that he won't lift a finger until she agrees to the repairs, Kat finishes the call and contemplates her workload for the forthcoming week. Stella wants her to illustrate a property in Devon, located on the banks of the River Tamar, and that morning she'd opened her laptop and researched its history.

In the medieval period, the property had formed part of the estate of the abbots of Tavistock, but the present house, built in the nineteenth century by the sixth Duke of Bedford for his second wife, is now a hotel. She's looking forward to venturing over the border and it will be interesting to see if there's a noticeable difference between Cornwall and its more English-influenced neighbour. If the illustrations go well and she has time, she may even visit the market town of Tavistock on the western edge of Dartmoor.

As Kat considers the week's commitments, working out which day is best to arrange a visit, a sailing boat enters her field of vision. Its distinct dark-blue hull immediately gives away its identity and she doesn't have to rely on the instinctive sensation bubbling deep in her belly. The yacht follows a course closer to the western shore rather than mid-channel and the occupants are fairly easy to identify. Mac and another man prepare to hoist the sails while a woman and two young lads sit in the cockpit. Sarah is at the wheel.

Kat's eyes dart back to Mac and her mind to the previous evening. His behaviour had been faultless; the perfect gentleman and interesting company, too. When he'd accepted her offer to come back for coffee and view her work, she'd been surprised by his intelligent understanding and observations of her illustrations, which are causing her to question her view of him. But, oh no, she's not going to allow herself to fall for him, despite the stupid responses currently assaulting her body. Without realising, Kat protectively crosses her arms over her stomach. It's easy to fancy someone who is gorgeous, but beauty is skin deep. It's the nature of the man that counts. Is it wishful thinking that makes her imagine he has something a little deeper, judging by his impeccable performance yesterday?

She watches a while longer. It's physical work sailing a boat and his toned body more than hints at muscular strength. No need for visits to the gym. She tuts when she realises she's blushing. What the hell is wrong with her? Anyone would think she was some young teenager fighting raging hormones. Next, she'll be drooling over pictures of naked men!

'For God's sake, Katherine Maddox, get a bloody grip,' she growls to herself.

Still, she can't drag her eyes away. As the yacht leaves the safety of the river for the English Channel, its sails billow in the gusting wind and *Windsong* rides the waves with ease. It looks *so* exhilarating! She'd been a fool to initially reject his offer. He was only being friendly. Perhaps she can accompany Steven when he sails with him. That's probably the most sensible plan, because however easy and delightful Mac's company was last night, it's obvious he and Sarah are a couple. She frowns, thinking of all the other women she's seen him with, and particularly the pretty brown-haired woman in Salcombe. Where does *she* fit into the scheme of things? She'd watched them walking hand in hand along the quayside. Where was Sarah then, and what would she have made of that? And what did she think of him taking her to dinner yesterday evening? Kat shakes her head. No, she is definitely not going to fall for him, however desirable he is. But then she remembers Jean's penetrating look as she'd said, 'But *of course* there are a lot of women interested in him. He's a charming and handsome man!' And she's right. He *is*, but that still doesn't make it OK to have a woman in every port. No, she's going to stand up for all women who find themselves at the mercy of charming and handsome men. She will *not* succumb. No, she won't!

Kat grimaces. She must stop having these internal debates with herself. It's exhausting! She will concentrate on the job she's here to do, get the illustrations done, enjoy the months in Fowey and then go back to her London life. But the thought of returning to her flat, with or without Gemma in residence, and the tight workspace they share at Bryanston Publishing feels less than exciting. What would Tara say? She hears her friend's voice in her head: *'Don't overthink things.'* Yes, blank it all out and focus on the task in hand. That's what she'll do. Back to work . . .

Kat peers through the side window, straining her eyes to follow the yacht's progress until *Windsong* is no longer in view. Sighing deeply, she walks from the room and enters the studio.

Mac prepares for poor weather, securing anything loose on deck and battening down the hatches. He looks out to sea. The tide rises and swells and a small fishing boat heaves and tosses not far off port. Working his way back along the deck, he relieves Sarah of her duty at the helm and peers at the sky with concern as the yacht lists and fights for the wheel. The westerly wind gusts at 30–40mph, and dark storm clouds circle menacingly overhead. He knows it will only be a matter of minutes before the rain comes. Even though he's set a course four or five miles offshore to avoid The Bellows around Dodman Point and attempt a calmer passage for his clients, the yacht's progress is taking much longer than expected.

Suddenly, a wave breaks across her bow and cold spray lashes their faces. *Windsong* is a bluewater sailing yacht, built to withstand extreme weather conditions and capable of taking oceans in her stride. She's handling well and behaving as expected, and Mac has complete confidence in her, but each time she heels over, one of the boys starts to whimper and the other turns green. He can't help but wonder if it would have been wiser for the Murrays to have enjoyed a caravanning holiday instead. Sarah catches Mac's eye and the look on her face tells him she's thinking exactly the same.

'Janine,' Mac calls out, 'I think the boys would be more comfortable below deck.'

The woman glances across at her sons. 'I think you may be right.' Rising unsteadily, she gathers them to her.

'Sarah, give the boys a drink,' Mac quietly instructs, 'and get them to concentrate on the horizon. The older one looks as if he's about to throw up.'

She nods and jumps into action.

Mac checks his watch. At this rate, they'll arrive in the Scillies with little time to do much more than turn around for the homeward trip. He glances across at the boys' father, firmly holding onto the guardrail. The man appears animated and excited by the thrill of the wind and spray coming off the messy sea. Well, Mac can understand that, but it's not about the adults. *Windsong* bucks as it rides a particularly large, cresting wave and Mac automatically bends his legs, absorbing the motion.

'Looks like this weather is set for the duration of the Bank Holiday,' he says, raising his voice above the sound of the wind.

Nick Murray's eyes gleam. 'How long before we reach the Isles of Scilly?'

Mac considers his answer carefully. 'Several hours. Twenty, possibly more in this weather. But I have to warn you, it won't be a comfortable crossing and I doubt we'll have time to explore the islands before the home run. Will the boys be OK?'

The man frowns, obviously irritated by this turn of events. 'Possibly not. Patrick can be very delicate.'

'We could sail down the coast to the Carrick Roads and moor up at Mylor – explore the River Fal instead?'

The man considers Mac's suggestion.

'There are several good facilities there, including a restaurant, bar and shop,' Mac adds.

Nick Murray pulls a resigned face. 'OK. Let's put Plan B into action. Kids!' he mutters with affectionate exasperation. Turning away, he watches the passing coastline.

With a revised destination confirmed, Mac concentrates on facing nature's challenges, safe in the knowledge that both he and *Windsong* are at one with the ocean.

33

Kat's car makes its way slowly along the tree-lined driveway towards the hotel. Across the border, the Devon countryside has a different feel and the undulating fields and extensive woodlands of the Tamar Valley promote an altogether softer landscape. Even the most casual observer would realise they were no longer in Cornwall, with its many *only just* hidden reminders of an industrial past.

Driving around the final bend, Kat pulls up beside a brand new Mercedes and switches off the engine. She sits for a moment, and surveys the charming, grey-stone property before her; its many little dormer windows and tall chimneys lending it a welcome, fairy-tale atmosphere . . . even on this dull day. When she'd left Fowey earlier that morning, the weather had taken a turn for the worse and there was a threat of rain in the air. However, the sky is lighter here. Hopefully the day will continue to clear and give her the opportunity to produce external illustrations without getting wet. Kat climbs out of the car. Extracting her drawing equipment, she locks the doors and walks towards an entrance porch where two massive stone pillars stand sentinel on either side.

A smartly dressed woman suddenly appears at the open door. 'Good morning.'

'Hello, I'm Katherine Maddox,' Kat says, extending a hand.

'I'm the manager, Theresa Gawton,' responds the woman, as she shakes Kat's hand. 'It's not the best of days to view the hotel, but I hope you will be able to get some idea of its splendour.'

'I'm sure I will.'

'If there's anything you require during your day with us, please let me know.'

Kat follows the woman into a softly lit, wood-panelled grand hall and immediately has the sense of stepping back in time. Huge, antiquarian shire maps line the walls and a welcoming fire crackles in an enormous grate. On a mahogany table is a large and exuberant floral display.

'Those are beautiful flowers,' she comments.

'They're picked every day from the garden to welcome guests.'

As Theresa shows Kat around the former fishing lodge, she points out its many wonderful period features including a number of original fire buckets, hose reels and telephones. The long corridors, wood-panelled walls, hushed tones and unhurried pace create a soothing atmosphere and Kat finds it easy to imagine how it would feel being the 'lady of the manor'.

'This Regency hotel is Grade I listed,' Theresa informs her. 'It's set amongst one hundred acres of wildly romantic gardens, full of follies and wonderful Champion trees. The landscape was designed by Humphry Repton, Capability Brown's successor.'

They enter a homely drawing room. In an ornate fireplace is another roaring log fire, and botanical paintings adorn the walls, while a selection of ottomans and plump sofas are strategically placed to take in the view. Standing at the window, Kat gazes out over flowerbeds full of rhododendrons and azaleas, and across lawns sweeping down to the meandering river, where, on the opposite, Cornish bank, swathes of forestry cover the hillside.

'The house was built in 1812 for Georgiana, second wife of the sixth Duke of Bedford,' says Theresa, coming to stand beside Kat at the window. 'At the time, a third of Devon was owned by the Duke and Duchess, and they looked for quite a while at what they had before deciding where to build. They thought this was the prettiest area.'

Aware of the hotel's past echoing in the air, Kat listens to the manager with interest.

'The building work followed a scheme by Jeffry Wyatville,' Theresa continues, 'while Humphry Repton was consulted on the design of the grounds. His proposals were accepted and an exciting, almost alpine terrain was developed with plenty of deliberately created viewpoints and a network of paths and steps, some leading up to a rockery or down to a pool, to – in his words, *add glitter to the scene* – with others fading mysteriously away into the undergrowth.'

'How tantalising,' Kat murmurs.

'Georgiana descended from Highland nobility and she employed artisans and tradesmen to create a faux Scottish landscape. On the Cornish bank, much of the deciduous woodland was replaced with conifers to remind her of her Scottish roots. There were, apparently, five-hundred thousand Scots pines standing by in the nursery.'

'Money was obviously no object,' Kat observes.

Theresa laughs. 'Not for the Duke and Duchess.'

Kat follows the woman into another wood-panelled room lined with shelves that groan beneath the weight of books.

'That's a charming feature,' she says, glancing back at the door decorated with faux bookshelves.

The manager smiles. 'There are dozens of comfortable little nooks for reading and we like to keep the library well-equipped. There's everything here from Zadie Smith to the complete P.G. Wodehouse.'

'I expect very few guests bother to explore the wider area with so much enticing them to stay put,' Kat comments, looking along the shelves and spotting several classics.

Theresa nods. 'That's true, many don't. There's no light pollution and all you hear is birdsong, the wind and nature. If you want to relax, read and walk, it's the perfect place.'

'I can imagine,' says Kat, dreamily. 'It's such a romantic spot.'

'Each afternoon, at teatime, the library table is laid with just-baked scones, pots of clotted cream and strawberry jam, cakes and finger sandwiches. It's the highlight of the day. You are welcome to partake.'

How much is that going to cost?

'All complimentary,' adds the manager, as if reading Kat's mind. 'It's our way of thanking you for featuring the hotel in Professor Marsh's book.'

'That's very generous.'

The woman gives a brief nod. 'Now, if you'd like to follow me I'll show you the original, panelled dining room with its display of crests belonging to family and prestigious friends of the Bedfords. We also have a private room in the Stable that seats up to eighty guests, but unfortunately it's not available to view today because it's being prepared for a wedding.'

'What a wonderful location to get married in,' Kat says.

'We receive many requests.' Theresa peers out of the window. 'Oh, that's good. It looks as if the weather's clearing up. After you've seen the hotel, I'll ask Thomas, our head gardener, to show you around outside. We have eight miles of riverbank, but I doubt you'll have time to explore every inch.'

Several hours later, during which she's enjoyed an indulgent cream tea, Kat surveys the illustration taking shape on her easel. Following a magical tour of the grounds, which are full of ancient trees, verdant glades, secret grottos, caves and waterfalls, her sketchpad is brimming with quickly drawn snapshots of fairy dells, wildflowers and rose-wreathed arches. Plus, of course, the charming shell house; a fairy-tale building with a mirror pool at its centre and decorated inside with shells, conches and coral. Now, she stands on a formal parterre, the raised border along its full length filled with an array of colourful plants. The gardener had pointed out *ipheion*, *muscari*, *alliums* and *camassia*, all backed by *Euphorbia characias,* adding an extra hit of spring green.

Already, perennial summer foliage bursts forth, ready to fill the borders with colour through the coming months.

Kat's large illustration looks up towards the house from halfway along the parterre, and she has added a couple of ladies wearing Victorian outfits. One sits on a bench; the other stands, holding the hand of a toddler clothed in an ankle-length dress. Another child sits on the grass and two dogs loll amongst the little group. It's high summer, all the figures wear wide-brimmed hats and the flowerbed borders are in full bloom. Kat glances over to where she's placed the bench. There's nothing there now, just a neatly manicured lawn, but as clouds scud across the sky, she catches a movement amongst the shadows on the grass. The scene *is* real; just hidden in a fold of time. It's as if she is there, enjoying a pleasant afternoon with these people. She wonders who they are. Is one of the ladies Georgiana Russell and those her children? They could be. After all, the Duchess had ten offspring with the sixth Duke of Bedford.

Glancing at her mobile, Kat is astonished to find she's been at the hotel for over eight hours, and she decides to call it a day. As she starts packing away her drawing equipment, the manager steps from the hotel onto the lawn.

'How's it going?' Theresa calls out, approaching across the grass.

'Very well, thank you,' says Kat, zipping up her pencil case.

'I've just finished my shift and thought I'd come and see what you've done and say goodbye.'

Kat smiles at the woman and unrolling the sketch that had been on the easel, she shows it to her.

'That's marvellous!' exclaims the manager. She turns to Kat with a curious expression. 'You've drawn the figures wearing Victorian dress.'

'I like to provide Professor Marsh with not only real-time illustrations, but also a few that address the past.'

'You've certainly captured that.' Theresa looks back

again at the large sketch. 'This woman here is definitely the Duchess. There's a remarkable likeness.'

So, it is Georgiana!

'Did you have her in mind when you started this drawing?' the manager continues.

'Not particularly. I just draw what I sense.'

'Well done,' Theresa says. 'You've managed to catch her exact likeness and expression.' She glances down at the bag and easel lying on the ground. 'Can I carry anything for you?'

'That's kind of you,' says Kat. 'Perhaps the easel. It's very light.'

34

Spring Bank Holiday Monday dawns wearing a sullen face, but at least it's not raining. A keen wind sweeps in from the sea, gathering up everything before it, and billowing clouds the colour of gunmetal race across the sky. Seagulls keep a very low profile, but two adventurous canoeists battle the choppy waters of the River Fowey, and the little Polruan Ferry bravely soldiers on as it chugs through the swell.

Kat turns away from the window. Hopefully, the rain will stay away for Jean and Stan's barbeque that afternoon. Crossing to the dining table, she rifles through the numerous sketches strewn across it. The ones of the hotel are coming along nicely, although she still has some finishing touches to do. She hopes Stella will approve of the historical illustration. Picking up one of her many filled sketchpads, she flicks through the pages until she comes to the drawing of Mac, standing in the bow of his yacht and wearing a beautiful smile that lights up his face. As with the first time she saw him, he still makes her catch her breath.

Mac . . . Where is he now?

Glancing up, she looks towards the river again. What had he said? He couldn't make the barbeque because he was sailing to the Scillies. You'd need to be in possession of a strong constitution to sail in this weather! No doubt that's one thing Sarah has, along with her many other obvious talents. Kat shakes her had. This won't do: thinking of Mac and being less than generous towards Sarah. She doesn't know either of them. Who knows, they may well be a match made in heaven. But as the thought forms, something tells her to keep an open mind. Checking her phone, Kat exits the room. There's just time for a shower before heading to the party.

Stan's property is a bijou Victorian house set in an elevated position overlooking the town, with stunning harbour views. Its rear-walled garden is the perfect setting for a party – with paved terraces, neatly mown lawns and regimented flowerbed borders – and a number of guests gather in groups, determinedly pretending it's the perfect day for an outdoor gathering despite the unpredictable weather. Outside a conservatory, in which a table is laid with plates, cutlery, salads and bread, Kat stands with Lisa and her family and recounts her recent walk from Polruan.

'The Hall Walk is said to be one of the top one hundred walks in the country,' Stan informs, as he replenishes her wine glass. 'It originated in Tudor times and was very popular.'

'There are certainly some lovely views along the way,' Kat says.

Stan nods.

'What did you think of Pont Quay?' Jean asks.

'Wonderfully tranquil, although I suspect it hasn't always been like that.'

'Indeed not!' Stan exclaims. 'Today, Pont Quay is Grade II listed and owned by the National Trust, but it's believed that Pont Pill was initially established as a small settlement when the parish's first Celtic saint, St Wyllow, settled in a cave there around AD 596.'

'The name "Pont" refers to St Willow's bridge at the top of the creek,' adds Jean. 'Today, the Cornish word for bridge is *pons* but in old Cornish it was *pont*.'

Stan smiles proudly at Jean, while Kat thinks admiringly that the two of them should work for the Cornish tourist board, since they have such a wealth of knowledge about the history of the county.

'The quay subsequently developed as an important area

of trade between farms in the area and other nearby coastal communities,' Stan continues. 'Several commodities were imported and exported. In the early nineteenth century, a number of working units were set up – a corn mill, a sawmill and a blacksmiths, I believe – and the farmhouse was once a beer house frequented by visiting barge crews.'

'Interesting,' Kat says. She'd sensed the bustling quayside of the past . . .

'Also, during World War Two,' he says, 'motor torpedo boats were repaired in the creek. The overhanging trees hid the boats from surveillance aircraft. Today, one can see hull parts and the remains of cradles for boat repairs preserved in the mud on the foreshore.'

'Come on, Stan,' Jean cajoles, resting her hand on the man's arm, 'let's not overwhelm Kat with history. I'm sure she will discover all she needs to know in the fullness of time.'

'Sorry. It's the schoolteacher in me,' Stan apologises.

'It's fascinating,' Kat assures him.

Turning burgers on the barbeque with a pair of stainless-steel tongs, Derek, Lisa's husband, says, 'We tend to gravitate towards the pub at Bodinnick after surviving the Walk.'

'Funny that!' comments Lisa, drily.

Kat laughs. 'It does help to be fit, doesn't it? I had to stop at the 'Q' memorial to catch my breath. As I looked across the river I saw Place House. I hadn't realised how dominant it is in the town.'

'It's been the Treffry family's ancestral home since the thirteenth century,' pipes up Steven, looking inordinately pleased with himself.

'Show off . . .' mumbles Jenny. 'Just 'cos you learnt that last week in history.'

Flushing bright red, the lad glances at Kat, as Lisa gives her husband a despairing look. But Derek simply shrugs and concentrates on the burgers.

'Well, it's a very handsome building,' Kat says, ignoring Jenny's putdown of her brother.

'Grade I listed,' says Stan. 'Most of what you see today dates back to the sixteenth century but the tower is somewhat older, fifteenth century – although it is largely rebuilt.'

'In 1475,' adds Jean, 'Dame Elizabeth Treffry rallied her household and successfully repelled French marauders by pouring boiling lead, stripped from the roof, onto their heads.'

'Quite some woman,' Kat exclaims.

'Yes,' agrees Jean. 'Sadly, though, because the French were thwarted they destroyed the church instead.'

'Is the house open to the public?' Kat asks.

'Unfortunately not,' Lisa replies. 'If you're interested I can show you Fowey's other hidden secrets. People tend to miss a lot.' She turns her attention to her children. 'Steve, Jen, make yourselves useful. The meat's ready. Grab some plates.'

As the afternoon slips into evening, dark shadows creep across the terraces and as strings of twinkling fairy lights spring to life, a collective 'ooh' resounds around the walled garden. Stan closes the lid to the barbeque, which has been on the go for most of the afternoon.

'Oh, good!' says Jean, waving at someone over Kat's shoulder. 'He's made it after all.'

A tingle creeps up Kat's spine, and she turns to see Mac and Sarah standing inside the gate, conversing with a huddle of guests. Ignoring the uninvited flutter assaulting her stomach, Kat watches as Mac laughs easily at someone's comment. Suddenly, he looks over and smiles as he catches her observing him. She doesn't have time to turn away and, instantly, her butterflies lift and swirl.

'So, Steven,' she says, quickly engaging the lad in conversation. 'Have you been sailing on *Windsong* yet?'

Excitement lights his eyes. 'Yes! It was brilliant.'

Damn! She's missed that opportunity.

'Do you think you'll do it again?'

'God, I hope so!'

Kat takes a deep breath. Her nerves are all over the place and she's desperate to glance back at Mac and see what he's doing, but she refuses to be *that* obvious. Not to mention, totally uncool . . .

'I meant to ask,' Stan says, pouring yet more wine into her glass, 'how did you get on with that traumatic adventure of yours over the border?'

Kat laughs. 'It was interesting. And even though the house has been turned into a luxury boutique hotel, it feels so comfortable that it's easy to imagine it's your own home. And the grounds . . . well, they are truly something else.'

Thankful for the distraction of Stan's conversation, she takes a gulp of wine. But Mac must be her default setting because she senses his approach, and then surreptitiously watches him out of the corner of her eye. Tousled dark hair, gorgeously tanned face, open-necked, teal-blue shirt, jeans that are just the right amount of worn-in . . .

'Hello, Mac.' Jean greets him with a smile. 'You made it after all.'

'I promised myself that come hell or high water I would be here.' He bends to kiss the older woman's cheek, though his gaze is firmly on Kat. 'And hell *and* high water it certainly was! We didn't make it to the Scillies, so we explored the Fal instead.'

'Well, I'm very pleased you are here,' Jean says warmly, giving his arm a pat. 'We were just discussing a hotel Kat visited last week. Stan very kindly treated me to a birthday luncheon there last year.'

'Where was that?' he asks.

'The Tamar Valley,' Kat responds formally, overcompensating for her nerves.

For God's sake loosen up.

'I could have quite easily curled up with a good book for the afternoon in one of their charming drawing rooms,' Jean continues.

'Yes, it was rather wonderful,' agrees Stan. 'Although I thought the hotel had a slightly collegiate feel, what with its long corridors, and those panelled walls studded with crests.'

'Well, either college or home, I think it would be a glorious place to live,' says Jean.

Say something! Don't remain mute . . .

'The sixth Duke of Bedford's second wife, Georgiana, fell in love with the valley,' Kat blurts out, her words tumbling over each other in a rush. 'She was the guiding spirit behind the development.'

Mac smiles and suddenly she feels foolishly comforted.

'And if my memory serves me well,' Stan says, 'it was Repton who designed the grounds.'

'Know anything about that, clever clogs?' Jenny gives her brother a sharp dig in the ribs.

'Ouch!' Steven grimaces and rubs his side.

'That's right, Stan,' Kat says. 'Repton designed the Duke's garden at Woburn and was invited to consider this project. Apparently, the hotel's gardens and grounds remain one of the most perfect examples of the *Picturesque style*.' She takes a sip of wine, making sure not to gulp. 'He also famously prepared red-linen bound portfolios containing beautiful watercolours to show his clients what their gardens would look like.'

'Sounds an intriguing place,' comments Mac.

'Oh, haven't you visited? You simply must!' Jean exclaims. 'It's definitely somewhere to take someone special.'

Kat glances sharply at her, but Jean's face is perfectly poised.

'What's that?' Sarah asks, suddenly joining them. 'Where are you taking someone special?' She wraps a possessive arm around Mac's waist.

An awkward atmosphere descends and as Mac steps subtly away from the uninvited embrace, a tremor of satisfaction courses through Kat.

'When I first arrived in Fowey,' she says, breaking the

mood, 'I saw the estuary full of boats. Could it have been a race?'

'Was it a Wednesday evening or a Saturday afternoon?' Sarah asks, not seeming to mind that Mac has distanced himself from her.

'Saturday.'

'Were they multi-coloured sails?'

'Yes, but some had white sails.'

'That would be the Troys and the Fowey Rivers,' Sarah states. 'They race during the summer months. The white-sailed boats with the bowsprits are the Troy class keelboats, built by local boat builders and kept within ten miles of the river. The smaller boats with the brightly coloured sails are the clinker-built, wooden, Fowey River dinghies.'

'That explains the 'T' and 'FR' on the sails,' Kat comments.

'Yes . . .' Sarah gives her a disdainful look.

Oh God! Why is she such a sailing ignoramus? Sarah is obviously perfect for Mac . . .

'You two must be hungry,' says Jean, suddenly taking charge. 'I'm afraid there's not a great deal left, but I'm sure we can rustle up something. Stan, what about drinks for our guests?' She sends him a meaningful look.

'Please excuse me. What a bad host I am! Now, what can I get you?'

All at once, everyone leaps into *busy* mode and Kat fights the urge to laugh out loud. She glances at Mac to find him watching her. His eyes dance in amusement, as though he perfectly understands what she's thinking, and a slow, sexy smile spreads across his lips.

As the first raindrops fall, the party hurriedly transfers inside. It's not a large house and the number of guests crammed into its space creates a cosy crush.

Kat finds herself standing in the living room with Mac. 'So, how was your *hell or high water* trip?'

He raises an eyebrow. 'Challenging. Not a good first sailing experience for one of the lads.'

'That's a shame. Do you think there will be a second?'
'The parents are keen, but I suspect the boy's stomach isn't!'
She pulls a sympathetic face.

'The Scillies are quite a sail from here,' Mac continues, 'especially if the weather is unfavourable, which is why we decided to explore the River Fal instead.'

'I don't know that area. I wonder if any properties on Stella's list are down that way. Perhaps I could explore it then.'

'If you like, we could sail there.' Mac's eyes meet hers. 'I'd be happy to show you the Fal. There are numerous interesting inlets.'

Kat hesitates.

But, this is what she wants, isn't it?

She opens her mouth to answer, but before she has a chance, Sarah joins them again.

'Mac, I think I'll head off now. Are you coming?'

He glances at his watch. 'Er . . . Not yet. You go on.'

Sarah's eyes shift accusingly to Kat. 'Well, don't be too long. We've some busy days ahead of us.'

Mac's left eyebrow arcs. 'See you later, Sarah,' he says in a level voice.

Wrong-footed, the young woman hovers briefly before turning away.

Kat frowns. There's something really odd about Mac and Sarah's dynamic, but she can't put her finger on it.

'We're off now,' says Lisa, approaching from across the room with her family in tow. 'It was good to see you again, Kat.'

Kat smiles. 'Likewise.'

Steven grins at Mac and, aware that the two of them need to discuss their next sailing expedition, Kat wonders whether to muscle in and suggest they include her. But, once again, she hesitates . . . And then the moment is gone.

'Well, I suppose I should also make tracks,' she says, looking around the room for Jean and Stan.

'We're going your way,' announces Lisa's husband. 'We'll walk you back.'

'It's OK, Derek. I'll see Kat safely home,' Mac interjects.

Kat turns and faces them. 'Guys, I'm perfectly capable of getting myself home!'

'Of course you are,' says Lisa, 'but when you have the option of being escorted home by a devilishly handsome man you'd be a fool not to accept.'

Kat's eyes widen. What can she say? If she refuses Mac again it will be downright rude. 'OK, thanks,' she says to him.

'All sorted,' says Lisa. 'Right, you lot . . . home!'

'Bye, Kat,' Steven says, giving her a lopsided grin.

'Come on, goofy.' Jenny grabs her brother's arm and practically drags him towards the door. 'See you again, Kat.'

As Lisa and her family depart, Mac turns to her with a smile. 'So, I guess you're stuck with me.'

She grins. 'I guess so.'

He laughs. 'Come on, let's find our hosts and say goodbye. Then I can see you *safely* home!'

35

Fowey has been busy with holidaymakers over the Bank Holiday weekend, but many of the tourists have already left and peace descends once more. As Kat and Mac make their way along Fore Street, the rain abates. A blanket of softly muffled silence enfolds the town, and Kat listens to the sound of their footsteps reverberating off the walls of the Medieval and Georgian buildings lining the narrow street.

It's never this quiet, or as dark, in London. There's always background noise and light pollution. It's such a different way of life. How lucky people are to live in this pretty harbour town.

Feeling at ease walking along the street with Mac, she glances across at him. He has such a comfortable presence, and neither feels the need to make conversation. Passing the bookshop and St Fimbarrus Church, they walk up the steep incline and turn into the Esplanade, when suddenly the heavens open.

Mac laughs. 'Knew it was too good to be true!'

Grabbing her hand, he breaks into a jog and pulls her into a deeply recessed shop doorway.

'Looks as if it's setting in,' he says, peering up at the dark sky.

Her hand is still in his and it surprises Kat to discover she wants it to remain there.

'Do you live aboard *Windsong*?' she asks, wondering why she's never asked that before.

He turns and looks at her. 'Yes.'

With Sarah?

The thought makes her pull her hand from his grasp, but instantly she longs for the warmth of his strong fingers.

'You must be very organised,' she says, somewhat stiffly.

He smiles. 'I have to be. It can be tough sharing with others in such a small space.'

So Sarah does *live on board.*

Kat straightens her back and gazes out at the street. A curtain of rain falls from the building above, creating a waterfall.

'What do you say we make a run for it?' Mac suggests.

Without responding, Kat propels herself out of the relative dryness of the doorway through the sheet of water, and sets off at a brisk jog down the middle of the empty street. A moment later Mac falls into step beside her, and when they reach Stella's house she hurriedly opens the front door and enters. He remains in the street in the pouring rain.

That's nice; he's not presuming anything.

'Come in, you're getting soaked,' she says, standing back from the door.

He steps into the entrance hall and shakes his head, sending droplets of rain in all directions. His shirt is soaked through and rivulets of water drip from his trousers onto the tiled floor.

'British weather, hey?' Kat says with a laugh. 'I'll get you a towel.'

Rushing upstairs, she grabs a large bath towel from the airing cupboard and then standing at the top of the stairs, calls out, 'Catch!'

Mac looks up as the towel hurtles through the air towards him. Dexterously, he catches it. 'Thanks.'

'You're welcome,' she says with a smile. 'If you want, I'll put your clothes in the dryer. Go through to the sitting room, it's the door opposite the studio. I won't be long.'

Five minutes later, having towel-dried her hair and changed into a fresh pair of jeans and a sweatshirt, Kat rushes downstairs, fills the kettle and switches it on. She walks along the hall towards the sitting room, but as she passes the studio she sees Mac is in there, standing in front of the easel by the bay window. Her face flushes vividly, not because he's checking out her drawing of the Devon hotel but because the towel, now wrapped around his waist, exposes a bare, tanned upper torso, beautifully muscled and with a light covering of swirling, dark chest hair.

Oh. My. God!

Composing herself, she enters the room.

Mac glances over. 'Once again, Kat, you've nailed it.'

She gives a half-smile, acknowledging yet another compliment, and forces herself to exhale.

As the sound of the kettle coming to the boil reaches her ears, she's grateful for the distraction. 'Would you like coffee or tea?'

'Coffee please.'

'Pass me your clothes and I'll put them in the dryer.'

He crosses the room, holding out the soaked garments, and though she attempts to avert her gaze, it's hopeless. There's a quiet, controlled strength in that body. Not overly worked-out, but still strong to the core – hardened from years at sea.

She dashes downstairs to the utility room and placing his wet clothes in the dryer, she sets the timer and switches on the machine. Then, for a moment, she stands perfectly still to gather herself. She just has to remember to breathe.

Heading back up to the kitchen a minute or so later, she makes coffee and carries the two steaming mugs through to the studio. As she enters, she sees Mac has found the sketchpad *again,* which is open at the drawing of him aboard *Windsong*. All at once, she wills the floor to open up and swallow her. Mac turns his head and regards her, and the look in his eyes makes her falter. Warmth and – if she's not mistaken – respect.

'Have you exhibited anywhere, Kat?'

'Oh no.' She laughs. 'I'm just a jobbing illustrator.'

Passing him a mug, she sits down opposite him.

'These sketches don't look like *jobbing* illustrations to me,' he says in a serious voice.

She smiles her thanks and her heart softens, then she remembers his consummate skill in charm. She has to find out what, if anything, he wants of her, before she can put her trust in him. And it's now or never. This not knowing is killing her!

'Mac, can I ask you something?'

'Fire away.'

'Since I first caught sight of you, I've seen you with a variety of women.'

He sits back in surprise. 'This is quite a change in conversation. What do you want to know?'

Everything!

Suddenly the room feels airless and glancing across the table, she catches the amusement dancing in his eyes. In response, she grows hot.

Is he going to make this difficult and toy with her?

'I like women,' he says simply. 'Is that a problem?'

There's nothing wrong with that, she supposes . . .

'No. It's just . . .' She hesitates, unsure how to proceed.

'Just what?' Mac gently prompts.

'You appreciating women isn't a problem, of course not . . .' Kat attempts to still her pounding heart. 'It's just that I've been messed around by men, and I'm wary being around someone who seems to have a different woman for every day of the week.'

He laughs. 'That's some exaggeration, Kat!'

'Not really.' She frowns, because this is not how she'd planned this conversation at all.

She meets his eyes. No longer do they twinkle; his gaze has turned grave.

She sighs. 'I know, I have no right to ask you to explain yourself to me.'

The atmosphere has suddenly turned from deliciously tense to uncertain. This could go either way.

'No, that's true, you don't,' Mac says, leaning forward and briefly covering her hand with his. 'But I invite you to ask.'

Taking a deep breath, Kat steadies her nerves. 'When I saw you at Tate Britain you were with a very stylish woman.'

'Yes, a very stylish *friend*! Next,' he says, as if ticking items off a shopping list.

Kat feels wretched. 'The dark-haired woman sailing with you in Salcombe. The one with the two teenagers.'

Mac frowns. 'A woman with teenagers?'

She nods.

Suddenly his face breaks into a look of astonishment and Kat squirms. But she's got to keep going if she wants peace of mind.

'She's a client,' he says. 'No, to be totally truthful, she is a client's wife. He'd been called away on urgent business and rather than cancel the charter he asked me to sail with his wife and kids instead. Next?'

Feeling slightly foolish, Kat steels herself. 'And Sarah?'

Mac sighs. 'Sarah is crew. She may want more, but she's definitely crew.'

Her eyes widen. *That's the relationship she couldn't put her finger on!*

But the way Sarah is with him, flirting and hugging at the slightest opportunity, it's obvious to everyone she wants to be *more*. Perhaps she considers she already is.

Mac picks up his mug and swallows a mouthful of coffee. 'Anyone else on your mind?'

She can hardly bring herself to ask.

He gives her a probing look.

'The other woman, in Salcombe.'

He doesn't answer immediately and she wonders if he's having trouble working out which one she's referring to.

'You were with her when you stopped and talked to me and my friend on the quay,' she prompts. 'While Tara's boys were crabbing.'

Kat watches as his eyes soften. He's generously answered

all her questions with dismissive humour, but she senses this woman is different.

'Francine,' he says, lowering his gaze. 'She's a good woman.'

Good woman or not, where does she stand in the scheme of things?

Kat waits.

A minute later, Mac looks up. 'For a while I thought Francine and I had something, but the relationship ran its course. I ended things with her recently, although we're still friends . . .'

Kat sips her coffee, mulling over all he's told her.

Mac watches as she grapples with her inner thoughts. 'Is that it, or is there anyone else you'd like to discuss?'

She hesitates. 'The silver-haired woman I saw you with at the tapas bar.'

Sitting back in his seat, Mac frowns. 'Jane? She is . . . *was* . . . a client. But she's since moved on,' he says in a bemused voice.

Embarrassed, Kat looks down at the table and shakes her head. She has her disastrous love life to blame for making her oversensitive and cynical, and causing her to second-guess everything. But when she glances up again, and her eyes tentatively meet Mac's, she's relieved to see a smile tugging at the corners of his mouth.

'So you see, I'm not some out of control Casanova.'

She gives a brief smile, feeling sick at the next question. 'What about the mother of your son?'

Deep emotion shows on Mac's face. When he speaks, he's so quiet she's not sure she's heard him correctly.

'She's not around anymore.'

What does he mean by that? Did the woman abandon them?

But Kat decides to end tonight's interrogation, even though she suspects there's much more to discover about this enigmatic man. 'Thanks for being so open to my questions, Mac.'

Without looking at her, he waves his hand as if it's nothing at all, although she can see she's stirred something up. She searches for another conversation tack.

'Would you like to come with me one day while I'm sketching?'

He raises his eyes to hers. 'I'd like that very much,' he says softly. 'I'm almost back-to-back with charters over the next few weeks, but I do have the odd day off here and there.'

In for a penny . . .

'I have to finish the hotel illustrations this week, but after that I plan to visit Penhallam Manor, or rather its remains. Perhaps you'd like to accompany me there?'

'Love to. Let me know which day and, hopefully, it will be one of my free days.' Mac smiles. 'As we need to coordinate things, I suppose it would be a good idea to exchange numbers.'

'Yes,' she agrees.

An hour later, after retrieving Mac's clothes from the dryer and directing him to the bathroom, Kat stands at the bay window gazing out over the dark river. On the opposite shore, the lights of Polruan shimmer across the water. When she'd left for the party earlier that afternoon she had no idea she'd be spending the evening with Mac . . . she raises an eyebrow . . . and a half-naked Mac at that! But she's not going to allow herself to get carried away and trapped by his spell. No, not at all . . .

At the sound of his footsteps on the stairs, she turns away from the window and walks out into the hallway.

'Once again, Kat, thank you for a very pleasant, if damp, evening,' he says.

She can't stop the smile spreading across her face. Mac's proving to be so *not* what she thought he was. He's defied her less than flattering theory of him, and his explanations for all the women she's seen him with have been plausible, going some way to dispelling her fears. They both take a step towards each other at the same time, and collide. Immediately he catches her arm to steady her.

'Sorry,' she says self-consciously.

His soft laugh is music to her ears. 'Don't forget to ring me when you know which day you plan to visit Penhallam. It sounds like an interesting adventure away from the water.'

He bends to kiss her cheek and, flustered, Kat looks up at the wrong moment; her mouth is so close to his that their lips brush for a second, and she instantly jerks away.

'Oh God, I'm so sorry!'

'Don't be.' His hazel eyes observe her, sexily. 'I'm not!'

'Honestly!' she says with a nervous laugh. 'If this was a sitcom there couldn't be a more embarrassingly laughable moment.'

'You're wrong there . . .' He raises a self-mocking eyebrow. 'Try sitting in close proximity to a seriously hot woman while you're trying to keep your dignity wearing nothing more than a towel!'

36

All that week, Kat concentrates on finishing her illustrations of the hotel. Although the Met Office has forecast favourable weather, it remains changeable, as if the start of summer has been put on hold. It's probably just as well, otherwise she'd be tempted to *down tools* and explore the beautiful area in glorious sunshine. She doesn't see Mac – he's busy with a last-minute, corporate yacht charter – but they speak on the phone and arrange to meet at Stella's house the following Monday to spend the day together. Hearing his voice does strange things to Kat, and despite her curiosity about James MacNamara, she is besieged with nervous energy as she realises what she's put into motion.

Saturday arrives quickly, and with the intention of spending an indulgent evening watching TV, Kat has settled in one of the comfortable armchairs in the sitting room when her phone rings.

'So, how's it going?' Tara asks, without introduction. 'Have you abandoned your London roots and applied for Cornish citizenship yet?'

Kat laughs. 'Highly tempted, although I doubt I'd be accepted. You have to be seventh generation or something before you're considered *local*.'

'Good to hear you haven't completely gone over to the other side.'

'I haven't, but I have to confess I haven't given Bryanston Publishing much thought, either,' Kat says. 'Each day this place feels more like home, and knowing I have to return at some point seems like someone else's concern.'

The friends fall into their customary easy banter.

'Any developments I should know about?' Tara enquires.

'Well . . .' Kat pauses, feeling the heat in her face.

'Go on, spill the beans,' Tara encourages. 'Don't keep me on tenterhooks.'

'Mac's accompanying me on assignment next Monday.'

'Excellent!' She can almost hear Tara punching the air. 'Tell me more. I mean, its so blimmin' obvious he likes you.'

Her enthusiasm is infectious and Kat finds herself smiling broadly.

'Not to me, it's not!'

'Don't give me that. You must be blind! Come on, details . . .'

Kat takes a deep breath. 'We were at the same barbecue and he walked me home, only we got soaked in a downpour and I invited him in and gave him a towel to wear while his clothes were in the dryer.'

The words tumble out in a single sentence, and Kat cringes. It sounds so contrived.

Tara, however, seems to be choking.

'Are you OK?' Kat asks with concern.

Tara coughs and splutters. 'For God's sake, Kat. If you're going to spring something like that, give me fair warning so I'm not drinking at the same time!'

'Teach you for drinking. Whisky, by any chance?'

'No, a rather fine brandy. I've had that kind of a day.'

'I may need a rather fine brandy before my day with Mac.'

Tara chuckles. 'So, tell me. What happened with the towel?'

'Sorry to disappoint. Nothing.'

'Oh, for goodness sake! I've never known anyone pass up so many golden opportunities.'

Kat laughs. 'I've told you, Tara, I've given up men.' Though as she says this, her inner voice asks whether she could make just one exception.

'And as *I* said, you two can't keep your eyes off each other,' Tara continues. 'Anyway, enough of your love life. I have an invitation for you. We're coming down to Salcombe next weekend and I thought it would be the perfect opportunity to meet up. Would you like to stay? Can you fit us into your busy schedule?'

'Yes to both. You know I'd love to see you all.'

Throughout Sunday night, Kat tosses and turns, hounded by an unnatural agitation that has consumed her ever since she and Mac finalised plans for their day together. She's hardly slept, and at 6 a.m. she finally gives up trying. With a sigh, she rolls over and watches a shaft of light pierce the room through a gap in the curtains. At least it looks as though good weather has finally arrived. She might as well rise and face the day. Perhaps a shower will help dispel the nausea claiming her.

By eight, Kat has already packed a cool bag with picnic food, cups and glasses, filled a large flask with coffee and checked her mobile several times to make sure it's fully charged. Her drawing equipment is already in the hallway and she considers whether to load the car while waiting for him to arrive. She glances around. Has she forgotten anything?

Exiting the kitchen, Kat picks up her art bag, opens the front door and steps out into the street. As she looks to her right she sucks in her breath. In the distance she sees Mac, walking towards the house with an easy but purposeful stride. There's nothing insecure about him – unlike how she currently feels – even the air around Mac seems to stand back in awe as he passes by.

Raising his hand, he smiles.

Just remember . . . breathe!

She smiles in return. Crossing the empty street, she presses the remote to unlock her car and places her bag on the rear seat.

'Morning.' Mac greets her as she walks back to the house. 'Looks like we're in for a good day.'

She glances up at the pale-blue sky dotted with white tufts of candy floss. 'At last!'

'Can I help carry anything?'

'Perhaps the cool bag; I've prepared a picnic. There's a rug already in the car.' She glances at his waterproof jacket. 'That's a good idea.'

'Just in case,' he says, following her into the hallway '. . . after my last escapade with you!'

Kat chuckles nervously as she enters the kitchen. Opening the fridge door she takes out a bottle of wine and two of water, and stows them in the cool bag.

'I think that's all.' She unplugs her mobile from its charger and glances up at the clock. 'If we're lucky and there aren't any hold-ups, we should arrive in good time.'

Mac walks across the room and picks up the cool bag as Kat grabs her jacket from the coat hooks in the hallway, and as she steps out into the street she sees him already stowing the picnic bag in the boot of the car. Briefly, her nerves settle. It's as if they do this all the time.

He looks across the road. 'All set?'

'Yes.'

She gives him a smile. Pulling the front door to, she crosses the road and climbs into the driver's seat, and lets out a silent, raggedy breath as she enters the location of the ruins into the sat nav.

The journey is uneventful, apart from having to negotiate commuter traffic around Bodmin, and ninety minutes later they pull into the small car park serving Penhallam Manor. There are no other cars.

As Kat switches off the engine, Mac gets out. Walking to the rear of the car, he takes out the cool bag and picnic rug from the boot, and she smiles to herself as she extracts her art bag from the rear seat.

It's so quiet. The gentlest of winds teases through the

trees as they approach a wooden combination five-bar and pedestrian gate, beyond which a track leads off tantalisingly into the forest. They stop to read an information board located beside the gates and learn that the grassed-over ruins they are about to see are of a medieval manor house, once home to the de Cardinham family for over three hundred years. Excavations carried out between 1968 and 1973 had revealed four ranges of buildings around a courtyard, surrounded by a protective moat.

'From research,' Kat remarks, 'I've discovered that moated manor houses are found mainly in central and eastern England. They're rare in the South West, so Penhallam is particularly unusual.'

'Perhaps the de Cardinhams were a questionable lot and needed added protection from invaders,' Mac suggests.

'Maybe,' says Kat, thoughtfully, as she opens the pedestrian gate and steps through. 'They also owned Restormel Castle and that was surrounded by a moat. Apparently, near here, at Week St Mary, there are remains of an earthwork castle that could have been the family's first home. The building of Penhallam may have represented a move to a more sheltered site, when the need for defence was no longer a primary consideration.'

'Interesting.' Mac follows her through the gate. 'Looks like we have the place to ourselves.'

'I hope so.' She glances back at him. 'I always work best left to my own devices but as soon as I start to sketch people tend to appear out of nowhere. They always want to ask questions, which is good, but it tends to interrupt the creative flow.'

'I'd best keep quiet then!' he says, walking beside her.

'Oh, I didn't mean you . . .' she says, flustered, but as his eyes meet hers she realises he's only teasing. 'It's far too early! I need at least two coffees before I get with it.'

'I'll remember that,' he says softly, under his breath.

Kat's stomach muscles tighten.

The track follows the course of a meandering shallow stream with banks covered in verdant ferns. On the opposite side is a darkly wooded area, eerie and silent; its many trees draped in lichen and moss. As if their voices would be too loud, or perhaps, disturb something hidden, Kat and Mac walk on in silence. Presently, they come to a clearing and reverently they stop and take in the scene. Growing undisturbed around the edge of the glade, red campion and spikes of blue bugle compete with the long grasses. Kat silently congratulates herself for identifying them.

At last, the work she did on those flower books has paid off!

In the centre, approached over a wooden bridge, are the low, grass-covered remains of the moated thirteenth-century manor house built by Andrew de Cardinham. Immediately, Kat senses its history. She can almost hear the sounds of daily life that would have once filled the air in this quiet, isolated spot.

Another display board shows an illustration of three men in flat caps excavating the area. In the background is a tractor with a digger attached.

'It's hard to believe the existence of the ruins went unnoticed until the 1960s,' says Mac, reading from the board. 'And then only when the site came under threat from tree planting.'

Kat joins him. 'Thank goodness a decision was made to save them for the nation. It's such a rare example of an early Cornish manor house.'

'Yes,' Mac says, glancing at her in thoughtful consideration. 'Especially in today's throwaway society.'

'It's a shame that stone-robbers removed many of the walls for building material,' Kat continues, scanning the information. 'That's a *takeaway* society!'

He gives a low laugh. 'It says here that the missing sections have been marked out by metal-framed cages filled with earth and topped with turf. It's a good way of showing visitors the full layout of the manor.'

'And great that English Heritage cares for the various wildlife here,' Kat adds. 'I think the moat is regularly cleared to encourage plants and things like dragonflies and water beetles . . .'

Aware that his gaze is still upon her, she shyly glances at Mac.

'What?' she asks.

'Nothing,' he says, though his hazel eyes are gleaming, and for a long heartbeat they assess each other.

Kat is the first to break eye contact. 'Come on, let's look around the site. I want to find the best spots to sketch from.'

37

As they cross the bridge – the site of the original drawbridge – the atmosphere is tranquil and serene. Halting at the entrance to the remains of what once had been the substantial and sophisticated manor of Penhallam, Kat and Mac stand for a moment and survey the ruins. The house was built around a quadrangle, then not inhabited for any great length of time and finally abandoned in the fourteenth century. Laid out before them is its full medieval ground plan, having survived unaltered by later building work. Immediately to the right of the entrance are low, grass-covered outlines of a room.

'This was the chapel,' Kat says respectfully, as she steps into its centre.

They are the only visitors at the site and yet she's aware of whispers in her peripheral hearing: shrouded and distorted.

'Look at this,' says Mac. 'Stone benches and what looks like the base of an altar.'

She nods. Taking out her mobile, she snaps a couple of photographs.

'I wonder what this was,' Mac considers, as he approaches an adjacent oblong area.

'I think it was private apartments. It's the oldest part of the site, circa late twelfth century.'

He turns towards her. 'How do you know that?'

'I did a bit of research, but also it's a feeling.'

Why is she being so honest with him? She *never* mentions her special gift to anyone!

She glances at Mac, bracing herself for a dismissive

response but, instead, she's surprised to find his attitude is curious and he's keeping an open mind.

'That's interesting.'

'This room here,' she continues, indicating a neighbouring outlined area, 'was the wardrobe, circa very-early thirteenth century.'

Mac folds his arms and considers her. 'You really have done your research. It's not just a case of turning up and drawing what you see, is it?'

She smiles. 'No. I like to get a feel for a place before I arrive. I take photographs on site to produce realistic illustrations later, because when I sketch *in situ* my drawings are not true of the buildings as they are in the present day.'

He frowns.

'You'll see,' she says.

Continuing their tour, they enter the northern end of the quadrangle of ruins.

'This is the hall and this is a hearth,' she says, pointing to a circular area void of grass. 'And those are the remains of the dais – the site of the high table – and do you see the stone-faced benches lining the east, north and south walls?'

Mac's eyes widen as he follows her finger. 'You can actually *see* the room, Kat?'

'It's hard to explain,' she says, taking more photos. 'It's not visible, and yet I sense an impression.'

He glances back at her, intrigued. 'What are these rooms?' He points to several oblong enclosures leading off from the hall.

'That one immediately adjacent is the buttery, which leads to the bakery and brewhouse, and then on to the pantry, which was probably a lean-to.' She indicates each room in turn. 'All are early thirteenth-century additions.'

'And that one there?' He motions to an area next to the pantry.

'The kitchen. It's a later addition, circa fourteenth century and probably rebuilt as a result of a fire. At the southern end, next to the entrance, is where the larder would have been. It had a stone-lined, cool-storage pit in its north-east corner.' She points to an area of ruins. 'That's where the two-storey lodging for household staff was situated.'

Mac gives her an incredulous look. 'That's quite a skill you have, Kat.'

'Skill?' She makes a sound in the back of her throat. 'I'm not sure I think of it as such. I mean, it's not something that can be put to good use.'

'I'd say it's being put to good use right now,' he says grinning. 'You shouldn't dismiss your gift so lightly.'

Kat stares at him. Whatever has happened to the all-action macho man who sails from port to port and can freely bed any woman who takes his fancy? Today, Mac's again showing a sensitive and insightful side, and her resolve to keep him at arm's length is being seriously tested. But old doubts still linger. Which version is the real James MacNamara?

'What are you thinking about, Kat?'

She shakes her head. 'Nothing of importance.' She smiles and glances at her mobile. 'I'd better get on, or at this rate I'll never get the work done.'

She turns away and walks back towards the entrance of the grassed ruins, knowing that an impressive tower once stood there. Heading towards the wooden bridge where they'd left the cool bag, Kat spreads out the picnic rug on a section of the grass-covered metal-caged infill wall and, sitting down, opens her art bag and extracts the sketchpad and pencil case. She considers which pens to use. Glancing up, she sees Mac has returned to the far end of the ruins.

'There's a slight impression here,' he calls out. 'I think it could have been a well.'

'Probably. It is in the general vicinity of the kitchen.'

She watches him take out his mobile phone and photograph the area. Half-closing her eyes, Kat stills her breathing, clears her mind, and allows the atmosphere to envelop her. And as her senses heighten and her fingers begin to tingle, the blood fizzes in her veins. Selecting a pen, she starts to sketch.

A while later, Mac joins her and she smiles at the look of wonderment on his face as he studies her illustration. On the sketchpad is a drawing of the impressive South Tower, with a traveller and horse at its entrance. She hears the distant sound of dogs barking and is unsure whether this is in the present, heralding the arrival of other visitors that will end their private viewing of the site. Spontaneously, she adds three dogs to the sketch and smiles. They complete the picture.

'Are you seeing that scene?' Mac asks incredulously, as he sits down beside her on the low wall.

'Yes . . . and no.'

Two lines form between his eyebrows.

'It's like a dream-vision,' she explains. 'Sometimes it comes to me vividly. Other times it's a suggestion, like a picture behind a veil – one that I have to try and grasp before it evaporates into the mist.'

'What's it like now?'

'Now it's strong. I can hear the sound of daily living – hammering, laughter, shouts, dogs barking.'

He gazes around the quiet clearing in amazement. 'Hard to imagine, looking at this peaceful scene.'

Putting aside her sketchpad, Kat opens the cool bag and takes out a couple of glasses. She passes them to Mac.

'If you could do the honours with the wine, I'll sort out the picnic.'

'How long have you had this ability?' he asks, extracting the bottle of wine from the bag.

As Kat places cutlery and plates on the rug she considers his question. 'I've been aware of another level of hearing and seeing for as long as I can recall, although I learned to keep those observations to myself. It was only when I started to draw that I couldn't hide it any longer. I was forever reprimanded for exaggerating and embellishing the facts.' She pulls a face.

Mac gazes at her thoughtfully. 'That's a shame.'

She glances at him. 'All part of building one's character, I guess.'

His lips twitch into a smile. 'Still, it must have been tough.'

'Yes,' Kat says quietly, 'and confusing too.' She takes a deep breath. 'But that's all in the past, thankfully.'

They enjoy an uninterrupted lunch. No dogs appear with their owners in tow and neither do any other visitors. Instead, they are blessed to have the serene tranquillity of Penhallam Manor to themselves for the day.

Over towards a marshy area of ground, Kat notices swathes of yellow iris, bur-reed and water crowfoot. Again she smiles contentedly, aware that her work at Bryanston Publishing has provided her with the ability to effortlessly identify the various flora and fauna. She watches a speckled wood butterfly flit from plant to plant before eventually selecting an iris. As it rests on the flower with wings outstretched, Kat picks up a pen and produces a quick sketch.

'You're so talented, Kat,' comments Mac, watching her replicate the butterfly onto paper. 'Not only can you capture the essence of historic ruins, but also nature too.'

She stops sketching and looks up at him. 'Did you know that the yellow iris is thought by some to be the original *fleur-de-lis*?'

He shakes his head.

'It's also believed to avert evil and was hung in bunches outside doors on the Feast of Corpus Christi in Ireland. Medicinally, it's used for its astringency, to stop blood flow.'

'Interesting what knowledge one accumulates over the course of a lifetime,' he says with a grin.

'Yeah, I'm a mine of useless information.'

He holds her gaze, and the way he looks at her makes her feel as if she's let herself down in some way.

'Why do you belittle yourself?' he asks.

'I don't, do I?' Suddenly she's alert and on edge.

He nods his head slowly.

Embarrassed, she quickly returns to sketching the butterfly.

'Tell me, Kat,' Mac says, leaning forward and balancing his elbows on his knees. 'What's your life like in London?'

Silently, she groans.

For pity's sake, let's not go there!

When she doesn't answer, he continues, 'Having seen you at Tate Britain, it's obvious you like to visit art galleries, but how do you fill the rest of your downtime? Lunch with friends? Or is there someone special waiting for you back home? I can't imagine anyone in their right mind letting you out of their sight for too long.'

She colours, not just because of his probing interest in her life but also because of the compliment.

'No one special,' she answers somewhat bleakly.

Mac straightens up, assessing her. 'Why is that?' he asks gently.

Oh God! Does she really have to go into all this?

'I have no idea. It's not as if I haven't had my fair share of partners over the years, but I tend to watch as friends get hitched and start families while I just continue on my merry way.'

He remains quiet for a while and silence hangs in the air between them.

'So,' he says carefully, 'given your previous messy relationship, shall I take it there is no one special back in London?'

She glances at him but he isn't looking at her. He's studying the ground around his feet.

'I thought there was. In fact, the day I saw you at the Pre-Raphaelite exhibition I'd just discovered he'd omitted to tell me about something rather important.' She grimaces as Colin's deceit, even though its effect has receded lately, still stings. 'Actually, *three* rather small but very important facts; two toddlers and the imminent arrival of a baby.'

His eyes meet hers and the complex look on his face confuses her.

'As it happens,' she continues with a bitter laugh, 'it was

while I sat on that bench in the gallery that I texted Colin and finished our relationship. I took the assignment in Fowey to escape London and all the reminders.'

Why, oh why, is she disclosing her relationship history?

Shifting her focus, she looks beyond Mac and notices how blue the sky has become; how all the clouds are puffy and full, as if solid enough to take the weight of a person stepping from one to the other. They appear to her as another beautiful landscape with columns and canyons, levels and layers, drifts and waterfalls – just waiting to be discovered. Suddenly, the sun breaks through and she hears the rustling of small animals traversing through the undergrowth and the glorious sound of birdsong in the surrounding woodland. As the world shows her its beauty, Kat's eyes widen.

'In my experience, there's always a silver lining to be found,' Mac says, 'in any situation.'

She turns her attention to him but he seems lost in thought. Instinctively she knows he'd had to dig deep to express what he just has. Time to change the tone of the conversation.

'It's turned into a beautiful afternoon,' she says lightly. 'I'll probably have enough sketches within the next couple of hours. Are you OK with that?'

It takes him a moment to come back from wherever he's gone, and she has the impression it was a sad place.

'Yes, I'm happy with that,' he says, giving her a small smile.

38

It's past seven by the time Kat drives down the hill towards Fowey. It's been a good day and a surprising one at that. Mac is nothing like the man she'd imagined him to be, though she's still not completely giving herself over to this new perception of him. What do they say about being once bitten, twice shy? Or, in her case, *many* times bitten.

'Thanks for coming with me today, Mac,' she says, as she turns onto the Esplanade.

He smiles. 'My pleasure.'

'I hope it wasn't too boring.'

'Not at all,' he says. 'It's been a real eye-opener.'

The tables on the pavement opposite Stella's house are full of tapas diners.

'Do you want to grab something to eat?' she asks.

He hesitates. 'As much as I'd like to say yes, sadly duty calls. I have a fair amount of preparation to do on *Windsong* before the next set of clients arrive.'

She battens down her disappointment. 'OK. I guess I've got quite a lot to be getting on with, as well.'

'Another time, Kat.'

'Yes.'

As they near Stella's parking bay, she watches in disbelief as a car reverses into it. Pulling alongside, she lowers her window and a woman in the passenger seat of the offending car gazes out at her. Kat motions for her to lower the window.

'Sorry,' she says, 'but that's an allocated parking space for my house.'

The woman turns to the man sitting beside her. He shrugs.

'You can't park there,' says Kat in a level voice.

The man shrugs again.

In the rear-view mirror she notices another car come to a halt behind her and she pulls over to the kerb in front of the offending vehicle.

She glances over at Mac. 'I know parking's tricky along this road but for pity's sake!' she says, and reaching into her bag, she pulls out her phone. 'It's as clear as day it's an allocated bay.'

She and Mac get out and walk towards the trespassing car.

She peers through the driver's window and raps on it. The man and woman are obviously having a discussion but he refuses to acknowledge Kat. Irritation bites. He can't possibly think he's going to get away with grabbing this spot. She raps on the window again. Deliberately slowly, the driver turns his head and a pair of steely eyes meets hers.

'You can't park here,' she says loudly. 'It's allocated to Dolphin House. Look!' She points to the plaque on the wall that clearly states the fact. The man doesn't react.

Anger mounts. Striding to the front of the car, she raises her phone and takes a picture of the number plate. The next minute, the driver's door flies open and the large man gets out.

'What the hell do you think you're doing?' he demands.

'If you can't respect the fact this parking bay belongs to my house then I'm taking it up with the police.'

The man's expression turns ugly and he takes a menacing stride towards her.

Immediately Mac steps between them. 'She's right, you know,' he says in an even voice. 'There's no getting away from it. It's in black-and-white.' He, too, indicates the plaque.

The man glares.

'There's a public car park at the top of the hill,' Kat says, 'and a few parking spaces further along this road. But you can't park here.'

The man's face turns crimson and he takes another aggressive step towards Kat.

'OK, mate.' There's an edge to Mac's voice. 'That's enough!'

The woman then climbs out of the car. 'Gary, leave it. We'll find somewhere else.'

'Yeah, another town. I've had it with this place.' He walks back towards the car but then turns. 'And I want you to delete that photo.'

'Of course,' Kat says politely. 'Just as soon as you vacate my spot.'

'No. *Before.*'

Out of the corner of her eye she notices Mac brace himself, preparing to defend her, and she feels another brick in her defensive wall dislodge.

'OK.' Calmly, she acquiesces.

'I want to see you do it,' the man demands.

Holding up her phone, screen facing him, Kat deletes the photo. The man grunts begrudgingly, and as he makes brief eye contact with her, she gives him a fake-sweet smile.

Mac comes to stand beside her. 'You OK?'

'Yes, thanks.'

As they watch the car swerve violently away from the kerb and roar off down the narrow road, Kat holds her phone out to Mac.

'He may have asked me to delete the photo, which I did, but he didn't ask me to get rid of the second one.'

Mac stares at the screen and back at her. 'You never cease to amaze me,' he says, with a grin.

Satisfied, Kat climbs back into her car and quickly reverses into the parking bay. As she extracts her art bag from the back seat, Mac opens the boot and removes the cool bag.

'I'll take that,' she says, as she gets out.

He smiles. 'It's OK. I'll carry it.'

Crossing the street, Kat opens the front door to Stella's house and immediately sets off down the hallway, calling out over her shoulder to Mac, 'Just dump the picnic bag in the kitchen. I'll sort it later.'

'OK,' he responds.

Having deposited her drawing equipment on the studio

table, she makes her way back to the kitchen. The contents of the cool bag are laid out on the counter and Mac stands at the window, running water into the sink. He turns as she enters.

'I've had a really enjoyable day,' he says. 'It makes a pleasant change to have solid ground beneath my feet.'

'It has been good,' she says quietly.

Switching off the taps, he leans back against the sink and considers her. 'You're a fighter,' he says. 'I like that.'

She flushes, the adrenaline from her encounter with that pig-headed driver having faded.

'I don't like it when people arrogantly flout the rules,' she says, 'I mean . . .' She trails off, and smiles at him. 'I guess I'd better let you get on. Thanks for your company, I had a great day, too.'

Crossing the kitchen, she picks up the empty bottle of wine from the counter and places it in the recycling bin, but when she turns back to Mac she's stayed by the look in his eyes. The moment stretches, and as if in slow motion she approaches him, rising onto her tiptoes and inclining her face up to his. Dipping his head, Mac kisses her softly on the mouth. There's nothing hurried about it, nothing unnatural or clumsy, and as Kat responds to the warmth of his lips she feels her body relax. Even though she instigated it, the depth of the kiss has taken her by surprise, although – if she's truthful – deep down she already knew it was coming.

Suddenly, Mac breaks the spell and steps away. It's as if they cautiously circle each other, both wary and guarded, but there's no denying the mutual attraction and shared primal urge.

Keep those barriers up, Kat Maddox. Just in case . . .

However, as she looks up into warm hazel eyes, lit with a promise, she feels her stomach slide.

'I'm away for the next six days, back on Sunday,' he says. 'But how are you fixed the following week?'

She forces herself to concentrate. 'I have a couple of venues to check out, but my time is very much my own.'

'Good.' He smiles. 'Would you like to come out on *Windsong* one day?'

Tara's words rings in her ears: *I've never known anyone pass up so many golden opportunities.* Well, her friend will be proud of her because this time she's not going to turn him down.

'I'd like that, very much.'

She watches as something shifts in his gaze. *Relief?*

'Great. How about Wednesday week?'

Without hesitation, she replies, 'Wednesday week's good.'

'I may not be able to collect you from the quay. Are you OK to catch the water taxi over?'

'Of course,' she says, though wondering why he can't pick her up. 'What should I bring with me?'

'Just yourself,' he says, eyes smiling. 'That will be more than acceptable.'

After Mac departs, Kat takes a long, leisurely bubble bath. Her mind buzzes with questions, and she knows sleep will more than likely evade her once again. But she has a number of useful photographs of the Penhallam ruins and decides to start on the illustrations the very next morning. She also has the few interesting sketches that had taken Mac by surprise, and then her mind casts back over the day they've enjoyed together.

She has no idea how long she's been lying there going over the day's events but when Kat sits up, sending the remaining bubbles swirling around her body, the bathwater is cool. Rising to her feet, she reaches for the bath sheet hanging over the radiator and instantly has a vision of Mac in the studio wearing nothing more than a towel. She smiles. Even in that potentially defenceless position there had been nothing vulnerable about James MacNamara.

She considers that now as she dries herself and wonders who Mac really is. He's told her little about himself. All she knows is that he's lived abroad for many years and his line of work is in yachts, that he has a son, that he has alluded to an estranged or ex-wife, but more than that she hasn't a clue. What she does know is that he's got under her skin and that even if she can't quite let herself go emotionally with Mac, her body has no trouble responding to him.

Kat purses her lips. Well, not *too* deeply under her skin . . .

Wrapping the towel around her body, she walks from the bathroom into the bedroom and stands at the open window watching the last rays of a setting sun paint the rooftops of Polruan in a magnificent, twenty-four-carat golden light.

39

On the Friday, Kat packs a bag and drives to Salcombe for the weekend to stay with Tara and her family. The town is heaving with early summer visitors, and to escape the hordes they spend most of the time out on the water, kayaking around the less-inhabited coves and trying out paddleboarding. Gulliver and Tyler take to the sport instantly, and the three adults enjoy it, too.

'Just think what great low-impact cardiovascular benefits we're getting from this,' Tara says, as she kayaks past Kat.

'Paddleboarding's certainly engaging my core,' Kat replies, standing on a board and trying not to twist her body while maintaining balance. 'And I know my heart rate has increased!'

Tara laughs. 'Apparently, you have to work as hard and burn about the same number of calories walking at a four-miles-per-hour pace as you do paddling a kayak at moderate intensity.'

'Well, I'm pleased you're burning enough calories to warrant our meal tonight at Dick and Wills Waterside Grill,' Kat calls out.

Tara laughs and heads the kayak towards the shore. 'I think it's time we pack up and return the equipment,' she calls out to Niles.

'No, Mum!' groan her sons. 'Not yet. Pleeeease!'

'The boys are having such fun,' says Niles. 'I'm happy to spend a couple more hours with them messing about on the river if you and Kat want to go back to the cottage and have a catch up.'

'Are you sure?' Tara asks.

'Absolutely,' confirms Niles. 'You girls go and have some uninterrupted quality time together. I'll get the boys back in plenty of time for dinner.'

Half an hour later, having taken the motorboat back across the water to the pretty resort town, Kat and Tara climb the steps from the Jubilee Ferry Pier to the street.

'We've time for afternoon tea, if you fancy it,' Tara says, checking her watch.

'Sounds like a grand idea.'

As they pass the gate to The Ferry Inn's riverside terrace, a loud burst of laughter drifts over the wall, reminding Kat of the last time she was there, when she'd seen Mac with Francine and before she'd made up her mind about accepting the assignment in Fowey. It seems an age ago, but it's only a few weeks.

Tara glances across at her friend. 'Shall we be totally decadent and take tea at The Harbour Hotel?'

'Oh, yes, let's,' agrees Kat. 'But will they allow us in dressed like this?' Her gaze drops to her cropped chinos and trainers.

Tara laughs. 'Only one way to find out!'

Mindful of the passing cars slowly manoeuvring along the narrow street, the two women walk up the hill and turn into the hotel's entrance. The foyer is bright and airy and there's no way of masking their attire, but Kat needn't have worried. Without hesitation, the receptionist directs them to the restaurant, where several people are already seated at tables. Floor to ceiling windows face the river but Tara requests a table on the outside terrace so they can enjoy the afternoon sunshine. The panoramic views over the Salcombe estuary are jaw-dropping and Kat gazes across the sun-kissed aquamarine water to the golden coves on the opposite bank.

'What are you going for?' Tara asks, picking up a menu.

Kat does likewise and considers the choices. 'It's got to

be 'The Traditional'. How can anyone resist freshly-baked scones with jam and clotted cream, served with a selection of delicious cakes and finger sandwiches?'

'I agree,' says Tara. 'Not sure I can get away with a dangerously good cocktail or two, but I fancy the Prosecco instead of tea or coffee. Care to join me?'

'Of course! Can't have you drinking alone at this time of day.'

When their food arrives, served on a pretty three-tiered porcelain cake stand, Kat is vaguely aware of other customers filling the tables on the terrace. As the two women relax in the sunshine – in Tara's case, briefly unencumbered by the responsibility of offspring – they settle quickly into the easy friendship they've enjoyed for almost four decades.

A while later, as Kat selects one of the remaining *petite gourmet* French macarons from the stand, she freezes.

'I'm so pleased we've managed to book a table at Dick and Wills this evening,' Tara says conversationally. 'We love it there. The boys do, too.' When Kat doesn't respond, she glances inquisitively at her friend. 'What's wrong?'

Putting the macaron down on her plate, Kat's stricken eyes meet Tara's. 'I think I'm going to throw up.'

'Are you ill?'

Kat's gestures to the end of the terrace, and Tara turns in her seat.

'What is it with us?' Kat sighs. 'We're like heat-seeking missiles.'

Tara glances back at her friend. 'You said it!'

Sitting at a table in the far corner is Mac . . . and Francine.

'Just when I was beginning to trust him . . .' Kat says with a sigh. 'I was even contemplating giving a relationship a chance. God, I'm such a bloody fool!'

Tara discreetly observes Mac and the woman, and watches their interaction with interest.

Despondently, Kat picks up her glass of Prosecco and knocks back a large mouthful. What is wrong with her? When he'd asked her to join him aboard *Windsong* she'd really thought they were progressing to the next level, but obviously their day on the water together is not going to happen now.

Why does she always attract the type of men who like to play around?

'I'm sorry, Tara, but I can't just sit here with them over there,' she says. 'I'm going.'

She makes to rise from her chair but Tara's firm grip on her arm stays her.

'Don't be in such a hurry. I think you're misreading the situation.'

Sinking back down, Kat lets out a groan.

'Just watch,' Tara insists.

Forcing herself to look, Kat's throat tightens as she fights the surge of emotions consuming her. Why had she allowed Mac to breach her defences? With her relationship history, she should have paid attention to her brain and not allowed her emotions to take the upper hand. Well, her heart is certainly getting a battering now.

But then she notices the body language between Mac and Francine. Francine is tense, agitated. Kat's eyes narrow.

What's going on?

A waiter approaches Mac's table with afternoon tea and the couple are briefly blocked from view.

'I think we may be witnessing a break up,' Tara says carefully.

'He told me he'd already finished the relationship,' Kat states flatly.

Tara frowns.

Kat returns her attention to the far table and as the waiter moves away she again, surreptitiously, observes the interaction between Mac and the pretty, brown-haired woman sitting beside him. If he is breaking up with

Francine, she's consumed with pity for the woman, knowing only too well how it feels when a love affair comes to an end. As Mac leans in close to his companion, his posture softens to one of concern as he speaks to her, and tendrils of jealousy work their way up Kat's throat. This woman obviously still means something to him. She tries to be rational and not imagine scenarios, or paint a history for the two of them without knowing the facts. She's been way off with her knee-jerk reactions before, after all.

Kat decides she *will* try to believe what he's told her.

Suddenly Mac sits back. Picking up the teapot, he pours tea into two cups and glances around, taking in his surroundings for the first time. Immediately Kat shrinks back, hiding behind a trailing fern, while Tara lowers her head and scrutinises the scone on her plate as if it's the most interesting specimen.

As Mac brings his attention back to Francine, Kat peers through the fronds of the fern and watches the scene unfold. She doesn't need to hear his words to realise he's encouraging his companion to eat, but Francine simply shakes her head and stares at the table. Putting his arm tenderly around her shoulders, he pulls her towards him and plants a soft kiss on her forehead. Suddenly the woman's face crumples, and tears stream down her face. After a moment, Mac removes his arm and stares out over the estuary.

Tara turns to Kat. 'Goodness, even from this distance you can feel the waves of emotion coming from her.'

Kat nods. 'Watching this doesn't feel right. It's verging on voyeurism.' She presses her lips together. 'I think it's time to go.'

'I agree,' says Tara, draining the remaining Prosecco in her glass.

As the two friends rise to their feet and discreetly withdraw from the terrace, Tara glances back at the good-looking, dark-haired man and the pretty woman sitting in the far corner.

Linking arms with her friend, she says, 'I know what you're like, Katherine Maddox, but don't go jumping to any conclusions just yet. Keep an open mind.'

40

Wednesday morning dawns bright and sparkly. Since seeing Mac with Francine in Salcombe, Kat has grappled with how to handle it with him. Should she abandon their day together or is she being overdramatic? Tara – good friend – has phoned daily, filling her head with positive vibes and telling her she'd be nuts not to at least get an explanation from him.

'Look, Kat,' she'd said, 'if we hadn't seen them you'd be none the wiser. You'd have gone sailing with him and enjoyed his company for what it is. You'd have made up your mind based on that, not on your imagination and this torture you're putting yourself through.'

Tara's right, of course. She always is.

As the water taxi makes its way towards Pont Pill Creek, Kat gazes out over the river. The water is a beautiful indigo-blue and she watches, mesmerised, as cloud reflections drift across its surface. A warm breeze ruffles her hair and half a dozen seagulls circle the motorboat, their screeching cries snatched away on the wind. All is sensuous, and excitement builds at the thought of seeing Mac again, although it's countered by the anxiety that nips at her heels. She takes a few deep breaths. Today will be make or break; she can't put herself through this *not knowing* any longer.

In a broad Cornish accent, the skipper calls over his shoulder, '*Windsong*, you say?'

'Yes. It's dark-blue-hulled.'

'Aye. I know the one.' He grins and turns away.

She knows it's her insecurity, but why the grin? Is he used to ferrying a bevy of women to Mac?

Kat grimaces. This internal chatter has got to stop!

As they reach the entrance to the creek, for a brief moment she forgets her apprehension. The water is turquoise here in the shelter of the quiet anchorage, where a variety of watercraft are peacefully moored. It's like a painting. Thickly wooded banks reach down to the shoreline, and in the shallows a heron stands stock still. It's as if she's entered a magical, alternative world – far away from the noise and bustle of the busy harbour town. But then Mac's yacht comes into view, and the knot in Kat's stomach tightens.

Is *this* a mistake? Will he have already seen the water taxi approaching? Is it too late to ask the skipper to turn around?

Once again, Tara's voice quells the questions in her head: *Don't go jumping to any conclusions just yet. Keep an open mind.*

Well, today she intends to find out, once and for all.

Windsong gleams in the early morning sunlight and suddenly Mac appears at the guardrail. Kat's stomach flips. He raises a hand as he watches their approach. She swallows hard. For God's sake, what is wrong with her? Anyone would think she'd never been on a date before!

A date? Is that was this is?

As the water taxi draws alongside the yacht, the skipper skilfully ties on a line.

Kat gets to her feet. 'Thanks,' she says, grabbing the sides of the boarding ladder and placing a foot on the first rung.

'No problem,' the man responds.

Glancing up, she sees Mac smiling down at her. She starts to climb and as she reaches the top, he takes hold of her elbow.

'I've got you.' His grip is firm and strong. 'Thanks, Sam,' he calls out to the skipper.

The man waves and turns the boat for the home run.

Kat steps neatly onto the deck and immediately notices the yacht's tender bobbing in the water, caught in the wake of the taxi.

Why couldn't Mac have picked her up from the quay?

'Welcome aboard *Windsong*.'

She glances at his smiling, hazel eyes. Despite her inner dialogue, as usual, her attraction to him makes her heart skip a beat.

'I'm here,' she says.

Jeez . . . What a foolish thing to say! Inwardly she groans and quickly averts her gaze.

'At last!'

'I've taken you at your word,' she continues awkwardly. 'I've just brought myself.'

'Perfect.'

Sneaking a look at him again, her anxiety eases a little and she glances around the yacht. The teak deck is uncluttered, and in the cockpit, protected by a dodger and Bimini, is a table, on which sits a bowl of cereal.

Perhaps he didn't want to interrupt his breakfast to collect her . . .

'Your yacht is stunning,' Kat says. 'Very elegant.'

He smiles. 'She's a bluewater sailboat, designed for extended voyages in open water. As soon as I saw her I liked her clean design. As the salesman said, *she has a peaceful and inviting style for sailing, dining and relaxing*.' His voice has taken on a warm, mellow tone, as if describing a lover. 'It's as easy living on deck as it is below,' he continues. 'The cockpit table is refrigerated, and opens out to serve six, while the dining area has banquette seating for eight.'

'I expect your clients greatly appreciate it.'

'I haven't had any complaints so far! The saloon is bright and airy and fitted with warm, cherry wood and light upholstery. There's also air-conditioning throughout.'

'Air conditioning,' she says. 'I suppose that's necessary in the Mediterranean.'

He nods. 'It makes it more comfortable. The swim platform is also useful for stepping on and off tenders and there's a hot and cold deck shower, which people seem to like.'

'So, this is your home.'

'Yes.' He pauses. '*Windsong* has been my home for a few years.'

'Well, from what I can see you keep it in pristine condition.'

He smiles graciously and dips his head.

From out of the corner of her eye, Kat sees a movement in the hatchway and she prepares herself, expecting to see Sarah emerge. But it's not the young woman who appears. Instead, her eyes widen at the sight of the lad she'd imagined standing with Mac outside the newsagents in Salcombe.

As he steps up into the cockpit, the boy gives her a shy smile. Kat turns enquiringly to Mac and catches the uncertain look in his eyes.

'This is my son, Alejandro,' he says. 'Alejandro, this is my friend, Kat.'

'Hello,' Kat says with a smile, wondering what Mac would think if she told him she already knew this boy was his son.

'Hello,' he says, walking to the table and climbing onto the seat. Picking up a spoon, he takes a mouthful of cereal.

There's no mistaking who his father is; thick, black hair curling onto his shoulders, and an open face, heartbreakingly familiar.

'Alejandro,' Kat says. 'That's Spanish, isn't it?'

The boy nods.

'He was born in Spain,' Mac explains, with a small anxious smile. 'We usually call him Alec, for short. It's the Scottish form and a nod to my heritage.'

She resists asking if Alec's mother is Spanish, though the lad's olive skin suggests he has some foreign blood. There's so much she wants to know . . . But now is not the right time to ask.

Kat slides onto the seat next to the boy. 'Are you a sailor like your dad, Alec?'

Beautiful, liquid brown eyes turn in her direction and the boy shakes his head, the action dislodging his fringe to reveal a long white scar extending from the top of his forehead to just beneath his left ear. Kat masks her shock.

'Sometimes.' Alec glances up at his dad. 'I wish I lived on *Windsong* all the time.'

'I know,' Mac consoles. 'I'd like that, as well. However, young boys have to attend school and it's best that you're settled, and that means living with Aunt Ariadne and Uncle Leo and your cousins.'

The boy purses his lips and frowns.

In an encouraging voice, Mac changes tack. 'We'll have fun today. We have lots to show Kat.' He turns his attention to her. 'I said we'd explore the river.'

She smiles. 'That sounds like a great adventure.'

'The upper estuary is well worth a visit. It's very tranquil, although we have to be aware of the tides. The Fowey Estuary is a flooded river valley – a *ria* – and the natural harbour is deep and accessible at all tides and in all weathers, and it's normally very sheltered, although there can be a fair bit of swell in the lower end during strong southerly gales. However, above Wiseman's Reach it dries out at low water.'

'Not a good idea to risk being left high and dry,' she says.

'No.' He turns back to his son. 'Alec, are you OK here while I show Kat around?'

With a nod of his head, the boy scoops up another spoonful of cereal.

41

Having checked the tide timetable and charts, Mac ensures Kat and Alec are suitably equipped with life jackets before they board the RIB.

'OK, Alec,' he says, as he starts the outboard. 'Cast off.'

The boy does as his father instructs and as the tender moves away from the yacht, he neatly coils the painter and lays it in the bottom of the boat.

'You like this, don't you?' Kat asks him.

He turns to her, eyes gleaming with excitement. 'I'm going to have my own boat when I'm older.'

'I'm sure you will.'

It's busy out on the water. Canoeists and paddleboarders weave in and out of the many small motorboats and dinghies, and Mac acknowledges various passing boats with a nod and a wave. As they make their way past the town, Kat gazes up at Place House, situated above St Fimbarrus Church. It dominates the scene and its parkland grounds with impressive Monterey pines stretch across the hillside as far as Caffa Mill. Soon they approach the village of Bodinnick and she turns her attention to Ferryside as they pass by.

Is it any wonder that Daphne du Maurier produced such wonderful writing from that stunning and inspirational location!

As the car ferry makes its way across the river towards them, with one eye on its progress, Mac opens up the throttle and powers on, keeping within the harbour's six-knot speed limit.

'All OK?' he calls out to Kat.

'Very,' she replies with a smile.

He regards her for a long moment.

And it is *very* OK, she realises in surprise. Being out on the water with Mac and his son, feeling the wind in her hair and the sun on her face, and listening to the sounds of the river . . . she can't think of anywhere she'd rather be.

Within minutes they reach the docks, and the industrial buildings and china-clay jetties stand out starkly against the beautiful, unspoilt backdrop. Pleasure craft mingle with working tugs, and moored alongside one of the loading bays – looking completely incongruous in its surroundings – is a large tanker. It's a profitable and important industry, but the commercial workings are a brutal shock to the senses in this natural environment, and Kat turns to face the eastern bank. A wide, concrete slipway leads down to the water where a number of boats sit quietly alongside a series of shore-linked pontoons.

'What goes on there?' she asks.

'That's Penmarlam Boat Park,' Mac says, following her line of vision. 'It provides storage and launching facilities to a wide range of boats.'

From out of nowhere, a long skiff suddenly passes by, its all-female crew rowing athletically.

Kat watches as it heads downriver. 'Goodness! You have to be fit to mess about on the water.'

Mac laughs.

It's not long before the more commercial aspect of Fowey is left behind. Taking his hand off the throttle, Mac brings the tender to idle.

'See that building over there?' He points to a small, tidal inlet.

Kat turns her head. Nestled in woodland and located at the water's edge is a sprawling house with its own pontoon.

'It's a seventeenth-century water mill,' Mac says. 'Once a recording studio where the likes of Oasis, Queen, Duran Duran, Coldplay, Robert Plant and many other famous musicians produced their magic. The inlet's private and the property can only be accessed by boat, or foot via the Saints' Way.'

'What a location!'

Mac nods. 'There wouldn't have been many interruptions to the creative process, I'm sure.'

'It's so secluded, set in amongst the trees,' she says.

'Did you know the Fowey Estuary has the highest concentration of ancient trees in Cornwall?'

She shakes her head.

'It's actually a collection of international importance.'

They sit quietly for a while taking in their surroundings before Mac opens up the throttle again. 'Remember to keep a look out for birds and wildlife, Alec.'

The boy nods enthusiastically and Kat smiles.

It is *so* tranquil in the upper reaches, and it has a completely different feel to the part of the river where Stella's house is situated. There, it's busy with sailing boats and ferries constantly criss-crossing the water, let alone the comings and goings of passenger ships and container vessels entering the harbour. A river of many faces . . .

As they approach a pretty, waterside village extending over the hillside, Kat spots a number of rowing boats and dinghies pulled up on the shoreline. In front of this, a rail track traverses a raised bank and crosses a small bridge, allowing the watercraft access to the river.

'What village is that?' she asks.

'Golant,' replies Mac. 'It's a great spot for canoeing and kayaking. There's also a good pub in the village, but if you park along the river in front of it, you must check the height and time of the tides. Anything over five metres tends to flood the road.'

'Thanks. I'll remember that!' She scrutinises the railway. 'I wasn't aware Fowey had a station. Is that line still in use?'

'It's for the china-clay industry. The line connects Goonbarrow to Fowey Docks. In fact, here comes a train now.'

Kat and Alec turn and peer along the track. In the distance, coming into view, a cheery red-and-yellow locomotive pulls a long line of loaded clay, hood wagons. She hears the boy counting them quietly.

'At low tide, you can see extensive sandbars and mud banks here,' Mac continues. 'They provide great feeding areas for wading birds – and local fishermen dig for sand eels to use as bait.'

'Forty-two wagons!' Alec exclaims.

They watch as the train draws nearer, transporting its cargo to the docks. Once it has passed out of sight, Mac turns the tender mid-channel and backtracking a short way, he navigates towards the mouth of a quiet creek on the opposite side of the river.

'This is Penpol Creek,' he says, as they enter. 'It's tidal, and home to ancient woodland and water meadows. It also has one of the largest heron-nesting sites in Cornwall. It's a fantastic place to explore.'

Floundering on the shoreline in varying stages of decay are several abandoned boats.

'Alec, see how many old boat wrecks you can spot,' Mac suggests.

As the tender meanders up the tranquil waterway, Kat watches the passing landscape. On the southern bank, the hillside is covered in trees stretching down to dip their toes in the water, while on the north shore, fields full of contentedly-grazing cattle slope down to the river. The sun sparkles on the water, and light, puffy clouds dot a sky the colour of speedwell. Kat closes her eyes and inhales deeply. She can't remember the last time she's felt so relaxed, and as she unwinds, any residual hurt from Colin's deception and uncertainty surrounding Mac evaporate into thin air. She's just drifting along, out here in nature . . . at one with the universe.

Opening her eyes, she finds Mac watching her, a thoughtful look playing across his face. 'It's good out here, isn't it?'

'You've read my mind.'

He smiles. 'Can you understand why I like to live on the water?'

'I certainly can.'

His eyes linger on her face.

'Look!' cries Alec, pointing upstream. 'Swans.'

And sure enough, gliding towards them in the centre of the creek are two beautiful, snow-white swans, their rippling wakes making perfect V's in the water behind them. For some reason Kat immediately thinks of Mac and her, and glancing back at him she has the impression he's thinking that, too, as he laughs softly.

The sound is like music to her ears, and all at once she realises this is exactly what she wants . . . to see and make him happy.

Hang on just a minute. She'll be hearing violins next! Don't get carried away. Don't forget Alec's mother. Who and where is she?

She turns away. Her resolve to be cautious is seriously slipping.

'What's that?' Alec suddenly calls out.

Both Mac and Kat turn to where the boy is pointing. A turquoise flash skims the surface of the river at the edge of the tributary.

'It's a kingfisher,' she says.

'Well spotted, Alec,' Mac praises his son. 'They go downstream on the high tide and like to fish by the bridge.'

Spellbound, Alec's eyes grow round with wonder as he attempts to follow the bird's flight.

He's beautiful, just like his father.

She steals another glance at Mac.

God, this is hopeless! She doesn't stand a chance . . .

'There's lots of wildlife here,' Mac continues. 'If you look carefully, Alec, you may spot owls, buzzards, goshawks, bats, herons or – if you're very lucky – a shy otter or even a pod of dolphins.'

'How wonderful,' Kat murmurs.

Although Mac continues talking to his son, his gaze rests firmly on Kat. 'Look down through the water and you may even see a shoal of mullet. There are also slow worms, newts, damselflies and butterflies, so keep your eyes peeled.'

'Alec, shall we see how many we can spot?' she suggests.

Animatedly, the boy nods his head.

Glancing back at his father at the tiller, Kat grows hot under his tender gaze.

Silently, he mouths, 'Thank you.'

42

After visiting Penpol Creek, they continue their journey upstream and explore the largest tributary to the Fowey; the River Lerryn. As the tender meanders alongside ancient trees bending low to touch the river and festooned in seaweed, Alec turns to Kat, his eyes full of excitement.

'That's where Mr Toad lives,' he says, pointing towards the riverbank.

'Mr Toad?'

'You know! He lives in Toad Hall.'

'Have you seen him?' she asks in a serious voice.

'No. He drives his car too fast.'

Oh what a glorious boy!

An overwhelming urge to protect this young lad from ever growing up and seeing the world with all its harsh edges takes her unawares. A warm, fuzzy maternal feeling comes over her. Is this what she's been missing out on all these years? She turns to Mac and is surprised to see tears in his eyes, or is it the breeze causing them to mist over?

Gruffly, Mac clears his throat. 'We're reading *The Wind in the Willows*. This waterside woodland belongs to the Ethy Estate and it's widely believed to be the inspiration for the Wild Wood in the book.'

Kat smiles, recalling Jean saying that Toad Hall itself was based on the Fowey Hall Hotel. Obviously, Kenneth Grahame's fertile imagination gained inspiration from many different locations along the river.

'My dad read that story to me when I was a child,' she says, gazing with interest at the passing woodland. 'Every night when he came home from work, my sister and I would beg him to read to us.'

Alec turns to her; his eyes huge.

'What is it, Alec?' she asks.

'I wish my dad could read to me every night,' he says quietly.

She glances at Mac at the tiller. His face is pained and quickly he turns away.

Kat gives Alec her warmest, most reassuring smile. 'But it's good that he's reading to you *now*, isn't it?'

Solemnly, the boy nods his head.

She bites her lip and wonders about father and son. Alec doesn't seem put out by her presence, but then, maybe if he's used to seeing Mac with different women it's normal for him. She frowns, and wonders again where the boy's mother is. She couldn't imagine abandoning Alec if she was his mother, but maybe the woman has her reasons. There's a story here, yet to be told . . .

It's not long before the river gives way to human habitation and soon another pretty, waterside village comes into view.

'Lerryn,' says Mac, answering the question in Kat's eyes. 'It's situated at the lowest crossing point, and when the tide flows out, stepping stones are revealed and people can cross the river on foot.'

He expertly brings the tender alongside a grassy quay where several people sit at picnic benches. Five minutes later, having tethered the boat, they head up the lane towards the Ship Inn and have lunch in the pub's garden. As they bask in the early afternoon sunshine, Kat gazes across the table at Mac and his son. It feels so natural spending time with them and a surge of satisfaction courses through her.

'It's a very pretty village,' she comments.

Mac nods. 'It is, although the inhabitants have to be mindful of the tides. The Lerryn River in Cornish is Dowr Leryon, which means *river of floods*. It's totally appropriate. High tides can be dangerous and during spring tides the cottages along the water's edge are liable to flooding.'

'It must be challenging to get insurance,' she says.

'I think so.'

All too soon, lunch is over, and as they walk back to the RIB Mac reaches for her hand. It feels safe and warm, and as he laces his fingers through hers Kat relishes the sensation his touch elicits. To passing strangers they appear as any other couple enjoying a day out with their son. Running ahead, Alec amuses himself tossing pebbles in the water while he waits for his dad and Kat to catch up.

As they make their way back downstream, the boy steers the boat, a broad grin settling on his face. Kat smiles to herself. It's wonderful to see the two of them together and how Mac involves his son, giving him the opportunity to have these new experiences, and not simply be a passenger. Mac is making life an adventure for Alec, and providing happy memories of time spent with his dad. She sneaks a look at Mac now. Seeing him in the role of father, another large brick in her defences dislodges.

When they reach the main river, Mac takes over and navigates upstream until they come to the Grade I riverside church of Saint Winnow. As he eases off on the throttle, a special calm and peace descends.

'I don't think there could be any more perfect setting for a church,' Kat remarks.

Mac nods in agreement. 'Saint Winnow is recorded in the Domesday Book, although the current church is mainly fifteenth century, it's reckoned to stand on the site of a seventh-century oratory dedicated to "Saint Winnoc".'

'Is that the village, over there?' She points to a clutch of rooftops.

'Yes. Or rather, a hamlet – it has a tiny population with just ten or so houses.'

After a while they continue on a little further. The valley suddenly closes in and the river meanders between mudflats, and water meadows, where a number of wildfowl root amongst the reeds.

'This is an important habitat and natural flood defence,' Mac explains, as they reach the salt marshes. 'It's a haven for wildlife, especially swans, mallards, egrets, herons and kingfishers. Apparently, Canada geese are regular visitors during winter.' He checks his watch. 'OK. Time to head back. We don't want to be stranded by the tide.'

He turns the tender mid-channel to return downstream on the turning tide. As the RIB skims over the water and they approach the docks, a sailboat tacks across the river. The young occupants are under instruction, and Kat watches as they dodge the boom and scramble across to the other side as the sail changes direction. It feels good out on the water. The skin on her face is taut – she's definitely caught the sun – and a comfortable atmosphere has accompanied them all day. Soon they pass Fowey town and as they turn into Pont Pill Creek, shouts and laughter carry across from the busy quayside. Mac steers towards the elegant yacht lying motionless on her mooring lines, and Kat looks back at him and smiles.

What would it be like to live on the water?

The thought takes her by surprise. It would be qute a contrast to her London life, the notion of which now induces a feeling of dread. Best not to think about it. She shuts off her mind to the inevitable return to the city.

The next minute, Mac brings the tender smoothly alongside and holds onto the yacht. 'OK, Alec. You know what to do.'

The young boy scrambles to his feet. Agile as a monkey, he climbs the ladder and loops the painter around a cleat. Once again, Kat marvels at the way Mac so easily allows Alec to get on with these tasks, without fuss or concern, as if there's no question the boy is capable.

'A competent sailor in the making,' notes Mac, again reading her thoughts. He presses the electric tilt switch next to the throttle and the leg of the outboard rises smoothly out of the water.

'Definitely,' she agrees, getting to her feet and grasping the boarding ladder.

Mac follows Kat up onto the deck, and unlooping the painter, he secures the RIB with a quick bowline knot.

'I'll put your life jacket away,' Alec says to Kat, as he wriggles out of his.

'Thanks, Alec.' She unbuckles hers and hands it to him.

As he dashes away to stow the jackets in a locker, Kat wonders if he's as tidy at home, or if it's just the novelty of being on the yacht.

'Right then, let's get tea on the go,' says Mac, crossing the cockpit and heading for the hatchway.

'What can I do?' Kat calls after him. She hasn't been much use up to now, but she's capable of making tea.

He smiles. 'You're our guest, you don't have to do anything.'

'But I'd like to.'

Hazel eyes assess her. 'Follow me then.'

In the galley, Mac fills a kettle and places it on the hob.

'You'll find biscuits and cake in that cupboard.' He nods to one at eye level.

The galley is cosy and as Mac sorts out the tea, he squeezes past Kat to the fridge. He's so close; she can feel the heat emanating from his body and she longs to be closer. But she mustn't forget there are still several important questions to ask.

Once at a safe distance and able to think straight again, Kat turns to him. 'Thank you for inviting me to spend the day with you. I'm so pleased I've met your son.'

A warm smile lights Mac's face.

Twinkling eyes, strong, white teeth, gorgeous tanned face, wild curly hair . . .

'I'm pleased, too,' he says. 'I wanted Alec to meet you.'

Heat floods her face.

Does this mean he really does view her as a potential partner?

Now's the perfect time to ask about Alec's mother, clear up any doubts about the woman in Salcombe and find out exactly what it is he wants from her.

'Dad!' Alec appears framed in the hatchway. 'A man in a boat wants to speak to you.'

Raising his eyebrows, Mac gives her a rueful grin before turning to his son. 'Tell him I'll be up in a minute.' He turns back to Kat. 'I know we have things to discuss,' he says softly.

She nods. Her heart beats so loudly she's sure he must hear it.

Taking a step towards her, Mac drops a gentle kiss on her lips. 'And I promise you we will, but another time.'

And then he's gone.

'So, how did it go?' Tara asks.

It's past ten and on the phone to her friend, Kat lies on the bed in Stella's house watching river reflections play across the ceiling.

'I met his son, he's called Alec.'

A sharp intake of breath. 'What's he like?' Tara asks.

'Gorgeous. He'll be a heartbreaker when he's older.'

'How old is he?'

'I'd say about the same age as Tyler.'

The ensuing silence is loaded.

'Go on,' Kat prompts. 'Say it.'

'I was just wondering . . .'

'About Alec's mother?' Kat finishes her friend's unspoken question.

'Yes.'

'It wasn't really the right time to get into that.'

'No, I can imagine it wasn't.'

'All I know is she's not around. But Mac has asked me to go sailing with him on Sunday and I intend to find out then, because I can't carry on like this. You know, the not knowing where I stand. Are we about to embark on a relationship, or is he simply considering me as an addition to his harem? Because if it's the latter it will be, "Goodbye, Mr Perfect".'

'Yes,' says Tara.

'Oh, God,' groans Kat.

'What?'

'Don't think we've ever had such a monosyllabic conversation!'

'No.'

The friends burst out laughing.

'It's late and I must catch some zeds,' says Tara. 'I've got a hellish day tomorrow, but I had to find out how it went for you today. And, Kat, please don't worry about Sunday. I'm sure it will be fine.'

'Well, one way or another, in four days' time I'll know for sure.'

'Yes.'

Kat groans. 'Let's not start *that* again!'

'No.'

Both women laugh again.

'Now go to sleep, my lovely friend,' Kat says, 'and thanks for checking in on me.'

'Always.'

Kat ends the call and wonders what Mac is doing right now. Is he asleep, or is he lying in his cabin also staring up at the ceiling and thinking of her? Rolling over, she places her mobile on the bedside table and gazes out of the open window, listening to the soothing sounds of the river and thinking back over her day with the MacNamara boys. As the sound of a passing boat drifts in on the night air, she smiles to herself. It has been a wonderful day, and she's enjoyed both father and son's company.

Suddenly her mobile pings, and she thinks it's probably Tara remembering something else she'd meant to ask. But as she scoops the phone off the bedside table her eyes widen.

Hope you had a good time on the water today. See you

Sunday morning at 9. I'll pick you up from your jetty. Sleep well. Mac x

She smiles at the kiss, but hesitates while contemplating her reply.

I did, thank you. Sunday at 9 it is. Sleep well yourself. Kat x

43

Over the next few days Kat works on the illustrations of Penhallam Manor. Despite the intense concentration it takes, her mind persists in transporting her to the elegant yacht moored in a quiet creek just across the river. What is Mac doing? Are he and Alec having fun? Is Sarah back on board and enjoying their company? Several times, Kat reminds herself to stop giving in to these distracting thoughts, and to stay in the moment if she wants her drawings to meet both her high standards and Stella's expectations.

By Saturday night she's a bundle of nerves, and as she chases sleep, a phrase plays over and over again in her head: *only a few hours before you see him and then all will be revealed.* As the mantra repeats itself throughout the long night, she resigns herself to counting down the hours until dawn.

At six-thirty she rises and showers; at seven she dresses in jeans, sweatshirt and trainers; at eight she attempts to eat a slice of toast and down a cup of tea. By nine she is ready. It's just as well she has her sunglasses because the early morning light is sharp and bright as she stands on Stella's private jetty watching *Windsong*'s tender traversing the water towards her. As Mac raises his hand in acknowledgement, Kat returns his wave and puts on a good show of solid composure, ignoring the butterflies in her stomach.

Manoeuvring alongside the stone quay, Mac's gaze lingers upon her as he holds the RIB steady. 'You're a sight for sore eyes this morning.'

'Thank you,' she says, stepping onto the boat, 'but if you knew what little sleep I had last night you wouldn't say that!'

His smile is unhurried. 'Hopefully you'll sleep better tonight.'

She gives a small, nervous laugh. Does he mean after a day's sailing . . . or something else? She can't help the sharp throb of excitement deep in her belly.

Pushing the RIB away from the quay, Mac slips the throttle into forward. Kat turns her face to the sun and closes her eyes, indulging in the sensations. Above the hum of the outboard she hears the shrill screech of gulls, and the bursts of laughter drifting across the water in the deep river valley. Just another day in the life of the busy Fowey Estuary . . . Only it's not *just* another day for her. Today she hopes to have answers to those burning questions, as Mac had promised.

Opening her eyes, she catches him studying her. He smiles before turning his attention to several approaching watercraft.

'Did Alec enjoy his time aboard *Windsong*?' she asks.

'He loved it.' He glances back at her. 'I was sad to see him go.'

'I expect he was sad, too.'

Anguish fleetingly clouds his gaze. 'He was. I don't get to spend a great deal of time with him, and the older he gets the more painful it becomes each time we part.'

She gives him a sympathetic smile, thinking that now would be the ideal time to bring up Alec's mother, but it's probably not such a good idea while Mac is navigating the river. She decides to wait until they have their *talk*.

Within minutes, the tender enters the creek. Sunlight glints off the moored boats in the deeply wooded inlet, scattering sparkles across the surface of the water. It's such a silent and magical, private place . . . but it's not that which makes Kat draw a sharp breath. This is her dream, the one in which she flew high above softly billowing, cotton-wool clouds and gazed down upon a beautiful river valley, its waters a deep shade of turquoise. She glances up at the sky. Yes, there are the clouds and, there too, the flocks of seagulls flying on invisible thermals. She turns her gaze towards Fowey. The town spilling down the hillside and hugging the river's edge is fast-awakening and she shivers as a keen sense of déjà vu overwhelms her. In her dream, a man had set off across the river in a rowing boat – OK, so she'd got that wrong – heading towards a handful of yachts peacefully moored in a hidden inlet. She turns and scrutinises *Windsong*. Small details aside, this is without a shadow of doubt the scene in her dream.

Goosebumps appear on her arms, and she briskly rubs them.

'Cold?' Mac asks, attentively. 'I'll lend you a jacket if you need one when we're sailing.'

She smiles. 'I'm fine, but thank you.'

The next minute they draw alongside and as Mac secures the tender, Kat climbs aboard. Crossing over to the starboard guardrail, she looks over the creek to the wooded shoreline. The trees are hung with shrouds of early Traveller's Joy, and in the shallows a heron stands stock-still. Without warning it lunges into the water, its action sending a series of perfect circles rippling out across the surface. The next minute, the bird resurfaces with a silver fish in its beak and with a jerk of the head, it swallows it whole.

She turns at the sound of Mac behind her.

'Have you had breakfast?' he asks.

'I have.'

'Then, shall we get going?' He smiles.' Your life jacket is in the locker over there.'

Crossing the deck, she puts on the life vest and then makes sure she keeps out of the way as Mac prepares *Windsong* for the forthcoming sail. She watches with interest as he operates the electric winch and the RIB is lifted out of the water and onto the davits. Once again, she is struck by his panther-like movements that waste no energy and display perfect control. It's an alluring combination of elegance and masculine power.

'You OK there?' he asks, as he secures the tender to prevent it from swinging.

'Very OK.' She smiles broadly. 'Apart from feeling a bit useless.'

He grins. 'Enjoy today without guilt, because if you take to it I expect you to accompany me on many a seagoing trip. Then, be warned, I will put you to work!' He gives her a wink.

An inescapable thrill of excitement courses through her that Mac is factoring her into his future.

Within minutes *Windsong* leaves the safety of the quiet inlet and as the yacht makes her way gracefully towards the mouth of the river, Kat watches the town swiftly retreat. Soon they pass the row of Victorian houses where Stella's holiday home is located, and as they approach Readymoney Cove, she gazes up at the property known as Point Neptune jutting out into the water. On the wild headland to the south are the ruins of St Catherine's Castle and on the opposite shore is the quaint village of Polruan. As Mac hoists the sails, she notices a solitary, white wooden cross below the cliffs at the entrance to the river, and asks what it is.

'That's Punches Cross,' he says. 'It's marked on very early charts – and there are numerous theories about its origins, some more believable than others.'

'Such as?'

'Well . . . the most widely accepted is that the cross originally marked the limits of jurisdiction of the Prior of Tywardreath. Another is that it's the spot where the boy Jesus landed with his uncle, Joseph of Arimathea, who was in the tin trade.'

Kat raises her eyebrows.

Mac grins. 'Other beliefs are that it's a corruption of the original name – the monk who collected the dues from the harbour lived at Pont, and so it was Pont's Cross – and another theory has it that Pontius Pilate landed there, and that Punches is a corruption of his name. Whichever story you choose to believe, the cross is now in the care of the harbour commissioners and it's an important navigational landmark for vessels arriving and departing the estuary.'

As *Windsong* sails out of the mouth of the river, Kat recalls Mac saying it could get choppy in the entrance in a strong southerly, though he'd quickly reassured her there were no significant hazards and the headlands were steep-to. From her limited knowledge of wind direction, she thinks it's a south-westerly today, but the weather is kind, the wind is light and the ocean is relatively calm. In no time at all, they are heading into open sea and as the yacht changes course, following the coast in a westerly direction, *Windsong* rides the waves with ease as she sails into the wind.

Prominent on the rapidly approaching headland is a red-and-white striped square tower.

'The Gribbin Headland Daymark,' Mac explains. 'One-hundred-and-nine steps to the top, although I admit to not having climbed them.'

'The views must be terrific from up there,' she remarks.

'Yes. We should check it out sometime,' he responds, eyes twinkling.

She loves the way he's being so inclusive of her.

'It's stood on the headland for nearly two hundred years,' he continues. 'It pinpoints the approach to Fowey's narrow entrance so that sailors don't mistake the treacherous shallows of St Austell Bay for the deep water of Fowey Harbour.'

Keeping the coastline to starboard, they pass Polridmouth Cove. It's so unspoilt. Apart from one family on the beach, there's no one else around.

'Over there, hidden from view in the trees,' Mac says, pointing inland, 'is Menabilly, once home to Daphne du Maurier.'

'So that's where it is,' Kat says, scanning the landscape in the hope of glimpsing the house. 'Menabilly was the inspiration for *Rebecca* and *The King's General*.'

'So I hear.' He nods.

She wonders if he's read either novel. She had the impression that nautical books and magazines were more his thing. But

'I guess, but in general the beach is pleasant and family-friendly. The next stretch of sand you see to the west is Carlyon Bay. Over the years, numerous development proposals have been put to the planners for residential properties, a hotel, leisure facilities, shops and restaurants, but nothing has been decided and it's still ongoing. Back in the 80s and 90s it had a great live-music venue, which attracted major bands.'

'You know so much about the area,' she comments.

He shrugs. 'Actually, I know the Med better, but I've spent a lot of time in Cornwall.'

'Sailing, I suppose?'

Or something else?

He gives her a probing look. 'Yes . . . And a girlfriend, from my dim and distant past, she lived in the county. I used to visit a lot, then.'

He says no more and Kat berates herself for her mounting irrational jealousy.

For God's sake, he said she was from his past!

'If you look left of Carlyon Bay,' Mac continues, 'you'll see the entrance to Charlestown Harbour. It's the last open Georgian one in the UK.'

She scans the coastline.

'It has a unique history and it immediately transports you back in time. It's also a dream film location for period dramas, most recently featuring in *Poldark*. At that time it had just nine fishermen, the main trade being pilchard fishing. It's still a working port, as well as home to classic Tall Ships. We should visit.'

Kat smiles. The way he talks, anyone would think they were a well-established couple. But before she allows herself to be seduced by this intoxicating idea, she reminds herself that she still needs to find out what his true intentions are.

Suddenly, the yacht heels over to starboard as a gust of wind hits.

'Whoah!' cries Kat, planting her feet squarely on the deck and instinctively leaning back in her seat.

Mac chuckles as he corrects the yacht's course.

'Don't be alarmed, Kat.' He flashes a reassuring smile. 'This is all part of sailing. *Windsong* has a keel with plenty of ballast, which keeps her upright . . . even in the most extreme conditions.'

'Well, that's OK, then,' she says, pulling an unconvinced face.

He laughs. 'All sailing boats heel over and we may even get a wave or two over the side, but that's the most exciting part.'

'I'll take your word for it.'

'You don't have to. Keel boats were designed using basic physics.'

'So what does a keel do?' she asks.

She's obviously said the right thing as Mac's eyes fill with pleasure. 'The keel has two main purposes. One, it prevents the boat from being blown sideways, and two, it holds ballast that helps keep the boat the right way up.'

'Very useful,' she says, drily.

He lets out a deep-bellied laugh. 'Yeah, I'd say so.'

'So tell me about the physics.'

A look of contentment spreads across his face. 'You have an enquiring mind, don't you?'

'I suppose so. I've never given it much thought!' She raises a wry eyebrow.

He laughs again, before launching into an explanation about wind pressure on the sails.

During a pause, Kat narrows her eyes, considering his words. 'Like if you're walking on a really windy day and standing upright, the pressure against you makes it hard to move forward, but if you bend at the waist it's much easier to walk as you have less surface area facing the wind?'

'Exactly that!'

She smiles. 'So, what else?'

Mac grins broadly. 'The ballast is located well below the waterline in the keel. If the boat heels over, then the leverage increases.'

Kat frowns.

'It's like this,' says Mac. 'Compare it to holding a weight in your hand with your arm straight out from your body. The weight feels heavier the higher your arm is raised. That's the exact effect the ballast has when a boat heels over.'

'I see.'

'A keel boat is very difficult to capsize when these two effects work together,' he adds. 'It's best to trust the science, Kat, and simply enjoy the experience.'

'One last question: how far is it safe to heel over?'

He smiles. 'Each boat has a different ideal heel angle. Generally, though, keel boats should be sailed somewhere between ten and thirty degrees. Keeping the angle consistent is important and this can be achieved by adjusting steering – as I've just done – along with sail trim and placement of weight.'

'Makes sense. Thanks, Mac.'

'You're welcome!'

Some time later, having crossed St Austell Bay and waved to the Fowey-to-Mevagissey ferry as it motored past, they sail around Dodman Point and into Veryan Bay. Kat takes the wheel once again and as before, exhilaration soon dispels any nerves. Relaxing into the yacht's movement, with a sudden thrill she realises she has never felt more *at one* with the elements. The weather has remained kind and as the landscape passes by, Mac points out Caerhays Castle and the charming, little fishing village of Portloe nestling in a cleft of rugged cliffs on the Roseland Peninsula.

'Are you OK up here while I go down and check the charts?' he asks, rising to his feet. 'I won't be long. Just keep a course for Gull Rock.'

'I'm fine,' she assures him.

His gaze lingers on her for a moment. 'You know, Kat, I believe you are.'

Kat watches as he crosses the cockpit and disappears below deck. She *must* ask those burning questions before too long. She glances up at the top of the mast. The pristine white sails stand out against a topaz sky streaked with high cirrus clouds, and half a dozen seagulls are following *Windsong*, ever hopeful of an impromptu meal. What a glorious way to spend the day. A smile spreads across Kat's face. Who'd have thought sailing would be such fun?

It's not long before Mac reappears. Pausing at the top of the hatchway, he gazes across the cockpit. 'You know, Kat, you look as if you were born to this way of life.'

'It's surprised me. I didn't realise how I love this experience.'

'People tend to fall into two categories after a taster session. Either they're head over heels, or they tick sailing off their bucket list and quickly move on to the next adventure. However, I get the impression you like a challenge.'

She laughs. 'I can't deny it, although I definitely like some challenges more than others.'

'Yes,' he says, his voice suddenly falling flat.

Sensing a change of mood, she glances at him sharply. His expression is hard to read. With a frown, Kat concentrates on maintaining course.

What has she said?

Mac steps up into the cockpit. 'I'll take over now.'

As he approaches the wheel she promptly moves aside. Instinctively, she knows he's distanced himself from her, and that even though they're in close proximity, they could be miles apart.

Mac takes the helm. Keeping the tall, prominent spire of Gerrans Church on the far headland midway between Nare Head and Gull Rock, he navigates *Windsong* through the six-hundred-metre wide passage. As the yacht glides by the rocky outcrop, Kat notices several cormorants striking their eerie crucifix-like pose. The long-necked black waterbirds stand facing into the wind, their bodies upright and wings partly outstretched.

Rounding Nare Head, they enter a wide, sweeping bay.

'This is Gerrans Bay,' says Mac, in a matter-of-fact voice. 'Those sandy beaches are Carne and Pendower but we're making our way to the fishing village of Portscatho over there.' He points across the water to a huddle of white-washed properties extending down the hillside from the church. 'The cove is east-facing and gives shelter from the prevailing south-westerly wind. What do you say to anchoring and going ashore? We can grab a bite to eat and look around the art galleries and shops.'

'I'd like that very much,' she says, wondering if his mood will lighten.

As the distance reduces between shoreline and yacht, yellow mooring buoys come into view. Mac anchors *Windsong* in the bay north-east of the harbour, leaving a clear passageway for small craft to come and go.

'We should be OK here,' he says, assessing the immediately surrounding water.

After releasing the RIB in the davits and operating the electric winch, Mac lowers the tender into the sea, and within minutes he and Kat set out towards the harbour. Whatever thoughts had plunged him into a sombre mode must have lifted because once again he is lighter, easy company.

But complex.

Kat casts her eyes over the rapidly approaching, pretty coastal village. An unhurried, holiday air prevails. Several families are picnicking on a small stretch of sand and half a dozen kayakers and paddleboarders navigate amongst the swimmers in the sea.

'Is the tide going out or coming in?' she asks.

'A couple of hours to high tide,' Mac says. 'If it was low tide or going out we'd land at Tatams Beach over there.'

Kat looks in the direction he indicates. Above the beach, behind a wall, she notices a group of people eating and looking out at the sea view.

'Do you know if that's a private home or a café?'

He glances across. 'Not sure. Why don't we check it out?'

She smiles her agreement.

'The approach to the quay is via a channel cut through the rocks around the head of the pier, which enables half-tide access,' he informs her.

Peering over the side, Kat checks the crystal-clear water. 'I can see a path!'

'Yes. Comings and goings of local boats keep the seaweed clear, so the exposed sand makes the path highly visible.'

'That's convenient.'

He gives her a half-smile, then, approaching the harbour wall, he brings the tender neatly alongside and ties on with a bowline knot. Immediately, Kat climbs the ladder onto the stone quay and gazes out over the ocean. It's a beautiful colour – dark turquoise, deepening to French Navy in the far distance. In the east, Nare Head and Gull Rock are bathed in a warm golden light. Opening her arms wide, she breathes in deeply.

'All right?' Mac asks, as he joins her.

She turns and gives him an open, genuine smile. 'Very.'

'Come on then. Let's find somewhere to eat.'

Heading in the direction of the village, they walk hand in hand along the seafront. On the opposite side of the quiet road is a row of well-maintained, double-fronted terraced cottages. Most have neat, front gardens filled with shrubs that thrive in the coastal climate, and an occasional palm tree. Silently, Kat congratulates herself as she identifies pittosporum, echium, mallow, valerian, sea holly, agapanthus and sea campion. Several gardens have strategically placed benches, tables and chairs – a perfect invitation to sit and people-watch. A black cat, basking in the early afternoon sun and sprawled out on a blindingly white, stone wall, casts a watchful eye over them as they pass by.

Next to the telephone box is a small, single-storey,

white-washed building with a pointed slate roof. As they draw near, a sign outside alerts them to an art exhibition taking place, and judging by the level of chatter and laughter emanating from within the tiny building, the event is in full flow.

'I'd like to call in, if you don't mind?' Kat says.

Mac squeezes her hand. 'Of course.'

45

It's nearing nine by the time *Windsong* enters the Fowey Estuary, and away to the west the setting sun continues its downward arc. As Mac lowers the sails, Kat maintains course, only stepping aside from the helm for him to navigate upriver. Once they enter Pont Pill Creek and *Windsong* is in position, Mac secures her fore and aft mooring lines.

Removing her life vest, Kat stows it away in its locker. Standing on a motionless deck feels odd after hours of constant movement embracing the sea conditions, and her ear has become accustomed to the sound of wind in the rigging.

She listens. It's *so* tranquil and still.

It's hard to believe she's been in Mac's company for twelve whole hours. Apart from that one blip, he's made it so easy, and the day has whizzed by. Though she remains cautious, when his arms encircle her waist she turns towards him and they share a long kiss – tender at first, then edging towards passion.

Before reaching its peak, Mac draws back. 'Thank you for coming with me today.'

'It's been such fun,' she says, stirring at the sensation his strong, toned body against hers has brought.

'Do you fancy opening a bottle of wine while I finish up here?' Mac suggests. 'We can have supper on deck. It's warm enough.'

'Sounds like a perfect end to the day.'

She thinks he's about to say something more, but he simply smiles.

In the galley, Kat opens the fridge and takes out a bottle of white wine. She pours two glasses and takes a sip from one. Then, having found a sharp knife and a chopping board, she starts to prepare the evening meal. Ten minutes later Mac joins her and she slides a glass of wine along the counter towards him.

'I see you've found the meats and cheeses.'

She nods. 'And some salad.'

He opens a cupboard and produces a crusty loaf and a pack of savoury biscuits. 'I'll take plates and cutlery up top.'

Sometime later, Mac and Kat sit in the cockpit gazing at each other across the remnants of the meal, listening to the various sounds of the creek settling in for the night. The other boats moored in the inlet are but shadowy images in the gloaming, and lights, soft to the senses, glow from a mere half-dozen. A moon hangs suspended in a darkening sky studded with stars, and the trees reaching down to the water's edge dim to black. Echoing across the river comes the haunting call of a waterfowl, and somewhere close by an owl hoots in answer.

'I'm so pleased you agreed to come sailing, Kat.'

She looks deep into Mac's eyes. 'I'm so pleased you invited me again, after my initial reluctance.'

He chuckles. 'No one can accuse you of being an easy nut to crack!'

Raising her eyebrows, she acknowledges the truth in his statement.

It's now or never. Go for it, girl!

Maintaining steady eye contact, she says, 'Mac . . .'

'Yes?'

'You said you had some explaining to do.'

His eyes widen. 'I did?'

She nods. 'You did. As you get to know me you'll realise there's little that passes me by.'

He exhales dramatically. 'Good to know!'

She laughs softly.

Sitting back, Mac spreads his arms wide along the top of the cushions. 'So what would you like to ask?'

She bites her lip. They've had such a great day together, is she now going to ruin it with her questions? But she has no choice. If they have any chance of moving forward, she needs to be sure she can trust him with her heart.

Reaching across the table, Mac gives her hand a gentle squeeze. 'Don't hold back, Kat.'

It's so distracting and hard to concentrate when he touches her. Gently, she slides her fingers out from beneath his.

'I know I don't have the right to ask you to explain yourself.' She gives a sigh. 'You can be with whomever you want.'

'That's true,' he tells her. 'And I want to be with you.'

Her heart stalls and her eyes open wide. Is she hearing straight? This gorgeous man *wants* to be with her? Picking up her glass, she knocks back the remnants of her drink.

Mac gets to his feet. 'I think we need another bottle, don't you?'

Incapable of speech, she nods.

While he fetches more wine, Kat attempts to assemble her thoughts. She can't believe he's laid his cards on the table. But if he really means what he says, she has to ask him now . . . just the once . . . about everything that's bothering her. Then, she'll never bring up the subject again. She won't let the insecurities of her past wreck her future.

As Mac steps up into the cockpit with bottle in hand, he tenderly observes her vulnerable, yet determined expression. Crossing over to the table, he tops up their glasses.

Hesitantly, her gaze meets his.

'Come on then, Ms Maddox,' he says, sliding into his seat. 'Ask away.'

Clenching her teeth, Kat closes her eyes and inhales deeply. Mac suppresses a smile.

'OK,' she says, opening her eyes and crossing her fingers

beneath the table. 'Last weekend I saw you in Salcombe with Francine.'

His eyes widen.

She hurries on. 'Tara and I were at the hotel, we were having tea on the terrace, and we saw you.'

His brow puckers.

'It . . . looked like you were breaking up with her,' Kat stammers, nerves rendering her tone a little high-pitched, 'but . . . I thought you told me you'd already ended the relationship.'

God. She sounds like some jealous lover.

His gaze is steady when he answers. 'I *have ended* the relationship,' he says, 'but, as I told you, Francine is not coping with that well. She's vulnerable at the moment and wanted to see me again, to talk.'

Kat considers his words. They're convincing enough, but then Colin had been pretty convincing, too, and look how that turned out. But she *so* wants to believe Mac.

'What you and Tara witnessed,' Mac continues, 'was me telling Francine that I would always care about her, and be there for her as a friend, but that I could no longer be more than that. What you saw was me gently breaking it to her that I've met someone; someone I want to get to know better . . .'

Kat holds her breath.

'And that person, if you have *any* doubts, is you, Kat.'

A lump forms in her throat and, feeling foolish, she smiles weakly. Uncrossing her fingers, she picks up her glass and takes a sip of wine. She hates asking these questions but he'd said there were things that needed discussing . . . and there's still one woman she *has* to ask about.

'One more thing, Mac. Alec's mother.'

He tenses.

She ploughs on. 'You say she isn't around. Who and where is she?'

Mac's face creases with emotion, and he turns away.

Dear God! He'll never want to be with her after this interrogation.

Kat reaches for his hand. 'You don't have to answer, Mac,' she says softly, 'but I would like to know, if you can tell me.'

He turns to face her again. 'I will tell you, Kat, because I want to be with you, if you'll have me. And I don't want there to be any secrets between us.'

If she'll have him! Is he kidding?

Her stomach ties itself into a knot as her heart starts to race. Why does she feel such a deep sense of foreboding? Sitting back smartly, she lets go of his hand.

46

Intense sadness pools in Mac's eyes and Kat fights the overwhelming urge to cry.

As though summoning strength from the depths of his soul, Mac says, 'I met Alec's mum, Ana-Sofia, when I was operating a yacht charter out of Barcelona. I'd only recently set up the business and Ana gave up her job to help me run it.'

He pauses for a long while, and Kat holds her breath, the dread increasing. Carried on the night air is the distinctive and plaintive call of a curlew.

'She was twenty-two when we got together. We married quickly and Alejandro came along the following year.' Mac pinches the top of his nose. Letting out a deep sigh, he meets Kat's stricken gaze. 'I was taking a client out on *Windsong*, and as he was an experienced sailor Ana had taken the day off from working on the yacht. She'd arranged instead to have lunch with her sister, Ariadne.' He pauses and Kat sees that he is trembling a little, which makes her heart contract. 'Ana was on her way to meet Ariadne at the restaurant, with Alec in his buggy, when it happened.' Tears now gather in Mac's eyes and he bites down hard on his lip. 'The car swerved and mounted the pavement without warning.'

Kat's hand flies to her mouth and she longs to reach out to him. Not only because what he's just said is so shocking, but because she can't bear to see this confident, self-assured man broken.

'Apparently, Ana didn't stand a chance,' Mac continues in a strangled voice. 'Witnesses said the car ploughed straight into her. She must have realised there was no way she was going to survive but she made sure Alec did. She managed to push him out of danger. That's how he got the scar on his forehead. The buggy tipped over when it crashed into the shop front.'

There's a moment of deep, impenetrable silence, before Kat wipes her eyes. Rising, she walks around the table.

'Mac,' she says, tenderly wrapping her arms around him. 'I am so very sorry.'

'Me too,' he says quietly. 'The driver was blind drunk and didn't have a licence. He said he never even saw her.'

Kat rubs his back. She has no experience of how this must feel, but it can't have been easy to recount this story to her. How brave.

Mac clears his throat and gently pulls away. 'There, you know it all now,' he says sadly.

'Thank you for trusting me enough to share it with me,' she whispers.

He nods. 'I don't broadcast it. Not many people know.'

She shakes her head. But Jean and Stan obviously do, and they're right: James MacNamara is a good man, through and through. How had she managed to misjudge him so badly? Her stupid, unfulfilling romantic track record and subsequent narrow prejudices had so readily cast him in an unsavoury light without really knowing anything about the man. Never again will she be so quick to judge another.

'Why does Alec live with his aunt and uncle and not you?' she asks softly, as she sits down beside him.

Rubbing his face, Mac expels air through his mouth. 'I had to make a quick decision. Obviously, I needed to earn a living, and yachts are what I know. The business was thriving but I couldn't run it with a toddler to look after, too. Alec was only three at the time. Ariadne and her husband were about to move to London and they offered to take him with them and act as guardians.' Mac pauses, his expression pained. 'It seemed like the right choice.'

'That must have been so hard for you.'

'It was . . . it *is* . . . But it's the best solution for him. He has routine and a settled home. I can't offer him that, as much as I would love to.'

'Does Alec have any memories of the incident?' she gently probes.

'No, thank God.' Picking up the bottle, Mac refills their wine glasses. 'The saddest thing is he doesn't really remember his mother.'

'I'm sure you can help him remember her,' Kat says. 'And children are very resilient,' she adds, thinking of Tara's two boys.

Mac nods. 'That's true. I try to have him with me whenever possible and he's taken well to being around boats.'

She smiles. 'It's in his DNA.'

Mac gazes at her. 'It is. Ana was also very competent around yachts.'

'Double DNA.' She smiles.

'And *you're* showing a lot of promise,' he says, with some semblance of a tease returning.

'Well, thank you for giving me the opportunity to find out.'

Mac takes hold of her hands. 'I think I've been in denial since the accident, and you have every right to ask about my lifestyle if you're considering taking me on. I've tried to bury my past and rebuild my life but I've been unable to promise anyone anything. Neither have I introduced Alec to any woman before. You see, I've never allowed anyone to get too close . . . I was too devastated.' He gives her an uncertain look. 'At least, not until I came to London for a meeting with my solicitor and caught up with Ariadne, who suggested an impromptu visit to Tate Britain . . .' He smiles at her through his tears. 'And there, amongst all those masterpieces, I found the best one of all sitting quietly on a bench.'

Tingles run up Kat's spine and she stares at him in disbelief.

'It's true.' His thumbs gently stroke her hands. 'I couldn't quite believe what I was seeing. You were like an exquisite statue – the most beautiful and complete work of art – and I was mesmerised. There was something about you that spoke to me, and then, when I had to leave – reluctantly I can tell you,' he raises an eyebrow, 'I thought that maybe this was some kind of sign and that I was slowly beginning to feel again and on the road to recovery, at last.'

Kat finds her voice. 'Whereas, in reality, I was sitting there completely screwed up and broken.'

He squeezes her hands. 'He's an idiot, Colin, for treating you like that.'

She's surprised he remembers his name.

'And then when I saw you in Salcombe . . .' Mac stares incredulously at her. 'I mean, what are the chances of that? I thought the gods must be smiling upon me!'

Bending forwards, Kat kisses him softly, then breaks away.

'It is odd, the way we were repeatedly in the same place at the same time,' she says. 'And here in Fowey, too!'

His look turns sheepish. 'Ah, that . . .' He clears his throat. 'I have a confession to make.'

She holds her breath.

'When your friend said you had the chance of staying here for a few months I took a gamble and arranged for *Windsong* to be in Fowey for the summer.'

Kat's eyes widen. 'You did?'

He laughs. Letting go of her hands, he raises his in surrender. 'I wondered if fate and destiny were possibly at play, and as we don't get too many chances in life I figured I should help it along a little. I had a yearning to investigate this . . . you . . . further.'

She can hardly believe what she's hearing. 'Oh, Mac, it could so easily have backfired!'

She'd always wondered about his being here in Fowey, but she can't deny the fact that no one has ever made such a grand gesture for her before. She shakes her head, wondering if she's imagining this.

'And I gave you such a hard time, too . . .'

'Yes . . . But then nothing worth having comes easily.' She shivers.

'Come here,' he says, pulling her to him and putting his warm arms around her.

As Kat nestles against his body, she attempts to comprehend the turnaround of events. All her doubts are drifting away. She has to give Mac a chance. She'd be a fool not to. And anyway, Tara will never speak to her again if she doesn't.

'Look at all the stars twinkling like diamonds,' she says, gazing up at the inky night sky. 'Perhaps they are aligning.'

'I'd say so,' he says softly, teasing a lock of her hair through his fingers.

She turns to him. 'Mac, whatever happens, please know that I want to be with you too.'

His gaze meets hers and slowly he smiles. 'You've missed the last water taxi back, although I can take you ashore in the tender.' He pauses. 'But there's another option I hope you'll consider.'

'What's that?' she asks, innocently.

'Stay,' he whispers.

47

The next morning, Kat stands on Stella's private jetty watching Mac motor upstream. The river, the colour of sapphires, sparkles in the early morning sunlight and she brushes stray tendrils away from her face as a warm breeze teases her hair. Never has she been in a more beautiful place, either physically or mentally. All is well with the world. Suddenly the sound of the outboard alters and the RIB slows to idle. Mac looks back. As their eyes meet he raises his fingers to his lips and sends a kiss out over the water towards her. Delightedly, Kat laughs and stretching out her arm, catches the kiss and holds it close to her chest. He smiles and pats his heart, before letting out the throttle and continuing on to Albert Quay.

Kat watches until he disappears from sight. Deep in thought, she turns and makes her way up the steps towards the house. Glancing up at Jerry and Sandy's property, she notices all the curtains are closed and there's no sign of her neighbours – obvious advantages to being retired. Unlocking the back door, she enters the house. It's cool in the lower hallway and briefly she leans back against the closed door and considers all that has occurred. Mac and she have discovered something deliciously unexpected and her face flushes as she recalls their intense passion. It wasn't just good sex. James MacNamara and Katherine Maddox had made *love* . . . and for most of the night. She smiles. Who'd have thought? Well, apart from her soothsaying friend, Tara.

Rushing upstairs, she strips off and steps into the shower, and standing under a cascade of hot water, she reflects on her night spent aboard *Windsong*. It was so wildly romantic, what with the secret sounds of the inlet and wildlife all around, and the gentle rocking of the yacht as it responded to the changing current. As she rubs shower gel into her skin, her body tingles at the memory of more insistent fingers exploring her curves. Placing the palms of her hands flat against the cool tiles, she stands motionless and relives the fire his touch had lit. As intense feelings had flooded her body, all she'd wanted was to weave a safe cocoon around him and protect him from his grief. She has *never* felt so selfless towards anyone before. Her previous, disastrous relationships have only ever been two people enjoying what the other could bring to the party, with a large underlying element of personal gain. Kat shakes herself out of her musings. Scary stuff, this giving her heart to another . . . and she'd made herself a promise never to do it again. This time, however, it feels different. Something about Mac makes her want to set her own concerns to one side.

Pushing herself away from the wall, she reaches for the shampoo bottle and vigorously washes her hair.

A short while later, Kat enters the studio with a cup of tea in her hand. Placing it down on the table, she approaches the bay window. On the easel is her large, unfinished illustration of Penhallam Manor as it would have looked in its heyday. She will complete it today. After all, there are no distractions. Mac said he won't be back until Thursday.

She's missing him already.

'Oh for goodness sake,' she says in exasperation. 'You've managed for thirty-eight years without James MacNamara in your life.' But even his name sends the butterflies in her stomach swirling into a vortex.

Extracting her mobile from her pocket, she composes a text to her best friend.

Lost my appetite.

Within a minute her phone alerts her to a new message.

That's not good . . . or is it?

She responds: *Think I may be a teeny-weeny, incy wincy bit in love!*

Hallelujah! Tara replies. *Mac, I presume?*

Kat laughs out loud and taps into her phone: *Of course, idiot!*

She has to wait five minutes for a further reply.

The only idiot here is Kat Maddox for taking so long to see what was so bleeding obvious to the rest of us! Can't chat now. In a meeting. Will phone tonight for the goss. xx

Kat smiles, then putting her phone to one side, she picks up a pen and gets to work on the incomplete illustration.

48

That evening, Kat wanders over to the tapas bar. Its interior is decorated in soothing, smoky Prussian blue and she chooses a table in a cosy, private corner away from the street-side diners.

'Hi there,' Mel calls out from behind the bar. 'On your own tonight?'

Kat looks over and smiles. 'Yes, just me.'

'No shame in that.' The waitress approaches and briefly hesitates. 'I . . . didn't know you knew Mac.'

'I didn't really, not when we came here the other night,' Kat says, truthfully.

But she knows him a little better now.

'He's such a great guy. Sarah was thrilled when he asked her to work for him again this summer.'

Good grief! Does everyone know everybody else's business in this town?

'When was he in Fowey before?' Kat asks.

'Let me think.' Mel purses her lips. 'He's definitely been around for a few weeks over the last couple of years, but normally later in the season.'

Despite the night she and Mac spent together, Kat can't help her niggling paranoia about him. Possibly it's *because* of that perfect night; she can't quite believe that Mac is for real. Maybe he's too good to be true.

She keeps her voice deliberately light. 'You know Sarah, too?'

Mel nods. 'Oh, yes.'

'Has she always worked with Mac?'

'Think so. At least, she crews for him every year.'

'But they're not . . .' Kat pauses, 'together?'

Mel laughs. 'Who knows? They're as together as anyone can be with Mac! He likes to be a free agent. You know, difficult to pin down.'

Even though Mac's explained the reason he doesn't get too close to women, Kat carefully considers this latest piece of information. He hasn't exactly lied to her – Mel has just confirmed Sarah *is* crew – and she could be a recent, past lover, but Kat still feels suspicious. They've spent a lot of time on that boat, alone together, it would make sense if they'd got close . . . or, as Mel says, as close as 'anyone can be with Mac'. Kat wonders how many other people in Fowey think Mac and Sarah are together?

'Oh well, we can but dream of being with the likes of him,' Mel says, raising a suggestive eyebrow. 'Are you ready to order or would you like a glass of something while you decide?'

Kat orders a selection of tapas, hoping the flavoursome dishes will persuade her appetite to return. 'And a glass of red wine please.'

'Goru Organic would go nicely with the dishes you've selected,' Mel suggests. 'Made from the Monastrell grape, it's a wonderfully juicy, intense, honest wine.'

'Sounds perfect.'

'Great. I'll be right back.'

Suddenly Kat's phone rings. She doesn't recognise the number and her eyes narrow.

'Hello, is that Kat?' says a woman's voice. 'It's Annabel from Carrington and Partners – the country property specialists. We met recently at the Palladian house.'

'Oh, yes,' Kat says, remembering how much she'd enjoyed Annabel's company. 'How are you?'

'Feeling guilty for not having contacted you before now, but work has been rather non-stop. Everyone wants to move to the county – not that I'm complaining!' Annabel chuckles.

'We did suggest meeting up for drinks, and it just so happens that I'm in the Fowey area tomorrow taking on a property. I wondered if you'd like to catch up over a spot of lunch.'

'That sounds really nice,' Kat says.

'What about meeting at Sam's for, say, twelve-thirty?'

'Perfect,' Kat agrees quickly, and they chat for a short while longer until Mel arrives with the food, and she finishes the call.

'Listen,' says Mel, placing the bowls on the table, 'I hope I didn't talk out of turn earlier.'

Kat glances up enquiringly.

'You know, about Mac and Sarah.' The waitress looks embarrassed. 'I hope I haven't spoilt anything for you.'

'Not at all.' Kat gives a resigned smile. 'We all come with baggage.'

Mel frowns. 'Well, as long as I haven't put my foot in it. I mean you two did have dinner here together . . .' She lets the sentence hang.

'We all have to eat,' Kat says, picking up a knife and smearing humous onto a finger of sourdough.

'I guess so,' Mel replies. 'Well, enjoy your meal. If there's anything else you want just catch my attention.'

All night, Kat tosses and turns. Despite her newfound opinion of and belief in Mac, the evening's conversation with Mel has unsettled her, and throughout the long hours she examines their every encounter in the minutest of detail. When she eventually falls asleep she dreams of a property, which she realises, on waking, must have been brought on by association with Annabel's telephone call, and which, other than the vivid image of the house, she can't quite decipher.

Kat rises early, intending to spend the morning photographing the recent batch of completed illustrations and emailing them to Stella, but as soon as she enters the studio her fingers start to tingle. She knows only too well what that means. Sitting at the table, she opens her sketchpad, selects a pencil and starts to draw.

Two hours later, Kat stares at the various sketches filling the pages. It's definitely the house from her dream, but something niggles and she frowns. What is it that tickles her subconscious? Picking up her mobile, she opens the gallery of images and scans back through the many photographs she's stored. Eventually she finds what she's looking for – a selection of house sketches she produced for the flower book series. And there it is – the handsome, period house with the granite quoins and mullioned windows. She hasn't thought about it since Hugo informed her he'd sent a couple of the flower books to Stella as examples of her work.

Amazing what the mind stores!

She checks the time. It's not long until she's due to meet Annabel for lunch. Getting to her feet, she walks towards the door, but at the threshold she turns back. Returning to the table, she re-examines the drawings she's produced this morning, and it seems to her that these illustrations of the house are full and complete, not the vague imaginings she'd sketched last year. Opening the camera on her phone, she photographs these illustrations.

Kat enters the bistro and glances around. The restaurant is busy and there's a throng of people at the counter waiting for tables to come free. She spots Annabel waving from a booth and makes her way over to her.

'How lovely to see you again,' the estate agent says, as Kat approaches.

'Thanks for suggesting it.' She slides into the opposite seat. 'You were lucky to get a table.'

'I was,' Annabel affirms. 'So, how have you been?'

'Good, thanks. I've been getting to know the highways and byways of Cornwall pretty well. I've even ventured as far as the neighbouring county.'

'Gosh, that's brave.'

Kat laughs.

'As they're so busy it's probably best to order sooner rather than later,' Annabel suggests. 'Are you working today or can you allow yourself a glass of wine?'

'I work better on a glass or two.'

'That's settled then. Let's order.'

Kat's appetite is still non-existent but she is tempted by the chargrilled salmon salad and a glass of house white. Annabel orders the Sam Burger Deluxe with blue cheese and a glass of merlot.

'Burgers are my weakness,' she explains, 'but I have to spend this afternoon getting the property I've just been to online, and it's going to be quite a challenge. I figured I deserved a treat.'

'It must be interesting visiting the different properties around the county,' Kat says. 'Where's this one?'

'Not far from here, between Fowey and Lostwithiel,' Annabel explains. 'Even though Gerald warned me about the state of the house, it was still a shock when I saw it.'

'Why is that?' Kat asks, her interest piqued.

They pause as a waiter arrives with their food and drinks, but once he's retreated Annabel picks up the thread of their conversation again.

'It *was* an impressive Grade II listed Georgian property, steeped in history. But, tragically, a fire broke out in the house last Christmas, and it was largely destroyed. Very little was able to be saved.' She bites into her burger.

'How dreadful! Were there any casualties?'

The estate agent shakes her head, chewing frantically, until finally she swallows and then continues. 'The owners were away at the time, and fortunately it was empty, although that meant the emergency services were only alerted once the neighbours spotted smoke rising from the roof. At first, they thought someone was having a large bonfire! I think seventy firefighters and twelve engines tackled the flames.'

'What an awful Christmas,' Kat says. 'Not only for the owners but also the neighbours.'

'Yes. It's such a shame. The house is little more than a shell now and covered in scaffolding and tarpaulin but a few rooms remain, and one can just about see what it was like. It's heartbreaking.'

'Can the building be sold?' Kat asks, picking up a fork and slicing off a small portion of salmon.

'Yes. That's why we've been instructed. The owners have decided to cut their losses and sell, as seen, rather than go through the trouble of rebuilding. They've already renovated the house once, and the catastrophic fire has proven a step too far. Obviously, the property will be valued accordingly but it will need someone with passion . . . a "vision", and very deep pockets – or possibly a grant from Historic England.' She takes a sip of wine. 'Or, if they're penniless but desperate for a project they could take their chances on the lottery.' Annabel sighs. 'If all else fails, I suppose they could set up a crowdfunding page.'

Kat chews, deep in thought. 'What's the likelihood of it selling?'

'I doubt it will be a quick sell. Possibly a developer may be interested. Shame, because it was a very handsome manor house and although it had lots of rooms, it gives the impression of once having been a well-loved family home. There *were* gable ends, numerous tall chimneys, different roof levels, wonderful stonework, arched windows, granite quoins and a couple of charming roof terraces with stone balustrading.'

'Have you taken photos of what remains?' Kat asks.

'Yes. It wasn't easy as there are very few elevations that aren't obscured by scaffolding, but I have partial shots. It's not really possible to visualise it from what's left, though.' Annabel cocks her head. 'Why? Are you interested?'

Kat gives a small laugh. 'Not to buy, but I'm interested in what it looked like.'

'I have the sales particulars from when the current owners

bought it.' Annabel delves into her handbag. 'Here you go.' She hands the brochure across the table.

As soon as Kat sees the main picture on the front cover, she feels light-headed, and a tingling sensation consumes her. In disbelief, she studies the photos on the other pages. She can't explain it, she's never visited the property, but this is definitely the house in her dream, and the one she'd featured in the flower book series. She glances up at Annabel who is watching her curiously. Will the agent freak out if she shows her the photos of her illustrations?

Kat bites her lip, considering.

'You look as if you've got a lot on your mind,' Annabel says.

'Can I show you something?' Kat asks, extracting the mobile from her pocket. She opens the gallery of photos she took earlier and passes the phone across the table.

Annabel focuses on the image on the screen and her eyes open wide. 'I don't understand,' she says, flicking through the various shots. 'What are these?'

'Sketches I did this morning. I had a dream about a house last night, following your phone call, and I felt compelled to draw it.'

'Goodness! This is giving me the shivers,' says Annabel, glancing up at Kat. 'Perhaps you are meant to buy it.'

Kat snorts. 'Chance would be a fine thing.'

Annabel thumbs through several more photos. 'The gardens are laid out the same and the sketch you've done from inside the doorway looking out . . . well, the floor tiles have survived and are still in situ.' She stares at Kat increduously. 'This is definitely the property! How did you do it? How did you *know*?'

Kat shrugs. 'It just came to me.'

'I think Gerald would be very interested in using your illustrations for our brochure,' Annabel says. 'You know, to show the property as it will look once restored. Would you mind if I showed them to him?'

'Of course not, if it helps.'

'Oh, I think it will. You'd be surprised how many people have no imagination whatsoever and find it impossible to see beyond the end of their noses. But with your help, we may find a buyer.' She looks at Kat and shakes her head in disbelief. 'I love things like this, but we won't tell Gerald these were produced from a dream you had. The man hasn't got a spiritual bone in his body, bless him.'

49

With lunch over, Annabel suggests they meet up again before too long and Kat heartily agrees. As the estate agent bids her farewell and heads off towards Caffa Mill car park at the far end of town, Kat turns in the opposite direction and makes her way along Fore Street. She has to dodge a party of chattering tourists, who are intent on weaving across the road in front of her, to peer in shop windows on the opposite side. It's been an interesting, if surprising, couple of hours, during which Annabel shared what she knew of the property's fascinating history, but Kat can't help feeling really sad that what now remains is a pale version of its former glory.

Life is fleeting, she muses, as she climbs the hill towards the Esplanade. *History is only as good as those who remember it clearly, and what happens when it's wiped out? Who will recall what once was and take the story forward?*

How depressing; time to turn her thoughts to something more uplifting. Instantly, Mac springs to mind and her face breaks into a smile. She checks the time on her phone and wonders what he's doing. Perhaps *Windsong* is anchored in a tranquil cove somewhere and he's enjoying a leisurely lunch with his clients. And Sarah, probably. She sighs. Three whole days until he returns. Still, she has plenty of work to be getting on with to fill those empty hours.

As it turns out, Kat has a productive afternoon and in the early evening she emails the latest illustrations to Stella, including her sketches of the property Carrington and Partners are about to market. She queries whether the professor knows the house. The historian replies almost instantly.

From Stella@ProfessorStella.com
To: Kat_Maddox1@Google3.com
Subject: Re: New Sketches

Kat

    Thank you for the consistently high quality of illustrations and their timely delivery. If only my students shared your hard work ethic!

    Your sketches of the property near Fowey are intriguing. I don't know it, but from the information you have provided I would consider including it in the book, if permission is granted. You say sales brochures are currently being prepared. Perhaps you could provide details of the estate agent handling the marketing and I will make contact. What a tragedy to have befallen the house. I feel compelled to redress the balance.

    Kindest regards,
    Stella

Kat responds immediately with Annabel's telephone number and Carrington and Partners' address. She doesn't know why, but she too feels driven to put right the tragedy that has occurred, in whatever small way she can. She looks again at her illustration of firefighters on ladders, directing hoses onto a roof engulfed in billowing smoke, and shivers.

Using her usual technique when summoning the past, she closes her eyes and stills her mind.

'Why did you make yourself known to me?' she asks quietly, thinking back to the previous year when the property first manifested.

But the answer doesn't come, and after a while she opens her eyes.

It's getting late, and as her appetite is still non-existent, she skips supper and turns in. Standing at the bedroom window, she gazes across the darkening river to the lights of Polruan and wonders how many people have stood on this spot and looked across the water over the centuries? How different was the view then? And what was here before the row of Victorian villas was built? She's keenly aware that history exists in the present, if only people take the time to scratch beneath the surface of what is plainly visible.

Strewn across the velvety night sky, pinpricks of diamonds wink at her. Is Mac also gazing at the stars? Comforted by the thought that he's under the same constellation, she closes the curtains and crosses the room. Climbing into bed, she plumps the pillows and picks up the book lying next to her phone on the bedside table. A bookmark highlights where she'd finished reading the previous night and she opens it to that page now. She hasn't read *The Wind in the Willows* since childhood, but the boat trip with Mac and Alec to the very inlet that inspired the author to write the story has spurred her on to acquire a copy from the town's bookshop. It seems only fitting to read the tale again here in Fowey, but also, she realises, it makes her feel closer to that special father and son.

Some while later her eyelids droop, but the sound of an incoming message on her mobile propels Kat back into the present. Reaching for her phone, she peers bleary-eyed at the screen. At once she's alert. Involuntarily, her stomach muscles react to the sender.

Missing you! Goodnight lovely lady x

Hugging the phone to her chest, Kat expels a ragged breath. *Never* in her thirty-eight years has she felt like this, but she has to be careful. Afraid to fall, she has to protect her poor beaten-up, battered old heart. She knows only too well how it feels when a relationship ends and even though this one is only just exquisitely unfurling, there's too much at stake this time. How should she reply? It's important not to unwittingly disclose the intense feelings Mac stirs in her too soon. She certainly doesn't want to come across as lovesick or needy, but neither does she want to appear cold and aloof. She decides to keep it comfortably light.

Counting the hours! Sleep well x

The following days drag by, even though much of Kat's time is taken up with busily researching the next property on Stella's list, but eventually Thursday morning dawns. It's a blustery day with a shy sun that hides behind thick banks of cloud gusting across the sky. In the sitting room, Kat stands at the bay window watching an ocean liner enter the mouth of the river accompanied by a pilot boat. It's an impressive sight, and as the passenger ship slowly passes Polruan, the fishing village is hidden from view. Out in the bay, the English Channel is battleship grey and angry under a bruised sky, which, dumping its load in the far distance, merges with the spume flying off white-capped waves. She wonders how Mac and his party have fared. Longing aches deep in her belly. Tonight he'll be home.

She instantly pulls a wry face, embarrassed at her presumption.

Home?

Yes, home! Somehow, it feels like that.

Kat watches for a while longer, marvelling at the way small watercraft dodge the liner that dominates the water. Regular as clockwork, the Polruan Ferry chugs its way across from the other side of the river, dwarfed by the passenger ship. It seems such a cheerful and friendly little soul; it could be a distant cousin to Thomas the Tank Engine.

'Anthropomorphism is alive and kicking!' she says to herself, with a wry smile.

Perhaps she's been spending too much time in the company of Mr Toad, Mr Badger, Ratty and Mole . . .

She turns away from the window and heads into the studio. Picking up her phone, she contacts the owners of the next property on Stella's list and, introducing herself, arranges a mutually convenient day to visit.

50

The wind has dropped and a palette of blue now replaces the sky's previous grey wash. Bravely, the sun shows its face. Kat steps out of the back door onto the terrace and quickly crosses over to the wall fronting the river. Breathing in deep lungfuls of salt-laden air, she attempts to calm her jittery nerves. The only sound is that of water slapping against the rocky shore below. Suddenly, a loud squawk makes her glance back at the house. Highlighted clearly against the azure canvas, a large herring gull struts its way along the ridge tiles of Stella's roof. Kat's artist's eye critically studies the bird, noting its white head, silvery-grey upperparts, black wingtips with white spots, pink legs, and, near the tip of its yellow bill, a red spot. She makes a note to feature it in one of her drawings.

Turning back to the river again, she scans the estuary for any signs of the elegant, dark-blue-hulled yacht. But the view is empty, apart from a solitary tanker crossing the far horizon and half a dozen Fowey River dinghies tacking across the bay, their vibrant multi-coloured sails billowing in the breeze out at sea. She sighs. All at once, the seagull swoops down from the roof and lands on the wall beside her. Cocking its head, it eyes her curiously.

'I know,' she says, 'it's a mug's game . . .'

She can't help it, but over the course of the rest of the day Kat checks the bay several times. Still no sign of *Windsong*. Mac said he'd be back today but he hadn't specified a time. For all she knows, the yacht may have passed by when she wasn't looking and is already moored up in the tranquil creek. She will just have to be patient. But how can she be when she's far from calm? A nervous energy has consumed her from the moment she woke up, and anticipation continues to build. But until she visits the next property, there are no further illustrations to distract her. She checks her mobile again. No message.

Looking around for things to do, she gathers up her dirty laundry and descends to the utility room. She loads the washing machine, adds a capsule to the drum, turns the dial to cool cycle and switches it on. Then she glances around and sighs. Now what? Walking upstairs to the kitchen she notices a half-full bottle of red wine sitting on the counter and pours herself a glass. It will settle her nerves . . . maybe.

Two glasses later, Kat checks her phone again. It's only nine-thirty but she decides to go to bed. After all, an early night won't do any harm and it means the morning will arrive more quickly and Mac will have returned. She tries reading for a while, but after she's read the same page four times she gives up in exasperation. Turning onto her side, she switches off the side lamp and closes her eyes. Before long, she's asleep.

It's sometime around midnight when the sound of knocking disturbs her. Disorientated, she gropes for the light switch and throws back the duvet. Climbing out of bed, she grabs her dressing gown and puts it on as she makes her way downstairs and opens the front door. There's no one there. She peers both ways along the darkened, empty street and frowns. The sound of knocking disturbs the night air once again and she turns. It's coming from the lower level.

Making her way to the staircase that leads below, Kat flicks on a light switch and instantly the area illuminates, sending shadows scuttling off to the farthest corners. As she descends the stairs, she ties her dressing gown more securely around her waist and reaching the backdoor, switches on the outside light. Through the glass she sees Mac standing in the lamplight. Quickly, she draws back the bolts and throws the door open wide.

'That's a bit of luck,' he says. 'I've got the right house!'

Immediately, he sweeps her into an embrace and Kat can hardly breathe. His body is firm and insistent against hers but his arms hold her gently, as if afraid he may hurt her. It's an intoxicating mix and her head spins. Fighting a bout of dizziness, she thinks she might even swoon. There's a freshness about Mac. His skin is cool from the night air and the smell of the sea lingers in his tousled, dark hair. It makes her want to grab his hand, run off to *Windsong* and sail away into the night. Escape the world together . . .

Drawing back for breath, she gazes up into his handsome face and her heart trips in her chest. There's loving in those hazel eyes that tenderly meet hers. It's subtle, but as he pulls her close again she knows it's futile to resist. She's definitely in trouble!

'I have missed you so much,' he says in a hoarse whisper.

He kisses her again and Kat willingly succumbs, but eventually she pulls away. They're still standing on the back doorstep. Taking his hand, she guides him into the hallway and bolts the door securely. Nothing is going to interrupt them.

'Did you come to Stella's jetty?' she asks.

'Yes. It was interesting working out which house was hers in the dark.'

She laughs and he kisses her again.

'Have you just got back?'

'No. We arrived at seven but the guys had organised a "thank you" meal in town. I couldn't duck out of it, even though all I wanted to do was come and find you straight away. I had to go.'

'Of course.'

'But, Kat . . .' He pauses, as if considering whether he should say what's on his mind.

Her heart flutters. 'What is it?' she asks urgently.

He inhales slowly. 'I haven't thought of anything else other than you these last three days. Sleep has not come easily, I can tell you.' He raises a sardonic eyebrow.

The breath hitches in Kat's throat. Can this beautiful man really be saying these things to her? Dear God, she could melt in a puddle at his feet! But she's not going to do that . . .

'Well, then,' she says, more confidently than she feels, 'I suggest you come to bed right now and catch up on some zeds.'

He laughs. 'I'll definitely take you up on the first part of that offer, but there's no way I'm in a hurry to do the second!'

51

The next morning, in the undefined space between sleep and waking, Kat stretches languorously, feeling unusually at peace with the world. Slowly, she opens her eyes.

Propped on one elbow, Mac is gazing at her. 'Good morning, beautiful.'

'Morning.' She smiles as the memory of their night of passion comes flooding back.

No wonder she feels at peace!

'I've been watching you,' he says softly.

Her eyes open wide.

Oh, no! She hasn't been snoring or sleeping with her mouth open, has she?

'You looked so blissed out, lying there with a wonderful smile on your face.'

She raises an eyebrow. 'I had much to smile about.'

He gives a small laugh and kisses her mouth. 'Then we must have both been smiling while asleep.'

She rolls over and faces him. 'Mac, how long have I got you?'

He answers without hesitation. 'As long as you want.'

Heat consumes her. 'I mean, when's your next charter?'

'Ah . . . That's a different question.' Lazily, he trails his fingers along the contours of her body, raising goosebumps on her flesh. 'I have to be on board for Sunday night.'

His hand is at her hip, and as his fingertips slowly work their way back up to her shoulder, he gives her body his full attention. As every part of her cries out to experience his touch, he raises his eyes to meet hers, and the desire she sees on his face makes her stomach slide.

'I love your curves, Kat Maddox,' he says in little more than a whisper.

She pushes herself up onto one elbow. 'And you know what, Mac?'

Slowly he shakes his head, as if drunk on feelings.

'I love it that you love them.'

Easing him down onto his back, she sits astride him and he urgently grabs her hips. She watches the emotions flicker across his eyes; vulnerability; longing; aching hunger; sadness. As their bodies respond to a mutually growing need, Mac's hands abandon her hips to cup her breasts.

Kat pinches herself. How lucky is she that this gorgeous man didn't give up on her? Despite her initial, hostile behaviour and her dismissive attitude, he has remained constant and unswerving in his belief of her.

Two hours later, they reluctantly emerge from the bed. Taking a shower together, under the pretext of applying soap, Kat and Mac continue to explore each other's bodies and, inevitably, this leads to other things. But, eventually, they get dressed and make their way downstairs.

'Would you like brunch?' she asks, glancing at the kitchen clock. 'There are croissants in the fridge – and I can do bacon and eggs if you like?'

He smiles warmly. 'To a famished man, that sounds like a lifesaver.'

'Now, why would he be famished?' She throws him a cheeky grin.

'I wonder.' He winks. 'Possibly something to do with the amount of recent exertion he's had?'

She laughs and turns to fill the kettle. 'Coffee or tea?'

'Coffee please. Can I do anything?'

'That's kind, but just relax. Perhaps you'd like to see what I've been working on?'

'I'd like that.'

She smiles. The fact that he's so interested in her work is an added bonus. 'Go on through to the studio.'

As Mac makes his way along the hallway she glances out of the window. The sun is shining and there isn't a cloud in the sky, but even if it had been a grey day it would still hold a magical quality. Something has shifted in her universe, and though she may try to apply caution and rein it in, her soul rejoices, as all remaining wistful thoughts of Colin, along with the baggage of her numerous failed relationships, disperse into the ether. It doesn't really matter what happens from here on in, because for this perfect moment in time she is at peace with the world. She can't remember when she's felt such a release. There's usually always some problem niggling away at her. But not today.

Is this how other people feel? Is it only her that worries and frets her way through the day?

Kat tells her inner voice to take a hike. It's too beautiful a day . . .

She turns on the grill. Taking a pack of bacon out of the fridge, she lays several slices on the rack and cuts a couple of tomatoes in half, adding them to the pan before placing it under the heat. She can do the eggs later; they won't take long. Quickly, she makes two mugs of coffee and joins Mac in the studio.

He turns as she enters the room. 'Where is this?'

She glances at the illustration on the easel – the one of the house engulfed by smoke.

'It's a property just outside Fowey,' Kat says, handing him a mug. 'It's for sale. I met the agent yesterday.'

Surprise registers on his face. 'Are you thinking of buying it?'

She laughs. 'Goodness, no! I couldn't take on anything like that. Annabel is a friend. She was looking over the house before we met for lunch.'

He turns back to the easel. 'Is this your imagination at play, or did the house actually catch fire?'

She pulls a sad face. 'Unfortunately, it did.'

'Has it survived?'

'Barely. Apparently, it's pretty devastated and only a few rooms remain. It's mainly walls and rubble now – the roof has completely caved in. But the current owners have already renovated it once, and they've run out of steam, so it's being sold, as seen.' She regards him curiously.

Mac studies the drawing again with interest. 'Did you visit the property, Kat?'

She shakes her head.

'So, how have you drawn this, if you haven't seen it?'

She takes a deep breath. 'I dreamt about it one night . . . and the next morning I had an overwhelming urge to draw the house.'

He directs his gaze at her. 'And your friend confirms it is the house she's selling?'

'Yes. She showed me an old sales brochure, and it definitely is the house,' Kat says in a matter-of-fact voice.

'But . . . That's incredible!' he says, staring at her in amazement.

She pulls a self-deprecating face. Then, crossing over to the table, she picks up her sketchpad and flicks through to a page. 'This is how it looked before fire consumed it.'

She shows him the illustrations.

'You know, Kat, if this is the house as it was, your ability to pick up on the past is extraordinary.' Mac regards her for a long moment. 'Have you considered taking it further?'

She shakes her head. 'I don't see how it could benefit anyone . . . or me.'

'I don't know.' He looks thoughtful. 'Maybe if people want to know more about the history of their properties, you could offer a service.'

She shrugs. 'Maybe, but I don't really want to draw attention to it,' she says, remembering all the times she's been accused of having an overactive imagination, and how the criticism had made her feel.

Mac smiles sensitively. 'Well, it was a handsome property that's for sure. One hell of a loss!'

'Annabel told me some of its history. She said the the house is listed. And I think there's the possibility of it qualifying for a grant from Historic England, for anyone wanting to take on the renovations – though whoever that is, they'll have to have plenty of energy and loads of dosh . . .'

She pauses to study Mac, who looks preoccupied, and then suddenly she's aware of the enticing aroma wafting along the hall and curling into the room.

'Damn!' she exclaims. 'I completely forgot about the bacon!'

52

Mac and Kat decide to have breakfast outside, and as they make their way out onto the terrace, she notices her neighbours, Jerry and his wife, sitting on their small balcony. Politely, she acknowledges them. The river is alive with watercraft and a gentle breeze wends its way in from the sea.

'It's such a beautiful day,' Kat says through a mouthful of croissant. 'What do you fancy doing this afternoon?'

'I know what I'd *like* to do,' Mac says, raising a suggestive eyebrow. 'But you're right. It's too beautiful a day to miss.' He considers her. 'I was thinking . . . Do you think your friend could arrange a viewing of that property near Fowey this afternoon?'

Her eyes widen. 'Really?'

'Yes.' Having almost finished his breakfast, he leans back in his chair, interlocking his hands behind his head and takes a deep breath. 'For some time now I've been thinking of ways to change things in my life . . . To be here for Alec for a start. Ariadne and Leo are terrific guardians, but it's increasingly becoming a compromise too far. I know my son wants to live with me, and I certainly want to care for him.' He lowers his arms. 'Not being a hands-on dad has been one hell of a thing to come to terms with, and hasn't been possible . . . up to now. But I've been giving it serious thought and there could be . . . no . . . *should* be changed priorities ahead.' He gives her a loving smile.

A warm, tingling sensation courses through Kat's body. Picking up her mug of coffee she takes a sip and observes him thoughtfully over the rim.

Changed priorities ahead. He's talking about Alec, of course.

But she'd stake her life on it he means something else too.

Mac then changes the subject. 'You know, Kat. That day you stood up to the idiot who nicked your parking space, well, you were magnificent.'

She purses her lips. 'I hate injustice and not just when it's directed at me. I'll stand up for anyone who's on the receiving end of it.'

He nods. 'That's what I love about you, Kat Maddox. Not only your curves but also your sharp edges.' He holds her gaze. 'And I've never been afraid to live life on the edge.'

Kat's breath catches in her throat. With every other partner *this* was always the 'rub'. Not one of them accepted her strength of character. She remembers Colin telling her to 'calm down', several times.

'That's just as well, then,' she says, bestowing him a swift smile. 'I'll give Annabel a ring and see if she's free to show us around the property this afternoon.'

Two hours later, Kat, Mac and Annabel stand in the grounds of the Georgian house, solemnly surveying its remains. The property is situated in a sequestered, sheltered, lightly wooded valley, amidst unspoilt rolling countryside – which in any other circumstance would be considered an enviable and sought-after location. However, a weighty silence hangs in the air, as if the universe, still in shock, attempts to process the catastrophic event that has taken place here. Huge tarpaulins hang listlessly from scaffolding, protecting the remaining rooms and architectural features against any further damage from the elements.

'How sobering,' Kat mutters.

Annabel nods. 'It's hard to accept so much history going up in flames.'

'Is it OK to go inside?' Mac asks.

'Yes.' She holds out a couple of hard hats. 'Firefighters

couldn't save the roof structure and the upper floors are unsafe, so it's my duty to advise you to take care and wear one of these.'

Mac puts one on, then drawing back a flap in the tarpaulin, he steps through what had once been the entrance to the house. Kat and Annabel follow.

'It was an important and outstanding country home of immense appeal,' says Annabel, gazing around at the remains.

'It certainly looked it from Kat's sketches,' Mac says.

Annabel nods. 'She did a great job portraying it as it once was.'

He glances proudly at Kat and without warning his heart pinches. She looks *so* cute in that hard hat.

'There were two large cellars,' explains Annabel, 'now mostly filled with debris from the collapsed house.'

'How was the accommodation arranged?' Mac asks, observing the remaining walls that indicate an extensive layout.

'There's a sales brochure back in the office. It's from when the owners purchased the property ten years ago, but it'll give you some idea. I'll send it to you.'

'Thanks. That would be helpful.'

'It's so tragic,' Annabel continues. 'The house had only recently undergone a refurbishment programme – a new kitchen, limestone flooring, new bathrooms, plumbing, rewiring and under-floor heating. It makes what happened so much more poignant.'

Mac stares at the charred remains of a splendid oak staircase. Deep in thought, he follows the estate agent into what had been the dining room. The devastation is apocalyptic. The only object remaining along one elevation is a row of full-length windows, the glazing either removed or shattered and the original shutters blackened with scorch marks. It gives the room the appearance of a tragic stage set.

Annabel gestures over to a corner. 'You can get an idea of the height of the ceilings from that section of ornate cornicing. It must have been a particularly impressive room. In fact, all the main reception rooms had high ceilings and beautiful, original features, such as oak flooring, Tudor-style plasterwork and ceiling roses.' She shakes her head. 'There was also an intriguing Victorian kitchen with the original spit, sadly no longer.'

Mac lets out a low whistle. 'The owners must be devastated.'

'Pretty much. They want the property gone in order to move on with their lives.'

Kat wanders through the shell of rooms towards the more untouched section of building. The atmosphere is intense, and whispered voices call to her – so palpable that she can almost feel them. As she listens, attempting to assimilate all the information filtering through, a chill skirts at the edges. She tries to block out Mac and Annabel's discussion and catch the suggestion, allowing it time to form. But it's no good. It was but fleeting, although the strangeness of it remains.

'It had two holiday apartments that provided a useful income, each with their own separate access,' Annabel explains to Mac, 'and an additional thirteen bedrooms. Upstairs was a large master suite, with views over the gardens and access to a roof terrace at the front of the house. There were also extensive attic rooms, which offered potential for conversion to further accommodation.'

'Plenty of options,' Mac responds. 'A lot to think about, for whoever buys it.'

'Yes indeed.'

He glances over at Kat, who is quietly gazing up at the remaining two-storey portion of the house. She looks pale and seems distant.

Making his way across the empty space, stepping over the pitiful remains of internal walls, he approaches her. 'Kat, are you OK?'

It takes a moment for her to respond.

'What?' She turns to him, eyes swimming. Quickly, she refocuses. 'Yes.'

He hugs her. 'Hey, you're cold. Let's go outside. There's nothing more to see here.'

Taking her hand, he guides her across the room and out through the flap in the tarpaulin onto the front lawn. It's good to feel the heat of the sun once again.

Kat glances around. The property feels so familiar; it's as if she's been here before. But, of course, she has . . . in her imagination. The grounds are exactly as she had drawn them, with the circular, granite pond in the garden to the south of the house. It's just the flowers that are missing, but she hadn't expected them to be here. They were the subject of the books, images she'd had to painstakingly create, but for some reason the house had appeared on the pages with ease. She gazes at a corner of the building where a sheet of tarpaulin has come loose, exposing a section of stonework. The granite quoins are exactly where she knew they would be as she'd featured that particularly attractive angle of the house, adding a profusion of billowing wildflowers in front of it.

'Good. The colour has come back to your cheeks,' Mac says, giving her a hug.

'I'm OK, Mac. Thanks for your concern.'

'I'm just going to check the rear of the house. Be back in a minute.'

She smiles. Suddenly, Annabel emerges through the flap in the tarpaulin, and together she and Mac disappear around the corner.

A flight of elegant, granite steps leads up to a grass-terraced wooded area and something in the trees catches Kat's attention. Swinging on a rope secured around the substantial branch of a large beech tree is a dark-haired boy. Should he be in the grounds? Is he the son of the owners? She should let Annabel know. Suddenly her eyes widen. As the boy swings round to face her, she recognises the lad; a gorgeous young man in the making.

Alec! Although an older version.

He calls out, and yet no sound intrudes upon the peace and tranquillity of the setting. Beside him is a wooden swing suspended on ropes, and Kat's jaw drops. A young girl moves back and forth, sweeping her legs through the air and effectively gathering momentum. Her long copper-coloured hair flows out behind her, and the joy on her face is evident as soundlessly she laughs. Tingles shiver up Kat's spine when a man enters the scene, giving a piggyback to a toddler. A little girl with dark chestnut-brown hair. Silently, he speaks to the children and all at once the boy points in her direction. As the man turns towards her, his features are dearly familiar and some sixth-sense calls out to Kat. Instinctively she knows what she's witnessing. Giving her a dazzling smile as he jostles the child on his back into a more comfortable position, he says something to the toddler who turns and immediately stretches out a pair of chubby arms towards Kat.

A lump forms in her throat. As tears well in her eyes she blinks rapidly, breaking the spell. The terrace is empty but the tree is still there, though no swing or rope hangs from its mighty branches.

This is a first. Never before has she been gifted a glimpse of a possible future.

She turns to see Annabel and Mac reappearing around the side of the house, deep in conversation.

'So . . . what do you think?' Annabel asks Mac, and Kat frowns.

What does Mac think about what?

'Well, it's a huge undertaking . . . quite a commitment,' he replies. 'The roof, alone, would cost thousands to replace.'

Annabel nods.

'But I've never been one to shirk hard work, and I'm

looking for a project. There's plenty of scope to recreate what once stood here.' Mac gazes around at the private setting. 'Kat mentioned there's the possibility of a grant?'

'Yes. I can put you in contact with the right people at Historic England. Their grants are an essential part in protecting the nation's heritage and there's a scheme that offers funding to owners of individual historic sites and listed buildings in need of repair and conservation.'

Mac turns and grins at Kat, who is still trying to make sense of what she's just witnessed, apart from being a bit blindsided by what she's hearing.

'What do you think?' he asks her.

Quickly she gathers her thoughts. 'It's one hell of an opportunity, but it would keep you busy for years. How would you run the yacht charter business?'

He smiles. 'As I said, change of priorities.'

Kat looks up into his soft, hazel eyes, the sunlight reflecting shafts of gold and green in their depths, and returns his smile.

'I think it's a fantastic idea, then,' she says, quietly, but sincerely. 'This house deserves passion like yours.'

'It could be *our* passion,' he says. 'Something we can share?'

Her eyes widen. What he's suggesting is beyond her imaginings. He's not just talking vaguely about a future with her, he's acting on it. So why does she feel so anxious . . . as though something is obscuring her happiness?

Mac eyes her shrewdly. 'What's the matter . . . There's something troubling you, isn't there?'

How can she explain what she's just seen and the feelings it has evoked?

She exhales slowly. 'It's just a little overwhelming. There's so much history here that needs preserving . . . and passing on to future generations.' She pauses.

Future generations . . .

She feels like crying.

'Don't be overwhelmed, Kat,' he says softly. 'A day at a time.'

Thinking of the odd sensation she'd picked up on in the house, she takes a deep breath. 'I think there was a dark period here during the Second World War.'

'What happened?' he asks quietly.

She shakes her head. 'I don't know, but I have the feeling something of importance took place here.' Her voice is little more than a whisper.

'There's light and dark in everything,' Mac says, putting his arm protectively around her shoulders and holding her close. 'But whatever took place here, it's all part of the property's story and it will be remembered. I promise.' He turns to Annabel. 'I'd be interested to learn more about the history of the house.'

Annabel's eyes narrow in consideration. 'Well, before the fire, what stood here was a very fine Grade II listed country house, originating from 1815. The Victorians added to it later.'

Mac nods.

'The site is within the Domesday manor of *Lantien Parva* and it has been suggested it's where King Mark of Cornwall had his domestic settlement. His stronghold was nearby at Castle Dore. It's also reputedly the site of the tryst of the doomed Tristan and Iseult.'

A deep silence weaves its way through the sheltered valley and it seems to Kat that the whispers, now quiet, are expectant; listening . . .

'There are various deeds and leases, dating from the mid-fourteenth century, that trace a fascinating pedigree from these ancient times to the more recent past,' the agent continues. 'The house was temporarily leased during the First World War to the Austrian Count Fabrice, who was reputedly a descendant of the Hapsburgs.'

'As you say, quite a pedigree,' comments Mac.

'Yes.'

Glancing with concern at the woman in the fold of his arm, he asks, 'Do you have time to show us the grounds, Annabel?'

'But of course.'

53

Later, Kat and Mac drive to the idyllic sandy cove of Polkerris and having parked in the village car park, they walk hand in hand down the hill to *Sam's on the Beach*. The sea sparkles beneath a warm afternoon sun and carried on the breeze is the happy sound of families enjoying a day on the sands. Kat gazes skywards at high cirrus clouds streaking across an intoxicatingly blue sky.

'Mares' tails and mackerel scales make lofty ships to carry low sails,' murmurs Mac.

'What's that?'

'A proverb sailors learned to warn of approaching rainy weather.'

'But it's such a beautiful day!' she says in surprise.

'Never trust the weather,' Mac says, with a wry grin, 'particularly the Cornish variety. Cirrus clouds typically occur in fair weather, but they can also form out ahead of warm fronts and large-scale storms, like nor'easterlies and tropical cyclones. Seeing them can indicate incoming storms.'

She ponders this as they approach the building. 'Landlubbers have no idea the extent of a yachtsman's knowledge.'

'It helps to know a thing or two if you spend most of your life on the water,' Mac says wryly.

Arriving at the entrance, they stop to read a plaque on the outside wall.

' "The old lifeboat station",' Kat reads, gazing at the information, ' "serving the Fowey area from 1859 to 1922." '

'Good of William Rashleigh to offer the RNLI money

towards a lifeboat for Fowey, and land and building stone for a boathouse,' comments Mac, scanning the board. 'No doubt it changed the nature of this community when it was relocated.'

Kat nods. 'It must have been exhausting handling the lifeboat during storms with just oars and sails.'

'Yes, very tough.'

They walk towards the entrance and Mac holds the door open for Kat.

Wood-panelled walls and a pebbled pathway lead past an open kitchen where a handful of chefs busily prepare an array of dishes, and as she walks by, Kat notices a custom-built, wood-burning oven full of pizzas, piled high with tantalising, colourful ingredients. They approach a pretty girl wearing the uniform black T-shirt, with *Sam's* emblazoned across her chest, her blonde hair tied back in a ponytail.

'Table for two?' she enquires with a smile.

'Yes, two,' Mac replies.

Inwardly, Kat gives herself a hug. *How gorgeous does that sound? She's so used to explaining her one-ness . . . and usually defensively.*

The waitress beckons them to follow as she turns and descends a short flight of steps to the dining area. Most of the tables are taken but there's an empty one in the window overlooking the horseshoe bay. A stone quay shelters the sandy cove and Kat gazes out at the mirror-like water gently lapping the shore. It looks so serene. It's hard to believe there may be a storm on the way.

'I'll be back in a minute when you've decided what you'd like,' the girl says. 'Specials are on the board.'

'Cheers,' says Mac.

Pulling out a chair, Kat sits opposite him and gazes around. The other diners are mainly young families, although there are a few couples among them.

'These large windows make it wonderfully light and airy in here,' she comments.

Mac agrees. 'It's probably where the original lifeboat doors were located.'

He opens a menu while Kat checks the 'specials', and when the waitress returns they ask about the seafood platter.

'The fish is exceptionally fresh,' she says. 'Our fishing boat, the *Emperor*, lands it daily. And shellfish such as lobsters, mussels and scallops arrive straight from St Austell Bay.' She smiles. 'I've worked my way through the whole menu and the seafood platter is my favourite.'

'That decides it then!' Mac teasingly says, giving her a wink.

The girl laughs. 'Have you decided what you want to drink?'

'A glass of the house white, please,' Kat says.

'And I'll have a pint of Betty Stogs,' says Mac, as his mobile registers an incoming message. Standing, he extracts the phone from his jeans pocket and peers at the screen. 'It's from Annabel. She's attached the brochure.'

Together, across the table, they study the sales particulars, only drawing apart when the waitress arrives with their drinks.

'It had thirty-eight rooms!' Kat exclaims. 'That's some house.'

Using his thumb and forefinger, Mac enlarges the brochure on the phone's screen. 'It says here that the land extends to approximately twelve acres, eight comprising pasture and the rest mature, well-maintained formal gardens.'

Kat picks up the glass of wine and takes a sip. Crisp, dry and refreshingly fruity, it's a perfect accompaniment to the seafood.

'They're *still* very well-maintained,' she says thoughtfully. 'I wonder if the owners employ a gardener, even though there's no longer a house. And that walled garden must have been a magnificent sight in its heyday. It looks so sad now with everything overgrown and abandoned. It's surprising that the original greenhouse is still standing.'

'It's a good size, that greenhouse,' Mac comments. 'According to these details, it measures sixteen metres by five.'

'Are you into growing vegetables?'

'Don't know, but I'm all for new experiences.' He gives her a deliciously wicked look.

'Here you go. Seafood platter for two.' The waitress places a selection of plates and bowls on the table. 'Scallops, sardines, tiger prawns, chilled shell-on prawns, salad, and not forgetting the *moules marinières* and bread.' She stands back triumphantly, as if presenting a prize-winning exhibit. 'Let me know if there's anything else you want. Enjoy!'

Turning away, the girl crosses to a party of diners on the far side of the room.

'Good choice, Mr MacNamara,' Kat says, picking up a slice of focaccia and dipping it into the bowl of marinière. As she bites into the bread, a dribble of the creamy, garlicy sauce runs down her chin. Quickly, she wipes it away with a serviette.

'Having fun there?' Mac teases.

She gives a quiet snort and dunks the bread again. 'This is delicious.'

Helping himself to a prawn, Mac peels it out of its shell.

'What would you do with the grazing land?' Kat asks.

'Not sure. Maybe rent it out to a local farmer for sheep or cattle.'

'Or you could put a couple of camping pods and yurts on it – or a few shepherd huts. They seem popular.'

'Not a bad idea.' Mac's eyes narrow as he considers her. 'No end of possibilities.'

'It's fortunate the fire didn't spread to the trees,' says Kat, spearing a sardine with her fork. 'From what we saw earlier, there's a profusion of mature trees and specimen shrubs. I noticed several rhododendrons, hydrangeas, camellias and azaleas, not to mention the yew, copper beeches and oak trees along the original, upper carriage driveway. And that monkey puzzle tree is simply wonderful!'

Wiping his fingers on a serviette, Mac swipes the screen on his phone. 'It says here that Edgar Thurston, in his 1930s survey, *Survey of the Select Gardens of England,* described several important British and foreign trees at the property.'

'Edgar Thurston!' Kat says in a voice implying she's well acquainted with the man.

Mac looks up and laughs. 'The one and only. Apparently, off the driveway is a sequoia *sempervirens* that he identified as "one of the largest redwoods in the country".'

'Goodness.'

He continues reading aloud. ' "In 1979, this tree was included in Alan Mitchell's *Champion Trees,* and it was still in existence at the time of these sales particulars." '

'When were they prepared?'

'Annabel said ten years ago. I expect the tree's still thriving, but there's only one way to find out for sure. Arrange another viewing.'

Kat stares incredulously at Mac. 'You're serious about this, aren't you?'

'I am, especially if Historic England approves a grant.' Closing the message, he looks across the table at Kat with a serious expression. 'A special country home could be recreated, befitting the one that stood there for centuries, and it would resolve my dilemma regarding Alec. I want to give him a secure childhood and it would be a great place for him to grow up in.'

She nods slowly. The boy would love it there. He could make dens in the trees, explore the fields and woodland, and also enjoy the coast and nearby river.

'But, Mac, wouldn't you miss your life on the ocean wave?'

Steadily, he holds her gaze. 'As I said, changed priorities. I can still moor a yacht in Fowey. After all, I'll need somewhere to live while all the work is going on . . . Although your idea of installing something on the land is a good one. Perhaps a converted horsebox, or a Winnebago, while the build's under way. Or, I could camp out in the stables and workshop.' Picking up his beer glass, he swallows a mouthful of the classic, smooth, amber ale. 'What do you think?'

It's a simple question, so why does it feel so much more?

'I think,' she says, carefully considering her words, 'it would be wonderful for Alec to live with his dad, and in such a natural environment too. I mean, let's face it, London is all well and good, but . . .'

She frowns. The air feels weighted with unspoken possibilities and the general noise from the other diners grows muffled, and sounds a long way off.

Mac smiles, but she notices a flash of uncertainty in his eyes.

'And that's where you come in,' he says softly, and for the first time ever, he sounds a little nervous.

'Me?' she says in surprise. A delicious tingling sweeps through her veins as she realises her soul already knows what's coming.

'Yes. I meant it when I said it could be our passion, our project together . . . And eventually our home.'

She listens, mesmerised.

Tendrils of vulnerability linger in Mac's gaze but, overridden by the strength of his spirit, the adventurer soon finds his pace again. Reaching across the table, he takes hold of her hand and raises her palm uppermost to his lips. Gently he kisses the soft skin, his eyes never once leaving her face.

'When I lost Ana-Sofia, I never thought I'd feel the same way about anyone again . . .' he pauses, taking a breath, 'but life has a way of throwing curveballs. I know we haven't known each other very long, but from the first moment I saw you, something about you stirred my curiosity. And then when we met in Salcombe I had the impression you were someone I could open my heart to – that it would be safe in your hands.'

Kat's vision blurs and she blinks away the threatening tears. 'Even though I was so foul to you?'

'Even though . . .' He bestows a tender smile. 'Actually, I respect that you put me through my paces. And though it's true that I've filled my time with female company, it was only ever an attempt to run away from the truth of my situation, from my emotions, I suppose. But I've been so alone . . . I was simply going through the motions of living, but hollow inside. It's you, and only you, who's managed to break through those barriers I put up . . . You broke into my heart. You're so smart and beautiful . . . talented, independent . . . and fierce.'

Kat swallows hard, her heart pounding at this stellar list of her qualities. She's aware that her hand is still resting in his.

'So,' Mac takes a deep breath. 'My proposition to you is this. Don't go back to London once you've fulfilled your assignment. Stay here, with me, and share this crazy adventure to return that house to its former glory.' His gaze is unwavering; dependable.

Kat's mind stalls, as a state of paralysis and fear consumes her. And then her inner voice kicks in.

Even though the thought of returning to London is not the most thrilling, how can she abandon her life there? It's all she's ever known! She has a job, a flat, friends . . . How can she?

'Breathe,' he says, gently squeezing her hand. 'I know it's a lot to ask and there's a great deal to consider, but I swear to you, Katherine Maddox, if you take me on I will never give you any reason to doubt that decision.'

He lets go of her hand and immediately all Kat wants is for him to take hold of it again.

They sit in silence for several minutes as she tries to absorb all he's said. Never before has anyone made such an honest declaration to her.

Eventually, Mac speaks again, and his voice is warm and tender. 'What's going on inside that lovely head of yours?'

'I . . . I'm a bit dizzy with it all, Mac,' she says breathlessly. 'You've dazzled me.'

And scared the hell out of her . . .
'That's . . . good, isn't it?'
She nods. 'But what if we don't get on? What then?'
'But what if we *do* get on?' He smiles affectionately. 'Kat, I know you've had a rough ride with men in the past but you have to keep trying. If you shut yourself off and never take another chance you'll always live with regrets.'
Is she brave enough to risk her heart again?
She looks up at him, her emerald-green eyes round with uncertainty.
'All I ask is that you think about it,' Mac says. 'I'll be away all week and . . . perhaps, if you're ready, you might have an answer for me on my return.'
Yes. That's good. That's what she'll do. She'll think about it while he's away.
'OK,' she says in a small voice, wishing her heart would stop fluttering and regain a regular rhythm.
'Come on then.' Pushing back his chair, Mac rises to his feet. 'I'll settle the bill.'

54

The time is fast approaching for Mac to depart but the thought of their impending separation is something neither he nor Kat wants to consider.

'I hope I've convinced you there's nothing to worry about,' he says, lovingly stroking her long, lustrous, chestnut hair.

She smiles through underlying panic. 'You've put in a good effort,' she says, nestling against his chest.

'Listen . . . Promise me that if you make your mind up while I'm away, you'll let me know straight away.'

She says falteringly, 'I promise.'

Leaning in, he kisses her. 'The thought of getting out of bed is not the most thrilling,' he says, glancing at his watch, 'but that time is sadly almost upon us.'

Trailing her fingers through the hairs on his chest, Kat looks up deep into his eyes. As her hands slowly move ever lower, Mac's breathing grows ragged. Her touch is both teasing and exquisite, and when he can restrain himself no longer he rolls her onto her back.

'Kat,' he says in a low, hoarse whisper, 'I think I'm falling . . .'

She cuts him off with a kiss and, once again, they are lost in the throes of a passion that neither seems able to sate.

At eight-thirty that evening, Kat phones Tara. She's proud she's managed to hold off this long.

'Hi, Kat. All OK?'

'Tara, I'm in a quandary,' Kat says, her throat constricting.

'Why?'

'I've been offered the chance of something so utterly unbelievable, but exceptionally scary at the same time.' Unsuccessfully, she attempts to mask the sob.

'Hang on.'

In the background, she hears a hushed conversation taking place, but a minute later her friend is back.

'Tyler's in the bath,' Tara says, 'and Gul's deep into *Minecraft,* so dear Niles has agreed to fend off any distractions. Kat, I'm here for you. What's happened?'

Kat gazes down at the pros and cons she listed on a sheet of paper after Mac left, and that she's spent hours considering. In the margins are a number of doodles of a certain man, which she can't recall drawing.

'It's Mac,' she says, manically weaving the pen through her fingers.

'I thought it might be! Come on, spill . . .'

Within ten minutes, Kat has brought her best friend up to speed, concluding with a general analysis of her disastrous track record with men and her lack of confidence in that area.

'I think there's something wrong with me,' she says sadly.

Tara lets out a groan. 'You know what, Kat? If I could herd all your previous partners into a room together I would give them a piece of my mind for reducing you to this state. There is *nothing* wrong with you. How many times do I have to say this? The only trouble with you is . . .'

'Oh no!' Kat interrupts. 'Not you too, Tara. Please!'

Tara hesitates.

'I've heard it so often – *"the trouble with you, Kat, is"* – and each time it's something different. I've tried so hard to remedy all my deficiencies that I now no longer trust my own judgement.'

'Oh you beautiful, misguided, wonderful woman!' Tara exclaims. Don't you see? Those idiots you've wasted your time on, they're the ones with the problem. What I was going to say was . . . the trouble with you is that you have a glorious shell and not one of those ridiculous men has been authentic enough to see beyond it. They couldn't move on from their lust and desire, and when they eventually saw *you* they were incapable of handling it. No, that's not quite right . . . saying that you had a problem *was* their way of handling it.'

Kat frowns. She knows Tara makes sense, it's something that's occurred to her before, but it's hard to break the lifelong habit of putting herself down.

'Now, Mac,' continues Tara, 'I would say he's the exception. From what you've told me, and what I've seen for myself, he's not easily caught in the spell of what a person looks like. He needs someone real. What he's seen in you from the start is the person you truly are, despite your best endeavours to put him off the scent!'

Kat rubs her temples. It's true. With Mac, it's not just physical, it's cerebral, too. He's different. Still, her head feels as if it's splitting from indecision.

'Tara. How can I give up my London life? It's my stability.' Her voice is raw with the effort of keeping her emotions in check.

'A life in London isn't going to feed your soul, is it? At best, it's transient. Visits to art galleries and museums with the latest fling – and that's assuming you're lucky enough to find one that's interested in culture – will only partially satisfy you. Getting your hands dirty and building something real for the future . . . I just know you'd thrive on that. Can't you see?'

When Kat doesn't answer, Tara carries on. 'Now listen to me. Mac seems steadfast and true and if you don't take this chance with him you will always wonder what could have been. *That* I am one hundred per cent sure of, Katherine Maddox.'

Kat smiles uncertainly. Tara never calls her by her full name . . . unless she has something of real importance to drum home.

'Do you hear me?'

'Loud and clear,' Kat says.

'Good.' Tara takes a deep breath. 'Of course, the decision is yours, and whatever decision you make, we will all continue to love you. Please know that.' She drops her voice to a whisper, 'But, my God, if Niles had offered himself to me on a plate as Mac has with you, we'd have got together several years earlier. We'd probably have half a dozen kids by now!'

Despite the tumultuous emotions consuming her, Kat laughs.

'You are my dearest friend,' Tara says, 'and all I want is to see you happy. So, for once in your life, do yourself a favour and let happiness in.'

Promising Tara she will consider just that, Kat ends their phone call and sits quietly with her thoughts for a long while. Eventually, they realign into something verging on calm, and all at once she knows exactly what to do. She glances at her phone – not far off eleven. Rising to her feet, she makes her way to the lower floor and Stella's office, and rummaging through the bureau, finds what she's looking for – a thick red, felt-tip pen. A wild energy possesses her and she runs up the two flights of stairs to the linen cupboard and pulls out sheets and towels, discarding several in a heap on the floor. Holding up a white sheet, she considers it. Yes, this will do! She'll buy Stella a new one.

Descending to the studio, she sweeps the table clear of sketchpads and drawing paraphernalia and lays the sheet out flat. Then, removing the cap from the felt tip pen, she draws the large letters in outline before carefully filling them in.

Kat can't sleep. The bedroom curtains are open – she doesn't want to miss *Windsong*'s departure – and her body is flooded with endorphins. It's five in the morning and she should be exhausted, but she's filled with a strange energy that makes her feel on top of the world. Getting out of bed, she crosses over to the window and watches the sky in the east lighten to a pale gold, touched by the first rays of a rising sun heralding the start of a brand new day. A shiver courses through her. She's not cold, and yet, she rubs her arms.

Dressing hurriedly, she makes her way down to the kitchen. It's doubtful the yacht will leave at this early hour, and she has time to make herself a drink. Filling the kettle, she switches it on and pops a teabag into a mug. Then, from a drawer she extracts a roll of string and a pair of scissors, and stuffs them in the back pocket of her jeans. When the kettle comes to the boil, Kat makes the tea and carries the mug through to the studio, where she gathers up the sheet before heading along the hallway to the balcony.

As Kat steps outside she feels the chill of the early morning air, and a seagull standing on the top railing of the neighbours' balcony gives a startled cry.

'Morning,' she says, and then laughs.

Setting the mug down on the small patio table, which is covered in a heavy dew, she removes the string and scissors from her pocket and unwinds the cord. As she cuts off a few lengths she's suddenly aware of being watched, and a prickle of apprehension raises the hairs on the back of her neck. For a moment, she wonders if Jerry and Sandy are about. She hopes not. It's paramount that nothing spoils this important and private moment. Glancing across at their balcony, she notices it is the large gull that's eyeing her curiously.

'Watch carefully,' she says, 'because you are witnessing Katherine Maddox taking a huge leap of faith and stepping up to her true self.'

Talking to a seagull? Crazy! But she doesn't care . . .

The sky in the east is streaked with warming shades of pink and gold, and she thinks she has never witnessed a more spectacular morning. Even at this early hour, the river is coming alive. *Windsong* could sail by at any moment.

Picking up the lengths of string, she winds them robustly around the top corners of the sheet and then looks around for something to secure them to. Unlike the neighbour's balcony, Stella's doesn't have the benefit of railings, so Kat considers the patio chairs. Moving one to each front corner of the balcony, she ties the string around their backrests and makes sure the knots are secure. Looking up, she sees the seagull is still watching.

'No messing on this masterpiece,' she says sternly. 'Understand?'

The bird cocks its head, its beady eye surveying her.

'This, I'll have you know, is the most precious artwork I've ever produced.'

It's shortly after eight when *Windsong* gets underway, and the sky is a cloudless blue as far as the eye can see. As the yacht slips her moorings, Mac spots a pair of swans and wonders if they are the same two birds he and Kat saw when they ventured up Penpol Creek. As he navigates away from the tranquil mooring and joins the main river, the water shimmers under a strengthening sun and something tells him it will be a good charter.

Still, there's somewhere else he'd rather be today. Both couples on board are experienced sailors, and for one insane moment he considers leaving Sarah in charge and diving overboard to spend the week with Kat instead. But he knows that's ridiculous, let alone unprofessional, and filling his lungs with air, he focuses his mind on the job in hand.

Windsong glides through the water, leaving barely a ripple in her wake and Mac can't resist looking towards Stella's house in the hopes that he might glimpse Kat. What he sees makes his heart leap, and finally the last of his long-endured sadness lifts and floats away.

She is standing on the balcony, bathed in sunlight and shielding her eyes. As the yacht draws level with the house, she waves and frantically gestures over the wall.

Mac smiles. How could he miss it? As his eyes mist over and a lump forms in his throat, he swallows hard. On a sheet draped over the balcony in huge red letters is her answer for all to see: YES!

Taking one hand off the wheel and raising his fingers to

his lips, he sends a kiss out across the water to her, and then watches as she stretches out her arm, catches the kiss of air and hugs it closely to her heart.

The seagull, disturbed by Kat's sudden movement, lifts into the air with an irritated screech. Spreading its wings, it swoops off to join the other birds circling on the thermals above *Windsong*'s mast.

As the yacht sails by, Mac gazes lovingly at the beautiful woman with the emerald-green eyes and the burnished-copper hair, and tenderly pats his heart.

Kat laughs with delight. Never before has she been so in love, and whatever the future may bring, this time she knows she will embrace it.

Acknowledgements

I wrote this book during several periods of lockdown and what a relief it was to escape the realities of Covid Britain and visit the popular sailing town of Fowey and the beautiful surrounding countryside, albeit in my head. How wonderful it was to cruise upstream and weave in and out of a multitude of boats, whilst hearing shouts and laughter echoing across the water from the bustling town mingled with the raucous cry of seagulls wheeling overhead. It was such a joy to be out in nature, navigating quiet creeks and peaceful backwaters, observing the varied wildlife along the riverbanks and experiencing the exhilaration of wind in my hair and spray on my face as the yacht raced along the south coast of Cornwall . . . all from my desk. As soon as lockdown eased I wasted no time in experiencing it in reality.

The beauty of writing is that an author has *carte blanche* to delve into his or her own memory and cherry pick what to include . . . or not. For my main character, Kat Maddox, I revisited my past and drew upon experiences of working for a London publishing house back in the day. However, I was intrigued by the sudden appearance of James MacNamara (aka Mac) as Kat gazed out of her office window and caught sight of him in the street below.

I never saw that coming! Nor did I ever spot a 'Mac' from my office window, however many times I gazed out of it, but I enjoyed every moment of Kat's discovery.

Cornwall and Devon have many historic manor houses that I could have included in the novel, and it was difficult to choose which ones to feature, but there was no confusion over the one that Mac considered buying. It is a property I know well, having stayed there several times when my sister and her family owned it. Tragically, in 2019 the house caught fire, and this event spurred me on, making me even more determined to include it in the novel. No one knows what's around the corner and this is my own small way of acknowledging and honouring its existence.

Thank you to my agent, Hannah Todd of the Madeleine Milburn Literary & TV Agency, for bringing about a new collaboration with Embla Books, and to editors Hannah Smith and Suzanne Clarke, who provided detailed constructive criticism that enabled me to hone the tale. And big thanks also to the wider Team Embla for helping to bring this story to the market. Very few people understand or appreciate the amount of work that goes on behind the scenes.

Heartfelt thanks to tour guide, Lucy Daniel, with whom I spent a very pleasant and interesting three hours online as she *virtually* showed me around Fowey and the surrounding countryside, and patiently answered my many questions. It was generous of her to spend so much time with me, and nothing was too much to ask. For those of you who decide to holiday in Fowey, I can thoroughly recommend her guided walks and tours, through her online website: www.lucydanielguide.uk

I consider myself lucky to have beta readers Sally Tunley and Helena Ancil on my team, as I can rest assured knowing the quality of their valuable insights and suggestions. Many thanks also to Shelagh Clowe, Mary Framptom-Price and Tony King for their guidance in all things nautical. Without you, despite the number of hours I spent watching sailing videos on YouTube, the hero and heroine would still be sitting in Mac's tender waiting for me to come to a decision about how best to describe them boarding a yacht! And don't get me started on knots . . . although I understand the bowline is a sailor's favourite.

And last but not least, thank you to my husband, Martin, who – blissfully unaware of what was in store for him when we first met – wholeheartedly supports me on this writing journey. But please . . . no more plot suggestions for zombies and aliens to appear in one of my novels!

Kate Ryder

Kate Ryder is an international bestselling author of romantic suspense and timeslip with a hint of otherworldliness/supernatural. Several years ago, she and her partner moved from the Home Counties to renovate a near-derelict cottage in Cornwall and, inspired by the ruggedly beautiful landscapes, she sets many of her novels in her adopted county. Today, Kate lives in a fully renovated cottage with her (now) husband and Bella, a rehomed Bengal-cross cat that insists on monopolising the keyboard and printer while she attempts to craft her next novel. Keep in touch with Kate:

Website: www.kateryder.me

Twitter: https://twitter.com/KateRyder_Books

Facebook: https://www.facebook.com/kateryder.author

Instagram: @kateryder_author

About Embla Books

Embla Books is a digital-first publisher of standout commercial adult fiction. Passionate about storytelling, the team at Embla publish books that will make you 'laugh, love, look over your shoulder and lose sleep'. Launched by Bonnier Books UK in 2021, the imprint is named after the first woman from the creation myth in Norse mythology, who was carved by the gods from a tree trunk found on the seashore – an image of the kind of creative work and crafting that writers do, and a symbol of how stories shape our lives.

Find out about some of our other books and stay in touch:

Twitter, Facebook, Instagram: @emblabooks
Newsletter: https://bit.ly/emblanewsletter